Scarlett and the Big Bad Billionaire

Scarlett and the Big Bad Billionaire

A SMALL TOWN ENEMIES TO LOVERS STORY

AN EASTPORT BAY BILLIONAIRES BOOK

TRU TAYLOR

Oxford South Press

Contents

About

SCARLETT AND THE BIG BAD BILLIONAIRE

In my *expert* opinion, every woman who's been left at the altar should follow up that singularly humiliating experience by spending a week in paradise with a totally inappropriate—and totally sexy—stranger.

Even better if you meet him at the bar of the resort hotel where your destination wedding and honeymoon were *supposed* to take place.

Even *even* better if he's hot and jacked and there are no names exchanged and zero chance of *ever* seeing him again afterward.

One week of no-holds-barred sex, sun, rum, and fun and your broken heart is on the road to recovery— or at least approaching the on-ramp.

Of course, the key to pulling off this surefire heartbreak cure is to make sure you don't fall for him during that amazing week in which you lived out every romantic fantasy you've ever had.

And whatever you do, *don't* run into your non-honeymoon fling three years later—at your matchmaking grandma's house.

Enjoy the read...

ONE

Second Wind

You can't really appreciate the meaning of the word "alone" until you find yourself standing at the altar in a wedding dress in front of all your friends and family... without a groom.
    --Scarlett Hood

Actually, I never made it quite as far as the altar—or in this case, the flower-covered arch embedded in the sand between the Aegean Sea and the thirty-five destination wedding guests all trying their best not to look at me as the tardy minutes ticked on.

I stood to one side of the wedding arbor, huddled with my bridesmaids and matron of honor, my sister Maddie.

Waiting.

Her husband Joey and the other groomsmen milled about on the other side in front of the rows of beribboned white folding chairs, some of the guys looking like they were ready to collapse into one.

Several of them were red-eyed and pale. *Must have been some bachelor night.*

"It was supposed to start fifteen minutes ago. Where is he?" I whispered, fighting back the tears threatening to ruin my meticulously applied wedding day makeup. "Has Joey heard from him today?"

Part of me was still hoping this was one of those "Hangover" movie situations and my fiancé would show up sunburned and repentant—but eager to stand by my side in front of the clergyman currently shifting from one foot to the other while shading his eyes against the already hot summer morning sun.

The more realistic part of me already knew the truth. Bryce wasn't coming.

"Joey said he walked him to his room when they got in at three this morning and called to make sure he was awake at eight."

"Why did they stay out till *three*?"

Maddie gave me a raised brow expression that said *You really have to ask?*

Right. Strippers, vodka, and any other vice he could get his hands on during his last gasp of freedom.

"How did he sound?"

She shrugged. "Like he was hung all the way over. Believe me, I've already read Joey the riot act—at three *and* at eight. But he said Bryce was up and getting dressed when he called."

"Do you think he could have fallen back asleep?"

While I hated the idea of my fiancé needing to be shaken awake on what was supposed to be one of the most exciting days of his life, I liked the idea of telling all these people the whole thing was off and they'd flown halfway around the world for nothing even less.

Maddie gripped my trembling hand with her warm, steady one. "I'll ask Joey to go check on him. You hang tight, sweetie. You'll be walking down that aisle in no time."

In a lower voice I'm not sure I was supposed to hear, she added, "Even if I have to drag the selfish prick here myself."

Before she could step across the aisle and speak to her husband, my four-year-old niece Trina ran up to us and embraced the baby bump that protruded from Maddie's long dress.

My mother was right on her granddaughter's heels. The

expression she wore, like everyone else in attendance, was tense with worry.

"Mommy, mommy, mommy," Trina said with breathless excitement.

"What is it honey?" Maddie bent down to level her face with her daughter's. "Do you need to go potty?"

"No, grandma just took me. We saw Uncle Bryce inside the hotel. He says he needs to talk to Aunt Scarlett."

Wrinkling her nose dramatically, the little girl added, "He looked raggedy, and he smelled funny."

My heart plummeted to the soles of my bare, freshly pedicured feet. I closed my eyes and swayed a bit.

Maddie put her hand on my shoulder to steady me. "Want me to go?"

"No. I'll go." I shook my head back and forth rapidly. My legs felt wobbly, like I was wading through pudding while on stilts.

"Where is he?" I asked my niece. "Where did you see Uncle Bryce?"

"Follow me," she said and turned to walk back down the aisle.

Unfortunately, she'd been a little *too* well-trained in the art of the wedding procession walk.

Trina took one slow step at a time, pausing dramatically between each of them to sprinkle flower petals onto the sand.

Spotting her and noticing me walking slowly behind while carrying my bridal bouquet, a few of the guests stood.

Which made more of the confused guests stand.

Which I guess made the string quartet I'd hired panic. They began to play the wedding march as my flower girl and I walked *away* from the arch.

A few guests whispered to each other, clearly wondering what was going on. I wish I could have told them. All I could do was try my best not to cry as I marched slowly toward my no-show fiancé.

Maddie caught up to Trina, scooping her up and apologizing profusely as we walked together toward the resort hotel. As soon as we stepped into the lobby, I spotted Bryce.

He really did look bad. He clearly hadn't showered after his night of debauchery, and he wasn't wearing his tux.

My ribs compressed, crushing my lungs and making it even harder to breathe than it already was in the dress's tight bodice.

Bryce didn't rush over to meet me. Instead, he stood there, holding his stomach and waiting for me to cross the lobby in my wedding dress and bare feet.

I must have been a spectacle, because everyone stared, from the employees to the guests checking in and out. All of them gave me sappy smiles, and some even applauded.

I raised a hand and forced a smile. "Thank you so much."

When I finally reached Bryce, Maddie took a step back, encouraging Trina to go check out the lobby fountain with her.

"What's going on?" I whispered to Bryce. He looked like he hadn't slept in days, and his eyes reminded me of a stray dog who expected to be kicked and chased away. He would barely meet my eyes.

"I had a talk with David before we left Anoka," he said.

"And?"

Had my stepfather secretly warned Bryce I was a nightmare or something? I doubted it—David and I adored each other.

It was more likely he'd threatened my husband-to-be within an inch of his life and scared the hell out of him. My stepdad, though a teddy bear to me and Maddie, could be intimidating to others.

He owned Mixitall, the manufacturing company Bryce and I worked for, and demanded excellence from all his employees, including his stepdaughter and future son-in-law.

Or was it *former* future son-in-law?

"He told me he's not going to give me the promotion to Operations Manager," Bryce said.

"Oh. Well, that's okay. With both our salaries we can easily cover our bills—especially once we move in together. We might have to put off buying a house for a while..."

Bryce's expression caused my rah-rah consolation speech to trail off into nothingness.

"Why are you telling me this *now*? Why do you not have your tux on? Just tell me what's going on in your brain."

Bryce twisted his mouth to the side and blew out a loud breath. "It's just that... I thought if we got married, I'd be a shoo-in for the position. I really wanted that promotion, Scarlett. I was counting on it."

For a few minutes I was quiet as competing sensations of a spinning head and a rolling stomach vied for my attention.

"What are you saying?" I finally asked. "You were only with me because you thought it would help you get ahead at Mixitall?"

"That's not the only reason," Bryce protested. "I think you're real cute and all. I really like you."

My mouth fell open, and for a minute I could hear nothing but a ringing sound in my ears.

"You... *like* me," I said.

"Yes. I do. And that's why I can't marry you, Scarlett. It wouldn't be fair to you. I'm sorry about the timing, but one of these days you're going to look back on this and realize I did the best thing for both of us. I think we should go back to being just friends."

Bryce's voice seemed very far away now, and his face blurred before my eyes. I didn't know how to respond.

Even if I could have found the words, my tongue seemed to have lost the ability to form them.

"Scarlett? You understand why I have to call it off, don't you?" Bryce was saying from somewhere deep in a hole. "I've already packed my stuff and moved it out of the room. Please don't hate me..."

* * *

Ten hours later

"I hate him," I said, not for the first time tonight. Wouldn't be the last either.

"We all do, honey," Maddie soothed. "He's a cotton-headed ninny muggins, and you're better off without him."

Maddie had replaced all her favorite swear words with toddler-appropriate variations since becoming a mother, but I appreciated the furor and loyalty behind the silly phrase.

I rested my forehead against the cool surface of the outdoor bar. It smelled like beer and pineapple.

"What I don't understand is why he even flew here with me in the first place if he knew he wasn't going to go through with it."

"He told Joey he didn't want to embarrass you since you'd already had your bridal shower. And he thought he could do it... up until this morning."

"It's like my dad and mom all over again."

They were never married?" my younger half-sister asked, clearly shocked.

"No, no, they *were*, but he left. They all do eventually."

"Not all of them," she said. "Not Joey. He knows I'll track him down and deep fry his Rocky Mountain oysters if he even *thinks* of leaving me alone with two kids under five."

"You wouldn't get the chance to mutilate him because I'd do it for you," I vowed before slurping what remained of the brightly colored drink in my glass. "Besides, you can't go to prison—you have to be there for the kids, whereas I will apparently never be having any."

Maddie gave me a chiding glance as she offered me a sip of her club soda. "Last cocktail, okay? You're not used to drinking so much. You're just piling misery on top of sorrow. Besides, I can't stay awake much longer, and Mom wants you to do brunch tomorrow morning before she and my dad leave."

Unlike me, our mother had managed to find a great guy after her marriage to my father ended. A couple years after she'd married David, Maddie had been born, and my life had become infinitely better.

At the moment though, I didn't want to face any of them—not even my sweet half-sister who wanted me to be sensible instead of ordering every umbrella drink on the bar menu.

"Nooooooooo," I whined. "No brunch. No Eggs Benedict and sad eyes and 'I'm sorry's' and 'better luck next time, kiddos.' I wish I could have gotten a flight out today. Then I wouldn't have had to spend two hours at my 'un-reception' assuring everyone how okay I am and trying not to spill on this dress so I can re-sell it."

My reception dress was a clingy red knit that matched the beautiful bougainvillea growing all around the property of the resort hotel. It was the only thing I'd packed for my destination wedding and honeymoon that wasn't beachwear or resort casual.

Come to think of it, maybe I *should* have just changed into a pair of shorts and a t-shirt. It wasn't like I was going to impress anyone at this point.

I guess I'd had some thought of maintaining dignity or some such nonsense. That concern was long gone tonight, thanks to Captain Morgan and the crew.

Maddie patted my back. "Well, for what it's worth, I think you should keep it. It looks amazing on you. Bryce didn't deserve that dress, and he didn't deserve you. He's boring—and he smells like hot dog water."

I lifted my head. "What?"

"He does. I didn't want to say anything about it when I thought you'd be spending the rest of your life with him, but it's true. I don't know how you stood it. I'll tell Mom and David you don't feel up to brunch. You can just see them when everyone gets home."

Ugh. I did *not* relish the idea of going back to face all my co-workers and friends who hadn't gotten the word yet about my canceled wedding.

But I would. Because I had to.

What was the alternative? Spending my honeymoon here alone? Maddie and Joe *had* to go back home—they both had work, and Trina had school. Mom and David were scheduled to go off on an excursion to the Acropolis tomorrow, not that I'd want to spend my un-honeymoon tagging along with them.

"What you need now is a hot bath and a good night's sleep," Maddie said.

"What I need is another drink." I raised my hand to get the attention of the young bartender who was looking more and more like Tom Cruise as the hours—and colorful drinks—accumulated.

He nodded at me and started mixing a replacement for my empty glass.

"Or maybe a lobotomy so I can't think about it anymore," I added.

"*Or...* a night with one of *those* guys," Maddie said with waggling eyebrows. "I'll bet you wouldn't even remember Bryce's name in the morning."

I followed my sister's pointed gaze to a group of guys on the other side of the bar. They were boisterous and loud as if maybe they'd started the party elsewhere and this was just one of many stops along their pub crawl tonight.

Every one of them was jacked, like bodybuilders—but then, no, they weren't puffed up and slickly styled.

Rather they were tough looking, their sinewy strength the kind that resulted from manual labor or old-fashioned bodyweight exercises. Several of them were tatted up.

"Don't be ridiculous. The last thing I'm interested in right now is men. You don't cure a hangover with more alcohol."

"Um... have you never heard of 'hair of the dog that bit you?'" she asked.

"I'm not interested in dog hair, horsehair, or sexily scruffy dark hair with a golden auburn streak," I said, checking out the attractive guy at the very end of the bar. He didn't appear to be drinking like the rest of his posse. "And I'm *definitely* not interested in a military guy."

"You think they're military?" she asked, studying them more closely now. "What's wrong with that?"

"My dad was a SEAL, remember? Ninety percent divorce rate?"

"Oh right. But how do you know these guys are military?"

"Don't stare at them," I hissed. "They'll take it as an invitation."

She grinned, talking through her teeth like a ventriloquist. "Too late. Incoming hottie alert. Look alive, soldier."

"Well, hello," the shortest of the guys said, flashing a brilliant smile at Maddie as he and his friends moved to our side of the bar.

His smile dimmed a bit, and his tone turned more respectful when he looked down and spotted her pregnant belly. "...ma'am," he added belatedly.

"Hi guys," she said. "I'm Madelyn. This is my sister—"

"No names," I interrupted.

One of the tattooed guys laughed. He was dark-haired and tall with piercing hazel eyes. "Why? Are you two on secret assignment?"

"Are you?" I snapped.

His grin widened. "Of course. But I'll tell you my nickname 'cause I know we can trust you. It's Wildman."

"The wild man," one of his friends echoed, raising his glass. The other guys raised theirs as well, bumping plastic cups and sloshing beer onto the counter.

Tom Cruise immediately swiped the spills with his bar towel.

"This is Badger," Wildman said, indicating the short guy who'd said hello first. "And this is Gandalf, Sharkbait, Volt, and the ugly one over there is Wolf."

Wildman hooked a thumb toward the hot guy I'd noticed earlier at the end of the bar.

Military. I knew it. Those were special ops pseudonyms if I'd ever heard them.

"How about it, ladies?" the short guy asked. "Can we buy you another round?"

Maddie glanced at me and took in my slight head shake and forbidding glare.

"Thanks, but I'm not drinking obviously, and we were about to call it a night." With a sympathetic glance in my direction, she added, "It's been a long day."

Looking at her pitying expression, I got a premonition of an even more depressing sight—the empty honeymoon suite that awaited me when I left this barstool. I wondered if anyone had thought to tell housekeeping to skip the whole flower petals on the bedspread thing.

"Actually... I think I just got a second wind," I said and raised the Ouzo martini Tom had just slid past Maddie toward my waiting hand. "Anyone want to make a toast?"

Sharkbait raised his glass.

"Here's to the times we'll never remember with those we'll never forget. Now who wants to dance?"

TWO

Designated Driver

Gray

Three martinis and counting—and I *was* counting since she didn't seem to be.

It was pretty obvious the Tom Cruise wannabe behind the bar had his eye on the knockout in the red dress, and he was the king of the generous pour.

If he came near her again with that bottomless Ouzo bottle, I was going to drop him.

No, red-dress wasn't my responsibility, but I was the DD for my squad tonight—might as well add her to the list.

Someone had to look out for her. Her sister, who appeared to be about eight months pregnant and dead on her feet, was apparently about to jump ship.

"Joey keeps texting asking where I am. Trina threw up from eating too much cake at the reception," she said, appearing flustered. "Apparently it's everywhere—he said it was like The Exorcist—flower girl version. And I have to get up at five a.m. for our flight home. Please let's just go."

Red hugged her and planted a kiss on her cheek. "Go. I'm fine. I've been telling you for an hour... just go to bed. I love you. I love Joey. I love Trina."

The pregnant woman had groaned and looked heavenward as if searching for patience or maybe superhuman strength so she could pick up her sister and carry her out of here.

"I'll look after her," I offered. "I'm the designated driver for my group tonight—well, actually the designated car-service caller since we don't have a rental. One of us always stays sober to look out for the rest when we're out together. I can keep an eye on your sister as well until she's ready to go back to her room."

The woman gave Red a glance then turned back to me with an exasperated expression. "She's not usually like this. In fact, I've *never* seen her like this. Today was—"

"Maddie..." came a warning voice from her sister.

"...a very bad day," Maddie finished. "I've realized since becoming a mother there are three things you can't *make* another person do—sleep, eat, and go potty. Now I've got a new one—go home before they're willing to. I'm afraid she'll stay till the bar closes."

"I have some bad news for you. This bar never closes." I shrugged. "It's Mykonos."

Finally, Maddie had given up and left after taking a picture of my driver's license and making me swear on my mother's life I'd see her sister safely back to her room and/or the ER, whichever seemed more appropriate at the end of the night.

My bet was on the stomach pump and IV fluids. "No problem. I'll make sure she gets there safely," I'd promised.

Now, observing Red Dress swaying on the small dancefloor, I tapped Gandalf on the shoulder.

"Cutting in."

"What? Why?"

"Don't argue with the DD." He frowned but walked away and went back to the bar, allowing me to take his spot as Red's dance partner.

Gandalf, AKA Greg Tolkan, was strong and had good reflexes, but like the rest of my buddies, our platoon commander was pretty well pickled himself. Even if our SEAL training had included drunken barfly mid-air catches, he probably wouldn't have done this girl much good tonight.

We never drank while deployed or even in the pre-deployment period—General Order Number One banned alcohol use for SEALS. But my squad and I were enjoying a few days of post-deployment R and R. We'd just carried out an operation in Syria where we'd conducted a hostage rescue of a team of global aid doctors.

Insertion and extraction had gone according to plan, unde-tected, and that was *always* cause for celebration. Sometimes blowing off steam was the only thing that kept us sane.

Apparently Red, as I'd come to think of her, needed to let off a little as well. She was going for some kind of record in the umbrella drink Olympics.

And the twirling competition. She spun in a circle, her beau-tiful curls swinging out around her head like one of those county fair chair swing rides.

Coming to a stop as the song ended, she gave me a half-lidded assessment. "You changed your hair. And your clothes." She blinked and craned her neck forward. "And your face."

"Yep. And my name." I offered my hand. "I'm Wolf."

"Wolf," she repeated as she shook my hand. "That's a fake name. Gandalf... Badger... all of you are using fake names. It's obvious. If you're not military or secret agents, you're all married and cheating on your wives."

I chuckled. "None of us are married. And *you're* the one who instituted the 'no names' rule. How about stopping for a glass of water, Red? You're gonna be pretty dehydrated in the morning."

Thankfully, she agreed and allowed me to lead her back to the bar where I ordered two waters.

"I'm not red. I was very careful not to get sunburned." She wagged a beautifully manicured finger at me. "Always wear sunscreen with SPF fifty or higher—especially in the Greek islands."

"I'll remember that." I chuckled. "But that's not why I called you Red."

My gaze dipped to the plunging neckline of her clingy red knit dress, and I forced them back up to safer territory.

Although her eyes were dangerous as well—almond-shaped with long lashes, they were the color of the Mediterranean sky.

Whoa there, cowboy. Not this one. Not tonight.

"Why then?" she asked.

Badger leaned over to us. "Because you're a red-hot fox. Hey, get it? Red Fox?"

"Better watch out for the big, bad gray wolf, little Red," Volt warned in a teasing sing-song. "He might steal all your goodies if you're not careful."

The rest of my squad except for Wilder, who was in deep conversation about American footfall with the guy next to him, cackled like hyenas.

"I apologize for my friends," I said. "They're actually great guys when they're sober. I'd trust any one of them with my life."

Red pointed a finger at me, her thumb raised as if she held a pistol. "I knew it. You *are* military, aren't you? Special forces, right?"

"We're all salesmen here for a convention," Badger said, insinuating himself back into the conversation.

She narrowed her eyes. "What *kind* of convention?"

Great. I knew why Badger had lied—we weren't supposed to own up to being a SEAL team when we were this close to the operation area. We'd all signed non-disclosure agreements, and besides, none of us wanted to find ourselves under investigation for sharing classified information.

But now I was involved in his stupid cover story, and I didn't know the first thing about being a salesman.

Glancing down at the colorful printed drink coaster on the counter, I said, "Promotional products. You know, stuff that's printed with company logos? Like napkins and t-shirts, and hats, and pens?"

"Uh huh. And what 'promotional product' do *you* sell?" Her tone was incredulous. "Embossed bullshit?"

She was actually pretty funny in that wasted, super-honest way some people get when overserved.

Sharkbait literally snorted with laughter. "Good one. Actually, we sell imprinted condoms."

"And sex toys," Badger added helpfully.

"They're kidding," I said.

"No, we're not," Gandalf said. "Wolf here is just being shy. He was salesman of the year. You wouldn't believe how many imprinted vibrators and dildos he sold this quarter."

Clearly my commander was exacting revenge on me for stealing his dance partner.

"You should see the trophy they gave him," he added with a snicker.

"Calling them 'sex toys' makes it sound trivial, but adult products are actually a huge business," Badger said. "And of course, logoed condoms have saved countless lives, so actually ol' Wolf here is a hero."

"Shit, you're making *me* want to sleep with him," Volt said.

Red slid from her barstool suddenly and tilted to one side as she struggled to find her balance. Immediately, I was off my own stool, extending an arm behind her back but not touching her.

Miraculously she managed to right herself and gave a salute to my friends and squad members.

"*I'm* not sleeping with anyone—ever again. I will be sleeping *alone* tonight... as soon as I can find my bed. Alone, alone, alone."

She fished clumsily through her purse then pulled out a key card and held it aloft in a triumphant pose. "*Here* it is. Goodnight gentlemen, to you and your dildos."

Raucous laughter met her slurred pronouncement. I glared at my friends then followed Red, who'd already begun to stagger down the sandy pathway to the hotel.

It wasn't until I dialed the car service for my friends and spoke aloud that she realized I was right behind her. She gave me an irritated look.

"Why are you following me? I don't *need* a ride—or any imprinted condoms, Mr. Dildo Salesman of the Year."

I cringed but didn't try to explain. The truth was off-limits, and she'd be too drunk to remember what I said anyway.

"I know. I'm not trying to sell you anything *or* pick you up. I promised your sister I'd make sure you got to your room safely."

"My suite," she corrected.

"Ooh fancy. Your suite, then. I didn't know I was dancing with such a high roller."

She laughed. "I don't usually roll that high. My fiancé booked the suite."

For the first time tonight, my gaze fell to her left hand, which indeed bore a diamond solitaire. "You're engaged."

For some reason there was a sinking sensation in my stomach. Must have been hunger—dinner *was* several hours ago, and the water I'd been drinking all night wasn't very filling.

"No," she corrected. "I. Am. Not."

"You're already married?" The hunger grew worse.

Now Red laughed out loud, throwing her head back, which threw her off balance and sent her swerving right into me. If I hadn't caught her, she would have toppled over sideways onto the dark beach.

"I'm *definitely* not married," she said into my chest. "I'm never getting married because men are a bunch of cotton-headed ninny muggins."

I couldn't help but laugh at the ridiculous insult. And the fact she'd just quoted the Elf movie. And because her breath was tickling my bare skin.

"Please allow me to apologize for the whole lot of us," I said.

Lifting her head, she pulled away from me and spun around, lurching back down the path.

"What floor is your suite on?" I asked.

Red wasn't listening. She'd wandered off the path toward the hotel pool, which glowed with inviting underwater lights as well as landscape lighting strategically placed among the lush plants surrounding it.

Closed at this hour, the pool area was deserted and quiet except for the steady rush of the artificial waterfall.

"Where are you going?" I asked.

"I want to swim. I didn't get a chance to swim yet. And the pool is sooooo pretty. It's why I picked this resort."

"I don't think that's a good idea. You can swim tomorrow. Let's just get you back to your room."

She ignored me, skipping toward the pool like a little girl. "Oooh, it's even prettier than it looked online. Let's swim."

"No."

I followed her to the edge of the water, where she dropped her purse, stepped out of her heels, and began stripping off her dress.

"Please don't do that," I begged.

She had no business swimming after drinking as much as she had tonight.

And *I* had no business seeing her with her clothes off.

That didn't seem to concern Red at the moment. She worked the dress—which had apparently required going braless—down her body, giving me a perfect view of her thong panties.

Whoa. Instant hard-on. A natural but completely inappropriate physical reaction, considering the circumstances.

The panties were spectacular, white and covered with sparkling crystals. Those she kept on, much to my relief.

And disappointment.

No—I was relieved. I did *not* need to see any more of that beautiful body, which was about as off-limits as it could possibly get.

She may look *like a hot woman, but at this moment she is ninety-nine percent alcohol and one percent herself.*

I picked up the dress she'd just stepped out of, hoping to convince her to put it back *on*, when she jumped in.

Shit.

This was bad. I looked around, hoping to see my friends passing by or maybe Red's sister coming back to check on her. She'd been right—you couldn't make someone else do something.

And apparently you couldn't keep someone from skinny dipping when they were determined to.

Red resurfaced, treading water and looking up at me like some kind of damn magical mermaid. The underwater lighting showed me an enticing outline of her figure, her bare breasts blurred just beneath the surface.

The inappropriate hard-on grew harder still. I took a seat on the end of a chaise lounge.

Better.

From this vantage point, all I could see was her head. I'd watch it like a bobber at the end of a fishing line. If it went under, I'd jump in and save her.

She splashed some water in my direction, wetting my toes. "What's the matter? Can't you swim?" she teased.

"I can swim," I assured her. In fact, swimming for at least an hour every day was part of my training routine along with running and weightlifting.

Naturally, I wouldn't be telling Red about that.

"I'm a great swimmer," she assured me in a slur that made the last word sound like *schwimmer.*

I chuckled. "I'm sure you are."

"Bet I could beat you in a race," she challenged with a cocky grin. "Loser has to jump from the top of the waterfall."

"No one's jumping from the top of the waterfall," I said in a firm tone. If she tried it, I'd forget politeness and pick her up and carry her half naked and wet back to her room. "And I'm not going to race you."

"Scared?" she grinned.

I couldn't help but laugh. "I don't have a swimsuit with me."

"Neither do I." she said, as if I might not have noticed she was topless. "I bought a new one for this trip. Too bad no one's gonna see it—it's a little much for the Y pool back at home. I got a spray tan too—and did body-pump classes *five days a week*... all for nothing."

She pushed off from the side of the pool, floating backward with a despondent expression.

"It wasn't for nothing. You look great," I assured her, and it was true. The girl was smokin'.

I wasn't sure if she heard me before going under. When she didn't immediately resurface, I stood and walked to the edge of the pool. She was swimming beneath the water toward the deep end.

She hadn't been lying—she actually was a good swimmer, and she could hold her breath a long time. Still, I was nervous. Even sober people could drown, and she was far from sober.

I was going to have to go in.

Great.

Keeping my shorts on, I pulled my shirt over my head and tossed it onto a lounge chair. I dove beneath the surface of the clear pool and swam hard from one side to the other, reaching her as she was on her way to the top for a breath.

When I resurfaced, Red was treading water. The gentle current she was creating caused the water to lap at her upper chest. She looked amazing.

She also looked pissed.

"You're a SEAL, aren't you?"

THREE

Honeymoon Suite

Gray

The question sounded so accusatory and so certain it caught me off guard.

I pretended ignorance. "You mean like a marine mammal? I guess I'm a pretty good swimmer if that's what you're saying."

"You *know* what I mean. You're an operator. You're on the teams. Look at those tattoos... those... muscles."

Now I had to smile. Her face was pure disdain, and her tone, which was meant to be threatening, seemed so incongruous coming from someone who stood barely five-three and sported turquoise toenails with shells painted on them.

"Oh..." I pretended to just get it. "You mean a Navy SEAL. Nah, just a good swimmer who likes to work out. Thanks, though."

She smirked in disbelief.

"Would it be so terrible if I was? I mean, some people think SEALs are brave and heroic—and hot."

"They are," she said. "It's just... my dad was a SEAL."

"No kidding? That's awesome."

"No, it's not." She turned and swam away from me, going to hang from the side.

I followed, gripping the lip of the pool surround and floating beside her. "Did he die on a mission?" I asked softly.

"No. But he was broken when he left the program. His body was a mess—his head was even worse. He wasn't able to handle coming back to mundane family life. He left us when I was eight and died a couple years later."

"I'm sorry to hear that," I said honestly. "It can be a grueling job—so I hear. I mean, that's what I read."

Keeping up the pretense was starting to feel shitty, but what else could I do? The rescue mission in Syria had made international news. Revealing myself and my teammates while we were still so close to the location of the operation was not only forbidden it would be stupid.

I should have hauled my ass out of the pool at that point and dragged her out too, insisting we call it a night.

But I wanted to keep talking to her.

Something about her raw vulnerability attracted me like a moth to a flame. It was probably just as dangerous.

"You know what else is grueling?" I said. "Peddling imprinted sex toys."

I gave her a smile meant to dazzle the sadness and all those inconvenient questions out of her head. "I mean, modeling all those different condom styles is brutal."

Red laughed out loud, a glorious sound that sank into my skin like sunshine.

"You're funny," she said.

"I'm serious. I can demonstrate like, twenty a day or so, but after that, I'm just wiped."

She laughed even louder. "Nobody can get hard twenty times a day."

"Wanna bet? Clearly, I'll have to prove it to you." I sank down, grabbing her ankle and jerking her beneath the surface.

We both came up laughing.

"I didn't see any anacondas while I was under there," she said. "Maybe just a teensy baby water snake."

"Oh, now you're really asking for it." I started to go under again, but she shrieked and kicked away, swimming toward the waterfall.

Naturally, I chased her.

She stopped just short of the cascade and swirled to face me, treading water and smiling.

With her eyes shining and her wet skin glowing in the landscape lights, the curtain of rushing water providing an almost otherworldly backdrop, she was the most beautiful thing I'd ever seen.

Without forethought or permission, the words in my head popped out of my mouth. "You are gorgeous."

I could see from her expression I'd surprised her almost as much as I'd surprised myself. Come-on lines weren't my style. Then again, it hadn't been a come-on. I'd only stated the truth.

"So are you," she whispered.

Then she surged toward me and wrapped her arms around my neck, pulling me under the spray of water with her and kissing me.

Wow. Her breasts were pressed against my chest, soft and full and fucking perfect.

For a few seconds I was so shocked I couldn't think. I just went with it, kissing her back. Her lips were soft and plush, and she tasted sweet, like lemonade and Ouzo.

Ouzo.

Right. She was drunk. And I was stone cold sober.

If we'd *both* been inebriated and decided to go for a little moonlit dip together, it might have been a different story. But I was supposed to be the responsible one here.

I broke the kiss.

She didn't act insulted, only sighed and lay her head on my shoulder. Her arms stayed locked around my neck as I treaded water, trying to hold her up without pressing her against my (inevitable) erection.

"Ready to go?" I asked gently. She seemed to be winding

down, her alcohol-fueled energy burst apparently expended by the swimming.

She nodded against my neck. "I'm so tired. This has been a terrible, awful, no good, very bad day."

"Okay. Hang on."

I swam to the side of the pool, climbing the ladder then hoisting her up and out of the water. Once I was certain she'd stay upright without my support, I grabbed our clothes from the lounger and offered her the red dress.

"There aren't any towels. You're going to have to put it on wet."

She nodded and wiggled herself back into the dress while I pulled on my t-shirt.

"Okay, time to get you in bed." I immediately corrected myself so there was no misunderstanding—on either of our parts. "I mean let's get you back to your suite so *you* can go to bed."

She nodded dreamily and slid her feet back into her shoes, tottering toward the open pool area gate.

I grabbed her purse and caught up, walking beside her in case she lost her balance. "Do you remember where your suite is?"

"It's not a suite," she said. "It's one of those little... little... what do they call those little houses?"

"Bungalows?" I guessed.

She laughed. "That's a funny word. Bongo, bungo, bungalow."

Oh boy. She was out of it, and she was going to be hurting in the morning. I needed to find this bungalow or suite or wherever she was supposed to spend the night—soon—or she was going to pass out on me, and I'd have no choice but to take her back to my room.

That would *not* be ideal.

Thankfully, as we passed the resort's luxurious, free-standing bungalows, something must have looked familiar to her. She headed toward the door of one of them.

"Oh—here it is. My room—suite—my suite-room, home

sweet bungalow home." She laughed again, attempting to swipe the key card in the lock.

After the third failed attempt, I took the card from her hand. "Let me help you."

The lock clicked, and she pushed the door open. When the light from one of the interior lamps hit it, I read the words painted on the outside of the door.

Honeymoon Suite

Oh. I was starting to get the picture.

Red stumbled inside and flung off her strappy heels one at a time. One smacked the wall just below a large mirror. The other somehow flew over her head and right at my face. I grabbed it just before it took out my left eye.

Thank you, sobriety.

The bed was strewn with red rose petals. On a small table next to it, an unopened bottle of champagne swam in a silver bucket of water. I assumed the ice bucket had held ice at one point today.

No wonder she hadn't wanted to return to her room.

Peeking into the dark bathroom, I saw what appeared to be an elaborate white rug then realized it was actually a wedding dress that had been left on the floor.

Well, that confirmed it. What we were dealing with wasn't a party girl but a jilted bride. It made sense. Based on the way she handled her alcohol she wasn't a frequent drinker.

Which concerned me. It wasn't safe for her to be alone in this condition.

She needed to be watched for signs of alcohol poisoning. Blood alcohol content could continue to rise while a person slept. I didn't know what her body weight was exactly, but it couldn't have been that much.

If she was unsupervised, she could choke or slip into a coma.

With that in mind, I stepped farther into the room where Red now lay face-down on the bedspread. Her bare feet hung off the end. She wasn't moving.

Rushing to the bed, I rolled her to her side and confirmed she was breathing. I gave her arm a little shake.

"Red, wake up. Don't go to sleep on me just yet. You need to drink some more water. Do you have any ibuprofen here?"

She rolled to her back, shaking her head from side to side. "Dunno... it might have been in Bryce's bag, but it's... gone. Gone gone gone."

A little whimper and she went quiet again.

I got up and checked the pockets of a small suitcase atop a luggage stand then moved to the bathroom. Several cosmetic products were on the counter along with a tube of toothpaste and a small toiletries bag. I searched through it, coming up with a couple of those travel blister packs containing ibuprofen.

Victory.

Now to get her to take them.

Returning to the bed, I attempted once again to rouse her. "Hey there, wake up. I need you to take this."

"Go away," she said softly in a much clearer tone than I'd expected.

"I can't do that. Not until you've taken this ibuprofen and had some water. Come on now, sit up for me."

"Tired."

"I know you are, and you can sleep as soon as you've taken this. Come on now, Red. Just a couple of sips."

Sliding an arm beneath her upper back, I pulled her up to a sitting position, supporting her slumping body against my own. I ripped the blister pack open with my teeth and shook the small orange tablets out onto my palm, holding it up to her mouth.

"Okay, here we go."

Thankfully, she cooperated, pressing her lower lip against my palm and licking the tablets into her mouth.

Um okay.

Once again I had to tell my dick not to get any big ideas.

It's not happening.

"Okay now take a sip," I urged, and once again, Red cooperated, swallowing several gulps of water.

"Good girl. Now you can go to sleep."

She nodded and reached for the shoulder straps of her dress, tugging them down in an attempt to strip again.

Fuck. I popped up from the bed. "Where are your pj's?" I asked as I ransacked the suitcase.

No answer.

Glancing back over my shoulder, I saw Red had gotten the dress off and turned over, putting the thong panties into full view once again.

God help me.

I whipped back around and resumed my spelunking expedition, moving from the suitcase to the bureau drawers, tearing through them like a twister across a Kansas plain.

"Don't you have *any* fucking pajamas in here?" I yelled in a near panic. It seemed like every garment I picked up was tinier than the last.

"It's my honeymoon," she said in a sleepy slur.

Right. I guessed there wasn't much of a need for pajamas on a honeymoon—not that I'd ever experienced one.

Finally, I grabbed the hem of my own t-shirt and pulled it over my head. It was reasonably clean—I'd changed into it before we'd gone out tonight. There might be some cologne on it, but I hadn't sweated in it or spilled anything on it.

Hell, even if it had been soaked in beer and sporting mustard stains it would have been better than letting her sleep in the (nearly) nude all night.

Because there was no way I could leave her here alone.

Not when there was a good chance those cocktails would be making a second appearance. I'd promised her sister to keep her safe, and that meant staying up all night to watch over her.

That part wouldn't be difficult—I was used to going without sleep. I'd stayed awake for stretches of seventy-two hours at a time during some missions and had remained lucid and alert the whole time. Life and death situations will do that for you.

Getting through *this* night might actually take *more* discipline.

Holding the shirt out in front of me like a talisman, I approached the bed. "Okay, I'm just gonna put this on you so you don't get... cold."

I swallowed hard then coaxed Red to sit up again. It wasn't easy, but I managed to get her head and arms through the appropriate openings in my t-shirt, then I scooped her up and moved her to the top of the bed so I could slide her under the covers.

As I lay her down, she wrapped her arms around my neck. "You're so sweet," she whispered. "Why are you so sweet?"

I was so shocked that for a second, I froze. Then I pried her hands from my shoulders. Quickly, I rolled her to her side, propped a folded pillow behind her back, and pulled the sheet and comforter up to cover her to her neck.

"You get some sleep now. You're going to feel pretty lousy in the morning I'm afraid, but this bed is the best thing for you."

"You come to bed, too," she said then gave me a half-lidded dreamy smile.

She wiggled her arms out from beneath the covers and held them up to me. "It's really cozy in here, and you're really, *really* nice. And cute."

I chuckled at her tone of voice, which was a mix of adorable little girl and full-grown temptress. I wasn't sure if in her altered state she thought I was her fiancé or if she really meant to invite *me* to her bed.

It didn't matter. As lovely as she was, there was nothing tempting about a nearly unconscious woman.

Her stark vulnerability made me feel protective. And while I was no altar boy, I'd never slept with a heavily intoxicated woman or one whose name I didn't know.

All of which meant I would be staying firmly on *this* side of the blankets tonight.

I stroked the backs of my fingers down her impossibly soft cheek, allowing myself only that minimal contact.

"Maybe another time."

She pouted. "You're going to leave, aren't you? Guys always leave."

"I'm not going anywhere," I promised. "You're safe. Sleep now. I'll be right here."

Settling into the incredibly uncomfortable chair in the corner, I watched her dream. Damn, she really was beautiful.

But what a mess.

If we'd met when she hadn't just been left at the altar, I would have been *really* into this woman.

Oh well, maybe it was for the best. My squad and I had a few days off, but it wouldn't be long before I'd be deployed on another mission, and with each one of them, there was always a chance I wouldn't be coming back.

It was better, in my opinion, to have no one to come back to.

FOUR

You've Got Yourself a Deal

Scarlett

Someone was shining a flashlight into my eyes. A strong one.

The red glow boring through my eyelids hurt—everything hurt, actually. My head felt like it had a heartbeat, and each of my limbs weighed at least six hundred pounds.

Cracking my eyelids, I determined the source of the irritating light wasn't a flashlight but an opening in the hotel room curtains. Hot morning sun streamed in, landing on my face and interrupting a heavy sleep marked by strange dreams of a wedding that never happened and a man who *wasn't* my groom spending the night.

I sat up abruptly, causing my brain to slosh in my oversensitive skull and turning my stomach.

It hadn't been a dream.

The wedding *had* been called off—and there had been a man. But apparently he hadn't (thank God) spent the night. Except for the spot where I'd slept, the bed was empty and still neatly tucked.

Looking around the room, I saw no sign of the disconcertingly hot guy from last night.

I had vague memories of vivid green eyes and white teeth that had gleamed in a wolfish smile so charming I'd actually forgotten for whole minutes at a time that yesterday had been the worst day of my life.

But it had.

And this afternoon I'd get on a plane, go home to Minnesota, go back to work, and try my best to forget about the whole thing.

Ugh. I dreaded the looks of sympathy coming my way—or worse, the friends and co-workers who *wouldn't* look at me, who'd find a way to be "busy" when I came into a room because they didn't know what to do or say.

Oh well. I had to face them sooner or later. What else could I do? Stay here in the Greek islands and hide forever?

Not only could I not afford to do that, the prospect of going on my pre-paid tours and dining at beautiful seaside vistas *alone* was enough to get my pitiful hungover ass out of bed and moving toward my suitcase to start packing.

The sound of a toilet flushing made me jump. Were the walls of the hotel room *that* thin?

Wait—this was a bungalow. There *were* no shared walls through which you could hear a neighbor's flushing. Which meant the sound—and the sound of running sink water that followed it—had come from *this* bungalow.

"Oh good, you're awake."

A man had rounded the corner and was now standing—shirtless—in my room.

Not *a* man, *the* man. The one from last night.

He looked even better than I'd remembered, with dark, messy hair and a body so fit and muscular it would have made me drool —if I hadn't been too dehydrated to produce saliva at the moment.

His eyes were arresting, and his face as a whole gave me serious young-John-Stamos vibes. Yes, I'd binge-watched every episode of Full House when I was younger—not sorry.

"I used one of the complimentary toothbrushes in there. Hope you don't mind," he said cheerfully. "I figured since Bryce wouldn't be using it, it was fair game. Unfortunately, he didn't leave any shirts, so whenever you're feeling up to it, I'm gonna have to ask for that one back."

I looked down at myself, only now noticing I was wearing an unfamiliar, and heavenly smelling—*good God what was that amazing scent?*—man's t-shirt.

And not much else.

I pulled up the hem and confirmed that yes, I was still wearing the ridiculously expensive, sequin-embellished "bridal thong" Maddie had given me at my shower.

"Yes, they're still on," he said.

I looked back up at the grinning guy.... what was his name? Fox? No, that wasn't it, though I'd heard that word at some point last night, and it was completely appropriate when it came to this guy.

Wolf. That's what it was. Also appropriate, considering the look on his face as he stared at the place where I'd drawn up the shirt for a panty-check.

I dropped it and tugged the hem down in a futile attempt to cover more of my thighs.

"I know. I just... um... did we...?"

I'd never had to ask a question like this before, having never been roofied—and never having drugged *myself* to the point of oblivion as I apparently had last night.

"Did you... sleep over?"

His smile widened. "I did."

My heart plummeted then fell further as he added, "But there was no sleeping involved."

"Oh my goodness, I can't believe I—"

Wolf interrupted, "At least on *my* part. You... were out like a light about five minutes after getting to the room. I thought you'd be up and down all night worshipping the porcelain god, but you actually did pretty well. How's your stomach this morning, by the way?"

My hand came involuntarily to cover it. "Fine. Well, not fine, but I'll live." I paused. "I'm confused. You stayed here last night."

"Yes."

"And you said you didn't sleep."

"That's right."

"But I passed out right after getting here?"

"You did."

"And we didn't..." I rolled my hand through the air, hoping he'd get what I was asking without my having to verbalize it.

"Watch a movie? Play cards?"

"You know, have... sex." I whispered the last word, as if that would somehow lessen the nightmare scenario currently playing out.

He laughed. "No. We didn't. Maybe it's just me, but the idea of screwing someone who has no ability to participate because they're *out cold* just isn't that appealing... no matter how beautiful and charming they might be when conscious."

My heart returned to its proper anatomical position, and I went to my suitcase, gathering some clothing with the intention of changing in the bathroom and giving this apparent Good Samaritan his shirt back.

Turning to face him again, I looked at him with new eyes. "Why did you stay? You must have been tired."

He smiled. "Not really. I'm used to getting by on little to no sleep when I have to."

"But you *didn't* have to," I argued. "You don't even know me. And I'm sure I was grossly unattractive last night in my drunken stupor."

Wolf laughed. "I wouldn't say 'grossly.'"

"Oh God." I covered my eyes with one hand.

"No seriously, you were funny." He shrugged. "You were having a bad day and self-medicating. We've all been there. Besides, your sister ordered me to watch over you, and she's scary as hell."

Now I laughed, thinking of my five-foot-one sister waddling around with a belly the size of a small country. "Oh yes. Terrifying. A total badass."

"A real Terminator. She came by this morning, by the way, to check on you and let you know she and her family were checking out."

"She knocked on the door?" I asked, horrified. "And you let her in?"

"Should I not have? I saw her through the security port and didn't want her to be worried."

Collapsing back onto the bed, I covered my face with my hands—which were full of skimpy resort wear and yet another pair of honeymoon panties.

"What did she say?" I asked through the fabric. Then I looked up. "Oh no—Joey and Trina didn't see me like this, did they?"

"No—they didn't come in. Don't worry. I assured Maddie you were fine, that I was planning to stick around and keep an eye on you while you slept it off—and that these..." He held up his hands in front of him like a surgeon who'd just done a pre-op scrub. "... would be getting nowhere near you."

There was a knock at the door. Wolf spun around and went to open it, speaking over his shoulder.

"I took the liberty of ordering some room service. I figured you might not be up to going out to a restaurant this morning, but it's important to get some food in your stomach. Best way to get over that gnarly hangover you're rocking. And I..." He opened the door. "...am starving."

We were both quiet as the room service waiter efficiently set up the breakfast cart then went back to the door. Wolf tipped him, and he left.

"I'll pay you back," I said.

He grinned and lifted the silver dome from one of the plates, snagging a pastry. "Don't worry about it. You paid for this over-priced resort breakfast—or maybe your fiancé did."

"Former fiancé," I corrected. "The room *is* in his name, and it's on his credit card, but actually I'm not sure who's going to pay for it now."

"Are you kidding? He should *definitely* pay," Wolf said.

He lifted the dome from my plate and an extra plate on the side of the cart. "In fact, I should have ordered the two-hundred-dollar-per-gram caviar for you."

My eyes bugged. "*Wow.* This is a lot of food. Why did you order so much?"

"Wolves have big appetites," he said, and proceeded to shovel astounding quantities of breakfast foods into his beautiful mouth.

After coming up for air, he said, "I was hungry last night when we left the bar, but I was afraid to leave you to go get some food."

That shamed me. "Thank you for staying—I'm not sure if I've said that yet."

"You're welcome."

"I really do want to do something to repay you," I said. "I've got some cash in my purse—it's in euros, and I won't be needing it since I'm leaving this afternoon."

He swiped the air with a big hand. "Nah, don't worry about it. I'm surprised you're leaving today. Old Bryce didn't spring for a very long honeymoon."

"Well, it was supposed to be a week, but... you know."

His eyebrows pulled together, and he gave me a compassionate look. "Right. It really sucks that he bailed on you. I'm sorry."

"Thanks. Yeah, well, what are you gonna do?"

I let out a helpless, humorless laugh. "The worst part is I've got all these tickets for museum tours, two island-hopping ferry passes—non-refundable, of course. You should take those, too. You and one of your friends could go see the 'wonders of Ancient Greece.' *Somebody* should."

For a few minutes, Wolf chewed his food quietly. Then he said, "Why don't you stay and see them?"

"By myself?"

"Would it be worse than going home right now?"

I had to think for a minute. "Maybe. I don't know. Maybe

not. No, actually I think it would."

We finished breakfast, chatting lightly about the resort, the food, the amazing climate. I *would* be incredibly sad to leave it all after waiting so long to see it.

"What time does your convention stuff start today?" I asked.

"What?" Wolf looked confused for a second. "Oh—the convention. Yeah, it's kind of, uh... winding down. The main stuff is over. We're just sort of in the... debriefing stage now. What time's your flight?"

"Three-forty-five. I'm gonna go ahead and get in the shower I guess and just head to the airport early. All my family and friends have left already."

Wolf was quiet another minute, chewing the last of his omelette. "I could go on the tours with you."

I put my fork down and swallowed hard to keep from choking. "What?"

"I could go with you." He lifted his shoulders and let them fall in a *no big deal* gesture. "Or we could just skip the tours and explore on our own. I've never seen the wonders of Ancient Greece. I've never seen the other islands. You said you had two non-refundable ferry passes, dinner reservations for two, two of everything. It would be a shame to let them go to waste. Instead of heading back home to—where'd you say you're from?"

"Minnesota."

"Instead of going home to Minnesota... you could stay here and enjoy your honeymoon. With me."

My belly flipped in an acrobatic move worthy of Circ du Soliel. "I don't know. It seems kind of..."

"Fun? Awesome? Adventurous? Exciting?"

"Weird."

"Why is it weird? Come on, Red, think about it."

He put his elbows on the table and leaned toward me.

"Why does that dickwad get to ruin your wedding day *and* your vacation? Whether you want me around or not, *you* should stay and have a good time. It'll be the perfect revenge against that asshole of a former fiancé. Order the caviar. Order the most expensive bottles of wine on the menu. Have the time of your life and charge everything to the room."

My breath caught in my chest as I tried to picture it. *Could* I really do that? The tiny hairs on my arms and the back of my neck lifted.

"But I don't know you. You don't know me. How do you know I'm not crazy?" I asked.

"You're not. I'm a good judge of character. And even if you are, a little crazy now and then can be a good thing."

"How do I know *you're* not some con artist who's going to take advantage of me?"

He raised one eyebrow and tossed a significant glance at the bed where I'd slept then gestured to the chair where he'd slept.

"We *don't* know each other very well," he said. "But what do you have to lose? If you're not having a good time, you can tell me to get lost and hop a plane back to the heartland."

The sound of a text notification had me reaching for my phone. It was from Maddie.

-Are you up? You okay?

I texted back.

-I'll live. Eating something now. Wolf ordered room service. He made me take some ibuprofen and drink water last night or it would be worse.

-Good. Is he still there? He. Is. So. Hot.

-He is. I mean yes, he's here.

I paused before typing the next words.

He wants me to stay in Greece and spend the week with him.

My sister's reply came a few seconds later.

-DO IT! You deserve a fling after what you've been through.

I put the phone away without responding.

"Sorry," I said to Wolf. "That was my sister checking on me."

"And what does the Terminator think you should do?"

"She's not sure," I lied.

"When I don't know what to do, I go with my gut," he said. "It's never steered me wrong."

"Oh really? And what's your gut telling you right now?"

The wolfish grin returned. "That your sister told you to go for it. *And* that we're gonna have one hell of a time together. What about your gut, Red? What's it saying?"

"Why do you keep calling me Red?"

His face brightened in a grin. "Your dress—from last night. You said, 'no names.' That's why you're calling me Wolf. You don't remember?"

"It sounds vaguely familiar." Much of last night was a blur. But I *did* remember not wanting to exchange names with the guys. It wasn't like we were going to form any lasting bonds at the resort bar on my super-sad non-wedding night.

"We can exchange real first names if it'll make you feel better," he offered.

"No," I blurted. "We don't need to do that."

So far, I'd done nothing but embarrass myself in front of this guy. I'd gotten blind-drunk, skinny-dipped with him, then stripped in front of him and passed out.

As I was not exactly my *best self* right now, anonymity was my friend.

Besides, what was the point? As nice as he seemed to be, I'd never see this guy again.

Which is why his suggestion that we spend my non-honeymoon together was actually kind of brilliant.

Maybe Maddie was right. A week of sun, fun—and possibly getting to know that incredible inked body *much* better—and my broken heart would be on the road to recovery.

Or at least approaching the on-ramp.

At the very least it was a great way to delay dealing with reality.

I still wasn't sure what my gut was saying, but my mouth said, "Okay, "Wolf," you've got yourself a deal. No names, no strings, one week of non-honeymoon fun, and then we'll go our separate ways."

He smiled and extended his hand for a shake. "Deal... with one addendum. If at the end of the week, we've fallen madly in love, I reserve the right to ask for your number—and your real name."

"That—is not going to happen," I assured him. "You should go back to your hotel and get dressed. Our first tour starts at noon."

FIVE

Flesh and Blood

Gray- Three years later (Today)

"You really shouldn't have troubled yourself," Mrs. Hood said as she watched me change a lightbulb in one of her Baccarat crystal chandeliers.

It seemed like every time I was here, another light in the old house had gone out. Finally, I'd made a trip to the hardware store and bought some LED bulbs guaranteed to last twenty years. I was in the process of replacing them all.

"I could have hired a handyman. Or done it myself," she said. "These old legs still have some life in them yet."

"It's no trouble," I assured her.

At eighty-nine years old, there was no way Mrs. Hood should be climbing ladders, and as a home security expert with Viridian Security, I shuddered at the idea of her inviting random strangers into her Eastport Bay mansion.

Not only did she have a houseful of priceless art and antiques she was physically helpless.

I'd been hired to install new security systems for her collection of old masters' paintings, Flemish tapestries, eighteenth century Qianlong Dynasty porcelain, and antique French furniture, but

I'd finished the job months ago. Since then, I'd been checking on her frequently to make sure she was okay.

"Well, you deserve an extra piece of blueberry pie," she said. "Had it delivered fresh from Nooky's this morning. Best pie in town."

"You're spoiling me now. You know how much I like sweets." I stepped off the ladder and grinned at the diminutive white-haired woman, elegant even in a pair of cuffed boyfriend jeans and a pink-and-white striped button down.

She patted my stomach. "You need some spoiling—and fattening up. Besides, I'm bribing you to stay around a little longer. I need you to help me write out some checks for my bills. My hands are so shaky it takes me about an hour for each check and still looks like chicken scratch. It's embarrassing."

"When are you going to sign up for online bill pay?" I asked.

"When pigs fly," she said baldly and let out a loud laugh.

I followed her to the enormous kitchen, where the checkbook and pie waited on a modestly sized wooden dining table. Serving myself a big piece, I dug in and watched Mrs. Hood leaf through her bills.

"It's getting to where I can hardly read these," she said. "Thank you for helping me, son."

"I'm glad to do it, but I feel kind of funny messing around with your financial stuff," I confessed.

"Pish tosh. You already know I'm rich. If I can trust you with my Renoir and my Colonial silver collection, then I think I can trust you with my checking account. Most of my money is in stocks anyway, though there is quite a lot of cash still upstairs in the safe in Stuart's old office."

I cringed and held out my hands. "Don't—I mean, you shouldn't tell people that stuff."

"I'm not telling 'people.' I'm telling you."

She was right of course—she could trust me. But still, I worried about her. There were plenty of people who'd be only too willing to take advantage of her trusting nature and vulnerable state.

Why was someone as kind as she was—and in increasingly fragile health—so alone in the world? I knew she'd had one son who'd died some time ago and her husband had passed away last year, but surely there were other relatives.

"Mrs. Hood," I began.

"Victoria," she corrected. "If you refuse to call me 'Vivi' then you must at least call me Victoria."

I smiled. "Victoria, I'm wondering if it might be a good time for you to ask your family to step in and help? Not that I mind. You know I don't, but there comes a time in all our lives when it's good to have relatives nearby."

"I'm afraid I don't have any. I've outlived my brother and sister. Their children and grandchildren live on the West Coast and barely know me. You're the closest thing I have to family now. You're like a son to me."

My heart contracted in a brief pulse, and I gave her a warm smile.

"Thank you. I'm very fond of you, too."

That was an understatement. Over the past few months, I'd come to love the old dame. She was funny and sweet and sharp as one of the MK 3 knives I used to carry as a SEAL. I'd told her on a couple of occasions that if she'd been sixty years younger, I would have proposed.

"You mentioned a granddaughter before," I said. "Where is she?"

"I wish I knew."

"She's missing?"

"Not exactly. I'm sure she's fine... wherever she is. We became estranged when my son and her mother got divorced," she explained. "My husband Stuart was... well, he wasn't the easiest person. He had certain ideas in his head about what our son should do with his life. When Charles decided to go into the military instead of join him in the family publishing business, Stuart was livid. Then Charles married a woman Stuart considered "beneath" the family pedigree. He wouldn't even go to the wedding. Stuart died without ever meeting our granddaughter, the stubborn old coot."

"But you did. You told me she was a lot like you."

"Oh yes. I used to think so. Now I might not recognize Scarlett if she passed me on the street. It's been so long. I haven't seen her since she was a little girl. I used to fly down to Florida to spend time with her whenever Stuart would let me get away. I wrote letters and sent birthday cards. They all started coming back marked 'Address Unknown—Unable to Forward,' and their phone rang and rang with no answer."

Her face brightened. "Perhaps someone at Viridian could look into it for me? I'll bet they could find her. I would so love to see her again before I die."

The words sent an unpleasant jolt through me. I'd noticed Victoria slowing down a bit since we'd met. Living alone probably hadn't helped, but the fact was she *was* elderly. I hated the thought of her not being around anymore.

I also hated the idea of inviting this callous, uncaring granddaughter back into her life. Yes, the family rift had occurred a long time ago, but Scarlett had to be almost thirty years old now—plenty old enough to reach out to the grandmother who'd been so good to her during the early years of her life.

I had a feeling what we found when we went looking—and we *would* find her—wasn't going to be pretty.

Anyone who'd leave this sweet old lady alone at the mercy of all the vultures out there had to be one selfish bitch.

Still, I couldn't tell Victoria "no."

"Of course. I'll take care of it. But no more talk about dying. You'll probably outlive us all—as long as you stay off ladders."

After all the checks were written out and sealed in envelopes addressed to their respective recipients, Victoria wrote one more. She handed it to me.

"What's this? Did we forget one?" I looked around for another bill envelope.

"That's for you—for your help today."

Immediately I pushed it back to her. "No way. I don't want it. I don't need it."

"Let me give you something, Gray. Please. It'll make me feel better. You spend so much time here doing things for me."

I stood and backed away from the table. "I appreciate it, but no thank you. I promise you, Victoria. I *don't* need the money."

My elderly friend walked me to the door. "You know, it's about time you made a family of your own to take care of."

"I haven't found the right girl yet."

That was my pat answer. The truth was, I wasn't sure there *was* a right girl for me. I dated women, but no one really held my interest. I had more fun with Victoria than with any of them.

Besides, my work and travel with Viridian kept me busy, and there was also the consideration of how much time my secret side gig took up.

It would be hard to explain to a girlfriend or wife why I'd often stay out all night long or disappear for days at a time.

"Besides, I'm not ready," I told Victoria. "I wouldn't be good for anybody right now."

"Pish tosh. You'd make an amazing husband and father, but if you want me to be able to dance at your wedding, you'd better get cracking on it," she said and winked at me.

I laughed out loud. I really was crazy about this woman, and I'd be damned if I'd let *anyone* hurt her... not even her own flesh and blood.

SIX

Big Girl Panties

Scarlett

"My mom said she had a really good time," Kevin said, shifting from foot to foot. "Thanks for being so nice to her."

"Oh, no problem." I backed toward the door of my apartment. "I hope you... two... have a good night."

My blind date took a half-step forward, collapsing the distance I'd (purposely) put between us. "I know she said she was sorry she couldn't walk you to the door with me, you know, because of the stairs—but I'm glad because if she was here, I couldn't do... *this*."

My date—my *thirty-year-old* date from a soon-to-be-deleted dating app—made an awkward lunge toward my mouth. I swerved to avoid the collision.

"Kevin... I really appreciate you inviting me out tonight and sharing all your top strategies for Clash of Clans... but I don't think we're a good fit."

"Mom doesn't come on *all* my dates with me," he assured me. "Just the first five or six. To make sure the girl is, you know, quality."

"I understand. And it's nice that your mom cares so much,

but I think three people on a date might be one too many for me. Good night."

I started to open the door to my apartment.

"Wait. What if it was just the two of us next time?" he said. "Could you give me just one more chance? I like you. Mom will be mad, but I think if it was just the two of us, we could have fun. You know?"

His face was so hopeful. And he *had* expanded my mind when it came to gaming apps. Also, I hadn't had any first dates in the past year that were measurably better than this one.

Unfortunately.

"I don't see why not." I sighed. "Let me check my schedule, and I'll get back to you."

I stepped inside, shut and locked the door, and heaved a long breath before walking into the living room.

My roommate Julianna was sitting on the couch with her feet on the ottoman, watching TV and stroking her cat, Hemsworth.

She swung her face in my direction and threw me a *kill me now* look.

"What?"

"You *know* what," she said. "'I don't see why not?' I'm surprised you got the words out past the yawn. Why don't you just tell the poor guy you're not interested and let him move on?"

I bristled. "I'm interested in Kevin." At her raised brow smirk, I corrected myself. "Sort of. I mean, I'm not *not* interested. He's very polite. He knows a *lot* about Clash of Clans. And he has a very... supportive... family."

"Why do you waste your time on go-nowhere dates with guys like Kevin, or what is that little guy's name who looks like he's still a college sophomore?"

"Henry. He doesn't look *that* young."

She rolled her eyes. "How many times has he been carded when you've gone out?"

"Every time," I admitted. "But when he's in his fifties that's going to be a good thing."

"Right. The point is, you'd rather waste your time going out with guys you have *zero interest in* than take a chance on a hot guy you might actually like."

"I like Kevin and Henry. They're... nice."

"Nice. You need to put on your big-girl panties and take some risks, Scarlett, or you're going to *nice* yourself into spending your life with the world's most boring guy. I've never seen anyone less excited than you are after you go on dates with these guys. That's not what you really want."

I plopped onto the couch beside her and pulled Hemsworth into my lap for a snuggle. He was a fluffy white Himalayan with blue eyes and the cutest little flat pink nose.

"And what do I really want, pray tell?"

"Besides to steal my cat? You want what all of us want—someone who's your equal, someone who's a challenge but also an ooey gooey delicious cinnamon roll. You want someone to thrill you."

"What I *want*—other than to steal your cat—is someone honest—completely transparent, someone I can trust to stick around instead of bolt for the door the first chance he gets. If that means he's a little boring, then so be it."

"Well in that case you're on the right track."

She held her arms out, and Hemsworth left my lap for hers. Even he didn't want to stick around.

"Neither Kevin nor Henry would *ever* leave you because they'd literally have no other options," she said. "And yet... you haven't gotten serious with either of them—or with *anyone* since Bryce."

I held up my hand palm out. "I don't want to talk about Bryce. I thought *he* was nice and safe—and look where that got me. That's why I'm taking my time, making sure I'm sure I'm sure. You have to date someone for at least a year before you can even *begin* to crack the surface of who they are, you know. Two years is better. Even then you never know—they could still end up deciding you're not worth staying for."

"If you say so," Julianna said.

"I do. Trust me, I know."

After Bryce I'd come to doubt my ability to recognize a wolf in sheep's clothing. It didn't help that I'd followed up *that* mistake by immediately making another one—agreeing to spend my non-honeymoon week with someone who actually *called* himself Wolf.

Admittedly, it had been an amazing week.

The problem came afterward, when I couldn't stop thinking about him and literally could do nothing about it.

Which led to my other dating rule—no casual sex.

Clearly, I was one of those people who just couldn't handle it. After only a week with Wolf, I had become unnaturally attached to him—or at least to his memory.

Even though we'd agreed not to exchange names or contact info unless we fell madly in love, it hurt to wake up one morning toward the end of the week and find him gone, nothing but a short note left on the pillow to remember him by.

Did I keep it? Yes, but only as a reminder of how foolish I'd been.

Anyway, the no-names policy was probably for the best. I hadn't been myself that week, wild and uninhibited and living out every sexual fantasy I'd ever had with a guy I barely knew.

Though I couldn't help revisiting those moments of forbidden pleasure from time to time, it kind of embarrassed me to think of them now. That week had been a feast for the senses. Since then, I'd been on a romantic starvation diet.

"Isn't dating supposed to be *fun*, though?" Julianna asked. "Isn't there supposed to be, you know, chemistry?"

"It can be sometimes, sure," I agreed.

Though I had no idea what Wolf's real first and last name were, his middle name had *definitely* been Chemistry. I'd felt it that first night in the hotel swimming pool, and it had only gotten stronger and more addictive as the week had gone on.

"But that's not what you want in the long term," I said.

"Chemistry, the 'spark,' the shivers—all those things are your body's response to danger—they're warning signs. Besides, that's not real life. *Real* life can't be that exciting and fun and pleasurable."

"Okay then, if you really want a spark-less, shiver-less, unsweetened oatmeal life, then there really isn't a reason not to go out with Kevin again."

"Exactly," I said, feeling like I'd somehow won the argument without actually winning.

"Oh—I picked up the mail." Julianna gestured toward the kitchen counter. "You got something."

I got up to go look at it. "You mean actual mail, not just junk mail?"

"Well, you got that, too, but one of them looks legit. It was Fed-Exed from Rhode Island."

I picked up the envelope. "That's weird. I don't know anyone in Rhode Island."

Once I had. Though I'd never been to the state, my grandmother used to visit from Rhode Island many years ago.

She was no longer in my life, though—yet another person who'd "loved" me then left. I had no idea if she was even still living. Besides, the return address had a man's name above it.

"Gray Lupine. I wonder what this is?"

Ripping the sealing strip from the cardboard envelope, I pulled out the neatly folded paper inside and began to read the typed words.

Dear Ms. Hood,

I'm not sure if you'll even care about this information, but your paternal grandmother, Victoria Hood, is in failing health. She has asked me to find you and request that you visit. Against my better judgement, as her friend, I am carrying out her request.

If you have any wish to reconnect with her, I'd advise you to arrange travel soon. I've enclosed a note from her as well as a check from my employer, Viridian Security, to ease the cost of airfare from Minnesota to Rhode Island. If you should need any further help making arrangements, contact Viridian at the number I've provided. I've also included Mrs. Hood's address and phone number.

It was signed simply with his name, Gray Lupine—no "sincerely," or "best wishes" and certainly no "yours truly."

I searched the Fed Ex mailer and found another piece of paper. This one written on light blue stationery with an imprint of red poppies.

I loved poppies.

The words were written in a light, shaky scrawl, but with a bit of squinting, I could make them out.

Dearest Scarlett,

I have written so many letters to you over the years. I am hopeful this one will actually reach you and find you in good health and happiness. I'm not sure if you even remember me—it's been so long since we've seen each other.

By now you're an adult with your own life, a job and perhaps a family to take care of. But if you could find the time, I would love for you to visit me. Not to be morbid, but I'm not sure how much time I have left, and I would really love to see your sweet face again.

There is so much for us to catch up on and talk about.

With much love,

Your grandmother, Victoria Hood

I stood there staring at the words, the paper fluttering in my shaking hand.

Julianna came into the kitchen. "Wow, look at your face. What is it? I can't tell if it's good or bad. Did you win a million dollars or something? Is someone dead?"

I looked up from the baffling letter. "No. It's from my grandmother. She wants to see me."

"Is this the grandmother you haven't heard from since you were ten?"

I nodded. "Yeah. I'm kind of in shock. I really thought she wanted nothing to do with me."

"Why would you think that?"

"Mom said my grandfather disapproved of my parents' marriage, and I assume my grandmother felt the same. She visited a few times when I was little and lived in Florida. I remember a few birthday cards with money in them. But after my dad left and mom and I moved here, I never heard from her again. My mom said it was for the best, that she didn't want me around someone who'd rejected us."

"It doesn't sound like she rejected you if she came to visit you. It's not exactly a short trip from Rhode Island to Florida," Julianna pointed out.

I shrugged. "I don't know. That's what my mom said. I was so young it's hard to remember. I do have a few memories of my grandmother—watching fireworks with her. She took me to Disneyworld once when she came down, and I think we went to some kind of botanical gardens where they had a butterfly habitat. One visit, she gave me some oil paints and these little canvases and tried to teach me to paint."

"I didn't know you painted."

"I don't. I was never any good at it. I think she was, though." I dropped the letter to the counter. "I don't know what to do with this. Does she really expect me to hop on a plane and fly out to Rhode Island?"

"Could be fun," Julianna said. "I hear New England is beautiful this time of year. You never take any time off—you must have a ton of vacation days stored up. You're way overdue for a trip, and you said you miss the ocean."

"But how awkward will it be to show up at my grandmother's door after, what's it been... almost twenty years?"

"So bring a little gift basket or something, flowers, local delicacies, some of your world-famous cookies."

"I'd hardly call them world-famous," I said.

"Well, Minnesota-famous at least. You sell out every day

during the state fair. They *could* be world famous if you'd expand your business past a few grocery stores and a booth at the fair. I bet you could make a living at it. Then you could leave that bookkeeping job you hate at your stepdad's company."

"I can't leave. David counts on me. Plus starting a business takes a lot of money—which I don't have."

Another obstacle occurred to me. "What am I thinking? I can't even go on vacation. Who'll do the bookkeeping while I'm gone?"

"They can get by for a week or two without you," Julianna said. "If they're really stuck, I can help out. I'm working the dinner shift at the Hot Dish for the foreseeable future—I could stop by Mixitall during the day. It might be nice to actually put my accounting degree to work for something other than balancing my checkbook."

"And as far as money to start a business, do what everyone else does—get a loan," she said, like it was the easiest thing in the world.

"I can't. I have too much student loan debt still."

"You never know. Have you even tried?"

"No." I went to the sink and started washing out the coffee cups accumulated there. "Even if I could, It's too much risk. What if the business expansion flopped? Then I'd be in even more debt and have no job."

Julianna picked up a dish towel and started drying the newly cleaned cup I handed her. "Well maybe old Grandma is loaded. You could be like, secretly a Kardashian or something."

"I seriously doubt it. Anyway, that's not why I'm going. I don't want *anything* from her," I said.

She stopped drying. "You've decided to go?"

"Yes. Maybe? I don't know. She sounded like it was really important to come soon."

"You should," Julianna said. "It'll be good for you—maybe she could tell you stuff about your dad, about what he was like before all the... you know. She's his mom after all. And she's your blood relative, too. You don't have many of those."

Turning my back to the sink, I leaned on it and dropped my head back to look at the ceiling. "That's true. But what if it's awful?'

"What if it's not?"

"What if it *is*?" I couldn't understand Julianna's optimistic expression. "If my mom wasn't good enough for the Hood family, how could I be?"

"If it's awful, then have some tea and crumpets with the old bag and get the hell out of there," she said. "Go see something new, do some things you've never done. You're always saying your life is boring. You could explore New England, tour the Eastport Bay mansions."

She waggled her eyebrows. "And meet another condom salesman."

My face hot, I turned back to the sink in search of something else to keep my hands busy. "I never should have told you that story. And he wasn't a condom salesman. He was a promotional products salesman who just happened to have condoms in his product line."

"And a very impressive 'floor model' to demonstrate them with," she reminded me—as if I needed a reminder.

My blush grew hotter. "I definitely never should have told you about *that*. Believe me, the last thing I want is to have a fling with another player. I'm lucky I made it out of that bad decision in one piece—I *won't* be repeating it."

SEVEN

Too Much Trouble

Gray

"Glad I'm not a player," I said to Wilder as the two of us sat watching the afternoon session of the New England Nauticals' summer training camp.

On the field in front of us, men of massive size and strength crashed into each other under the blazing summer sun while on the next section of the field, others ran wind sprints in their pads and helmets.

I was sweating just sitting still on the grassy hillside overlooking the summer practice fields located in Eastport Bay. The team's games were played at their stadium in the state capital of Providence, about a half-hour's drive away.

"Yeah, I don't miss this part," Wilder said. "Though looking back on it, training camp two-a-days were nothing compared to BUD/S training. Whenever my brothers give me shit about declining to go through the NFL draft, I politely invite them to see how long they'd last during basic underwater demolition training."

We both laughed. Wilder had played college football but decided to join the Navy and become a SEAL instead of going pro in the sport.

All three of his younger brothers were big bastards and tough as hell, but still, to make it through SEAL training, you had to want it more than anything—and have a brain that could override the torturous twenty-four-week assault on the body.

Out of forty thousand Navy recruits each year, only six percent qualified to even begin the training program. Out of those, only one in four completed it.

Still, these Nauticals' players were no joke. Two of Wilder's brothers were on the team. Presley had been drafted by the Nauties, as they were nicknamed, right out of college. Dylan had just been traded from Tampa.

"Your parents have to be thrilled about this," I said. "Three of you living in Rhode Island now."

Wilder nodded. "Oh yeah. My mom is back to cooking massive amounts of food every Sunday trying to lure us over there, and Dad bought season tickets. All we need now is to get Merc here and they'll have to change the team's name to the New England Lowes."

His middle brother Mercury, Merc for short, played for San Francisco. He was as fast on the field as his name suggested, a wide receiver with an all-time regular season touchdown reception record approaching those of Randy Moss and Jerry Rice.

Word had it he was even faster *off* the field. Honestly, none of the Lowe brothers were hurting for female attention.

All of them were tall, jacked, and good-looking, and all of them had been named after classic rock musicians—except for Wilder, who as the firstborn had been given his father's name.

Reportedly he'd lived up to it when he was younger, though now that he was married to Jessica, he'd proclaimed himself "tame."

The hillside around us and the stands below were packed with Nauties fans dressed in jerseys or t-shirts bearing the team's logo, a heavily muscled sailor wearing a "let's enjoy some shore leave" expression.

The local fans were just getting to know Dylan, but they

already loved Pres—especially the women. I couldn't help but notice the proliferation of females, young and old, in attendance.

Some of them held signs with Presley's name on them. One read, "Ready to get Nautie anytime you are."

Another wore a shirt with his picture, and the words "Nautie by Nature" beneath it. A few had those blow-up pics of his head, which they held up while screaming declarations of love anytime he ran over to this side of the field.

During one of the breaks, Pres looked up to our position and gestured to the two of us, motioning for us to come down to the fence separating the field from the crowd.

As we reached him, he stretched an arm over the fence to clasp hands with his brother then with me.

"You candy-ass SEALs come to see how the real men do it?" Pres teased.

"When I see some real men, I'll let you know," Wilder said, and the brothers laughed.

"You guys are looking good," I said.

"Thanks man. It's always hard at the start of camp after a summer off. But I think we've got a good team this year."

"How's Dylan doing so far?" Wilder asked.

"Great. He's learning the plays fast, putting in the full effort on the field—of course you know him. The coaches love him."

"Good, good," Wilder said. "I can't wait to see a game. It'll be almost like being in the back yard on Fairfax Street again."

"Only we won't have *you* there to run circles around our asses and make us look like untalented hacks," Presley said.

It was clear he idolized his oldest brother, and Wilder had just as much affection for him.

A player jogged toward us, grinning ear to ear.

"Speaking of untalented hacks…" Pres said.

Laughing, Dylan Lowe stopped running and swaggered up to the fence. "You guys here looking for autographs? You'll have to wait till after the practice—and get in line behind *them*."

He tossed his head toward the flocks of women in the stands.

"No thanks—I've seen your handwriting," Wilder said. "How you feeling? Adjusted to the new system yet?"

"Not gonna lie—it's a lot. The Nauticals' play book's as thick as a dictionary. I'll get it though. I'm just so fucking happy to be here, you know?"

Turning his attention to me, he said, "Gray, it's good to see you man. How's the security business treating you?"

"I can't complain," I said.

It was true. I was lucky to have a job where I could actually use some of the skills I'd acquired as a SEAL. I'd been the one in my platoon who went in first to disable a security system or conquer a particularly challenging lock.

When I left the military, I wasn't qualified to do much in the civilian world—unless I wanted to embark on a life of crime as a cat burglar. But then Wilder had started Viridian and hired me and the rest of our platoon to work for him in security.

Some of the guys worked as bodyguards for celebrities and other high-risk targets, while I used my considerable knowledge of home and commercial security equipment—and the tricks burglars and other home invaders used to defeat it—to help our clients protect their homes and businesses.

It wasn't glamorous like a career in pro football, and it wasn't exactly my passion, but it was good, honest work, and I liked the feeling of helping people.

"You guys gonna stick around till the end of practice?" Dylan asked.

"Sure," Wilder said. "Wanna go grab a bite afterward?"

"Definitely."

"That'd be great. We'll have a couple hours before evening meetings," Presley said. "Meet you back here in about an hour."

Wilder and I walked back up the hill to the general area where we'd been sitting. As we did, I noticed several sets of female eyes following us. They were probably wondering how we knew Pres and Dylan and trying to figure out how to get invited along on our dinner plans.

Wilder must have noticed them, too. He smirked. "Lots of very *enthusiastic* fans here today."

"Oh yeah. Plenty of number eight-seven jerseys. And I'm sure it won't take long until Dylan has his share of 'Nautie girlfriends' as well."

"No doubt." After a pause Wilder asked, "So, how's *your* girlfriend doing?"

I looked over at his expectant expression, confused. "I don't have a girlfriend."

He laughed. "I'm talking about Victoria Hood. You spend so much time with her, I thought maybe you two had made it official."

Now I laughed. "Well, she's a hottie alright, but I'm keeping my options open. I'm not quite ready to settle down and have babies with her."

"You should, you know," Wilder said in all seriousness. "I mean about the settling down part—Jess and I are still working on the baby thing. Marriage is the best."

"That's because you finally get to have sex with the girl you've been lusting over for half your life. Oh, and she happens to be a super-hot popstar."

"I can't argue there, but it's more than that," Wilder said. "I mean, not to get all deep and everything, but it's pretty unbelievable to wake up next to your best friend every morning, to have a house that actually feels like a home, and to know that someone has your back not just now but for the rest of your life."

I looked out over the field, only marginally paying attention to the action. "Yeah, well, I'm happy for you man—truly—but I never had anyone like that. I'm starting to doubt I'll *ever* feel that way about anyone. I'm not even sure I'm capable of it. I think something's wrong with me."

Wilder sounded concerned. "A lot of vets get that, you know. Emotional detachment can be a sign of PTSD. Have you thought of seeing a therapist? Mine helped me a lot."

Looking down at the grass beside me, I plucked a strand. "It's not that. I mean, yeah, after what happened in Iraq and then the trial, I was pretty fucked up right at first. But I saw someone and learned some coping mechanisms. I'm doing great with that actually."

At the suggestion of my therapist, I'd taken up an old hobby when my career as a SEAL ended. Well, it had been *more* than a hobby when I was young. I'd dreamed of becoming a great artist, of making an impact on the world with my painting.

For various reasons—including lack of tuition money—I'd shifted gears, left art school, and gone into the military, leaving those old dreams behind.

Now I used art to help me get in touch with what I was thinking and feeling, to process it all in a way talking about it couldn't seem to do. I'd discovered that when I transferred the more troubling thoughts and feelings from my brain to a canvas, they couldn't spin round and round inside and torment me.

Not that I'd talk to Wilder about that stuff. My art was private, not exactly compatible with my image as a hardass ex-SEAL.

"I'm not numb or anything," I assured him. "I care about the job, the guys from the team. I care about Victoria. It's just relationships, I guess. I want one—in theory. What you have with Jessica seems great. I'm just not interested in getting to know any of the women I meet, and I'm not interested in letting them get to know me. It all seems like too much trouble."

The last time I remembered having any *real* interest in a woman was that crazy week I'd spent in Greece comforting a jilted bride on her un-honeymoon.

In fact, it had been one of the best times of my life—I'd been stupid-crazy about the girl—but moments like that one weren't meant to last. They were like flares, burning bright and hot, lighting up the night sky for only an instant before they flamed out.

Wilder grinned. "Things with Jessica and me weren't exactly

smooth sailing at the start, if you remember. She was trouble with a capital T."

"I remember."

"I wouldn't worry about it," Wilder said. "Sounds like you've got your head on straight. When the time is right and, more importantly, when the *person* is right—boom, it'll happen. You'll find the one who's *worth* the trouble."

"Yeah, maybe."

"She's out there," Wilder assured me. "And I can't wait till you meet her, and I get to say, 'I told you so.'"

EIGHT

You

Scarlett

The cab pulled to a stop in front of 254 Oceanview Drive, and all the air left my lungs. I blinked rapidly, fumbling for my phone.

"Hold on a second, please,' I said to the driver. "I need to double check the address in my email."

No, this was it—the street address I'd been given for my grandmother's house.

But this was no mere house. It looked more like a national monument, with soaring marble exteriors and giant columns and so many windows across the front the cleaning staff must have gone through gallons of Windex every week.

Tall, ornate iron gates separated the expansive property from the sidewalk.

My, my, Grandma, what a big house you have.

I got out of the car and walked through the open gates down a long pea gravel driveway lined with oaks and red maples, taking in neatly manicured gardens complete with water features and hedge animal topiaries.

The grounds were enclosed by wrought iron fencing with

flowering rhododendrons, mountain laurel, and dogwoods just inside it, serving as a natural screen from the street traffic.

At one point where the driveway curved outward, I caught a glimpse of blue ocean in the "backyard."

This *couldn't* be the right place. Maybe it was a ritzy retirement home, divided into apartments to house numerous elderly residents?

But I hadn't seen any signs to that effect.

When I reached the massive front step, I pushed the doorbell and waited, staring up at the enormous iron and glasswork front doors and listening to the peels of rich melody ringing through the mansion.

I half expected the door to be opened by a man in a tuxedo, the kind of butler you saw in period dramas, or maybe a security guard who'd tell me to get lost, that I had the wrong address after all and didn't belong here.

That last part was certainly true. I'd never even seen a house like this one, much less been inside.

When the door opened there was no butler but a smiling middle-aged woman standing inside. She wore a navy cardigan over a navy pinstriped top and khaki pants with black flats.

"Hello, you must be Scarlett," she said.

"Yes, I must be—I mean, I am. That's me."

The woman didn't seem to notice my nervous stammer. "Come in please. Welcome to Indigo Point. I'm Stephanie Felman, the housekeeper. Mrs. Hood is expecting you. She's in the informal parlor."

Of course she is.

As if a house with a name like Indigo Point could have any less than *two* parlors. As I followed Ms. Feldman through the gleaming corridors and up a staircase so dramatic it put Jay Gatsby to shame, the nerves in my belly danced like a 1920's flapper from his era.

No wonder the Hood family had considered my mother

beneath them. You'd have to be a Vanderbilt or Rockefeller *not* to be.

Mom was a simple woman from a firmly middle-class family in Anoka, Minnesota. Her dad had been a farmer, and her mom had worked in a sock factory. Though she'd graduated high school and gone to one year of college, my mother wasn't what anyone would consider "sophisticated."

To my father's apparently wealthy society family, she must have seemed barely qualified to be the help, much less a suitable wife for the heir to a massive family fortune.

Mom had told me my father had come from "means", but I'd pictured a nice four-bedroom house with a pool. Maybe she hadn't known the extent of it.

Dad had certainly never mentioned to me that he'd grown up extremely wealthy. In fact, I remembered him speaking of rich people in disdainful tones.

This is bound to be a short visit.

My skin crawled in dread as I pictured the haughty look that would overtake my blue-blooded grandmother's face when she met me. She'd probably be dripping in jewels and sitting in some kind of fancy gold-plated chair like a queen on her throne.

Stephanie finally stopped at one of the doors along an impossibly long hallway.

"Here we go," she said and opened it. "Have a nice visit. I'll bring along some refreshments for you two in a while."

"Well, I may not be staying that long..."

My protest died off as I got a look inside the room. It was bright and cluttered—and noisy. A big screen TV on one wall showed a fit young blonde woman doing squats and chirping, "You can do it! Just four more," in a cheery tone. Her teeth were so white they were almost blinding.

In the middle of the room, a tiny woman in 1980's style workout clothing—spandex bodysuit, sneakers, and legwarmers —squatted along with the video.

Well, they weren't full squats, but she bent her knees, moving slightly up and down as she pumped her arms over her head then out to the sides. The dumbbells she held were hot pink and labeled as one-pound weights.

For a minute I just stood there, paralyzed by shock and uncertainty. Judging from the white hair and thin, shrunken frame, the woman was at least in her mid-eighties if not her nineties.

I wasn't sure what to do. If I spoke up and surprised her while she was already exerting herself, I might give her a heart attack.

She must have seen my reflection in the television because she whirled around and dropped her weights to the floor with a thunk.

"Scarlett," she exclaimed, looking delighted.

"Hi. I'm sorry to disturb your exercise."

Mrs. Hood started moving toward me, waving one hand in front of her as if swatting away a gnat.

"Not to worry. I was just trying to squeeze in my Denise Austin before you got here. I would have skipped a day, but Gray says it's important to keep moving every day if I want to maintain my flexibility. I'm working on building some muscle so I can go out and stroll on the Bluff Walk like I used to. He also has me doing art therapy. Gray says it's good for dexterity and peace of mind."

Gray. The man who'd written to me.

He must have been her new "gentleman friend" or maybe some kind of caretaker—a doctor or physical therapist or something. I knew he wasn't her husband because the information I'd gotten from Viridian indicated Mr. Hood had passed away about a year ago.

When my grandmother reached me, I stuck out my hand for a handshake. She moved right past it, embracing me. I was so surprised all I could manage was a stiff hug and an awkward pat on her arm.

She pulled back, beaming. "Look at you—my how you've grown and changed. But I still see that sweet little girl in your face. You're even more beautiful now."

"Uh... thank you. I... like your house." Well, that was lame, but I was in shock.

This was not the haughty grand dame I'd expected. This woman was more Golden Girls than Cruella DeVille. And when I looked into her face, recognition bloomed inside me.

She had changed a bit, but I did remember her—the sparkly, blue eyes, the beauty mark on her left cheek, the mischievous smile that suggested pajama parties and blanket forts and late-night cookie jar raids.

Cookies.

"Oh. I brought you something." Belatedly remembering the gift basket I'd brought from Minnesota, I held it out to her.

She clapped her hands like a five-year-old. "You brought me goodies. Thank you, dear. Let's sit down and have some. All that exercise has worked up my appetite, and all Stephanie will bring us is cucumber sandwiches and fruit salad and tea."

With a wink, she added, "She's so old school."

My nerves were displaced by a genuine chuckle. This lady was a hot sketch.

"Want to bring the basket out to the loggia so we can enjoy the breeze while we eat?" she asked.

"That would be lovely," was what I said. Inside I was thinking, *What's a loggia?*

I soon found out. Mrs. Hood led me from the parlor down a hallway to a set of glass doors that revealed blue sky and even bluer water. Pushing through them, I realized they led to the largest balcony I'd ever seen.

Balcony wasn't even the right word, as the covered outdoor space was wide and deep and would have easily held fifty or more people. The floor was covered in tiny tiles forming mosaic images of shells and mermaids, dolphins, and crashing waves. It was stunning.

The view past the loggia's half-wall was even more breathtaking. The open Atlantic Ocean stretched to the lighter blue of the horizon.

As she'd promised, a pleasant breeze stirred my hair and the skirt of my dress.

Mrs. Hood walked all the way to the front of the structure, stopping at the safety wall and throwing her arms out to the side like Leonardo DiCaprio in Titanic.

"Isn't it glorious, dear? You absolutely must see the sunset from here. The ones we watched together in Florida were pretty, but Eastport Bay sunsets aren't too shabby either."

"I'm sure. Where would you like me to set up the food, Mrs. Hood? Is this table okay?"

She turned to face me, hands crossed over her sternum. "Oh no, this breaks my heart. Do you not remember me at all then?"

"No, I remember you. A little."

"Do you remember what you used to call me?" she asked.

"Vivi," I answered shyly. The word felt foreign on my tongue, I hadn't said it in so long.

She smiled. "I'd love for you to still call me Vivi... if you wouldn't mind."

"Okay." I swallowed. "Vivi. Would you like to sit here and eat?"

"That would be fine, Scarlett dear." She made her way slowly to the small round table. "Now let's see what you've brought for me."

"I thought you might like to try some Minnesota classics." I removed the flatbread from its packaging. "This is lefse—it's flatbread made from mashed potatoes, a Scandinavian traditional food. So is this... it's called krumkake."

"Those look like ice cream cones," she declared with amusement.

"They'd probably make good ones. These are usually filled with whipped cream, but they're delicious just as they are."

Mrs. Hood—Vivi—picked up a krumkake and nibbled on it while I withdrew the final item from the basket.

"These are Sweet Scarlett's cookies. They're chocolate chip, and they're pretty popular in Minnesota. People buy them by the bucketful at the State Fair every year. Just recently, a few grocery stores in my local area have started stocking the dough."

I stopped short of telling her Sweet Scarlett's was actually my company. I wasn't ready yet to share things of a personal nature, and the small side-business I'd poured my heart into was the definition of personal.

"Well, they have your name, so I know they'll be sweet," Vivi said as she took one from the mini-bucket.

After eating three and declaring them delicious, she seemed ready to get down to the reason for my visit.

"Thank you for coming here today, Scarlett. I was so excited when Gray told me he'd managed to track you down. I know you haven't had much interest in keeping in touch, but as we are quite literally running out of time, I thought I'd make one last effort."

I shook my head, confused. "Track me down? One last effort? What do you mean *I* didn't have any interest in keeping in touch? You're the one who vanished from my life when my parents split up."

Though her eyes were encased in wrinkles, they managed to pop wide open. "Not at all, sweetheart. I continued to write you and call."

"I haven't received any communication from you since I was ten."

"That explains why I never got any replies. Then at some point my letters started coming back as undeliverable. 'No forwarding address,' they said. I went down to Florida to try to find out where you and your mother had moved. I even had an investigator do a nationwide search for a phone number or address in her name. He came up empty."

"Well, mom and I moved in with her parents in Minnesota when I was about that age. The house and the phone were in their names, and then she married my stepdad, and her name changed. I don't understand why the letters weren't forwarded though."

"I don't either. It wasn't until I met Gray that I was finally able to find you. He'll explain everything when he gets here. There are several things I'd like for him to speak with you about."

"He doesn't live here?"

She gave me a funny look. "No. But he should be arriving any minute."

"Well, I'm looking forward to meeting him."

It would be nice to see what kind of man my grandmother was keeping company with, and maybe this old gentleman would be able to shed some light on the mystery behind our estrangement.

Popping a cookie into my mouth and chewing, I thought about what Vivi had said. It was so contrary to what my mom had told me about the two of us being rejected by Dad's family.

"So... you *didn't* cut off Mom and me after the divorce?"

Vivi's expression was wounded. "No, sweetheart. I felt like you might need me even more after your father left. I'm so sorry about that, by the way. It broke my heart to see the changes in Charles. Toward the end he was like a stranger. I guess there are some things human beings just weren't meant to see. It must have been very scary for you as a little girl to watch your father become so different."

"Honestly, I can hardly remember him. He was deployed so much when I was little, and when he was home, he was closed off in his room alone much of the time. I'm sure it was PTSD or maybe the effect of too many concussions from being near explosions? No, I didn't understand why he seemed so distant when I was little. When I got older, I did—at least somewhat. I'm sorry for your loss, too. He was your only son, right?"

"My only child," she confirmed, adding, "though I've come to think of Gray as a son—or a grandson."

My head jerked back in surprise. "So Gray Lupine isn't your boyfriend then."

And apparently, he wasn't the elderly gentleman I'd been picturing either.

"I'm a little old for a boyfriend, sweetheart, but thanks for the compliment. No, Gray is a dear friend, and I've come to think of him as family. We have so much in common and so much fun together."

I tried to imagine what a man young enough to be her grandson might have in common with Vivi.

And what they could possibly do for fun together. I was starting to get a bad feeling about this young man who seemed to be *so* involved in her life.

"Vivi, how long have you known Gray?"

"Oh, let me see... about six months, I think. He's so good to me. He comes by all the time to check on me. You're going to love him."

She glanced up and over my shoulder to the space behind me. "Speak of the devil and he appears... here he is."

I stood and turned around then nearly choked on thin air when I saw the man standing in the doorway.

"You," I nearly shouted.

A wide wolfish grin spread across his handsome face.

"You."

NINE

I'll Be Watching

Gray

What the hell was *Red* doing here?

I recognized her immediately. It was impossible to forget a face I'd spent so much time fantasizing over.

When she'd stood up and turned around—*boom*.

All that stuff I'd said to Wilder about being unable to feel anything for anyone? Problem solved. Sensations I hadn't felt in years deluged me.

My eyes roamed over her, taking in the details that had changed or managed to slip my memory in the past three years.

Her blonde, wavy hair was a little lighter than I'd remembered, and there was a new spray of freckles across her nose and cheekbones that added just the right amount of cuteness to her beauty and kept her from being unapproachable.

The incredible blue eyes stared back, appearing a little dazed at seeing me again. How had she managed to track me down to Eastport Bay?

Even if she had, how'd she known I'd be coming *here* to Victoria's house?

"Gray, dear, I'd like you to meet my granddaughter, Scarlett Hood. Didn't I tell you she was lovely?"

That's when the pieces clicked into place. My vacation fling hadn't tracked *me* down—I'd found *her*... and invited her here via Fed Ex.

What were the odds? It seemed impossible, but the woman I'd had the most unforgettable sex of my life with was Victoria Hood's long-lost granddaughter.

I could barely manage to gather enough air to respond. "Yes, uh... you did. I mean, she is."

Victoria gave a little laugh. "Well come say hello. I've never seen you act bashful before."

Moving to stand beside Red—uh, Scarlett—Victoria put her hand on the younger woman's arm.

"Scarlett, this is my friend Gray. He's the one who helped me find you. He's been wonderful these past few months, helping with things around the house and with my checkbook, making sure my art and other valuables are taken care of."

Instead of extending her hand for a polite handshake, Scarlett folded her arms across her chest. Her eyes narrowed, and her pretty lips curled in a scowl.

"I'll just bet he has."

What the fuck?

That was a weird way to say thank you to the guy who'd been watching out for her elderly grandmother—something *she* should have been doing, by the way.

It was also a rather cold greeting considering how much time we'd spent naked together.

Not wanting to upset Victoria, who was obviously delighted at her reunion with this unfriendly young woman, I managed to paste something resembling a smile on my face.

"Scarlett, it's nice to... see you again."

In truth it was more than nice. She looked so good it almost hurt to look at her. Somehow she'd gotten even prettier in the past three years.

"You look great," I said, unable to help myself.

The eyelids narrowed further. "You look... the same."

Victoria glanced back and forth between us. "Oh, I didn't realize you two had met. I thought you'd only corresponded by mail. Did you go by Gray's office at Viridian first then, Scarlett?"

Instead of answering her grandmother, Scarlett stared at me. "*You* work at Viridian Security? How did you go from selling condoms and vibrators to working in security?"

"Vibrators?" Victoria asked, clearly confused. "Is that some sort of electronic security device? Did you put those on my art collection, Gray?"

My face heated in a flash that moved from the neck up. Looking down at my shoes, I cleared my throat.

"No, I... didn't feel your pieces would benefit from those. Why don't I help you inside to your room for a rest, then maybe Scarlett and I can take a walk and discuss some of the things you wanted me to address with her."

"I think that's a *great* idea," Scarlett practically growled. "Vivi?"

She offered her arm for support, calling Victoria the nickname my friend had so often invited me to use. Not wanting to overstep the bounds of our relationship, I'd declined.

Scarlett apparently had no qualms about using the endearment, even after basically abandoning the woman to fend for herself in her old age.

After making sure Victoria made it to her bedroom for her afternoon nap, the two of us stepped into the hall.

The instant the door shut behind us, Scarlett whirled to face me. "What are you doing here?" she demanded.

"I'm here because Victoria invited me over. Why are you here?"

"Same." She glared at me, chewing on her lower lip. "Did you know it was me when you sent the letter?"

"No. I had no idea you were her granddaughter. I didn't know your real name—remember? She asked me to find her granddaughter, so I did."

"Do you *really* work for that security company?"

"I do." Pulling out my wallet, I extracted a Viridian business card and handed it to her. "That's how I was able to locate you. Actually, *I* didn't do the locating—there's someone in my office who specializes in that sort of thing. He did it for me. I just wrote the letter."

"She said you've been 'helping' her. Why?" Scarlett's face was a portrait of distrust.

"Because she needed help." I waited a significant beat. "Because she *has* no one else to do it."

"She has me."

"Oh really? And where have you been for the past twenty years, miss suddenly devoted granddaughter? Do you have any idea how defenseless and alone your grandmother is? She's easy pickings for predators."

Scarlett harumphed. "Tell me about it."

"What's that supposed to mean?"

She leaned closer, stretching up in a futile attempt to go chest-to-chest with me. "You tell me, *Wolf.* You're the one who preys on vulnerable women in resort bars."

I felt like I'd been slapped. "*Prey?* You think that's what I did? I wasn't even there trying to meet women that night. All I wanted was some R and R with my buddies. But I couldn't leave you alone. You were so drunk you might as well have been wearing a sign that said *Rob and Rape Me—Please.* I was walking you back to your room to keep you safe. You *begged* me to swim with you. You begged me to stay overnight."

"And then you decided to spend the rest of the week eating and drinking on my tab before vanishing."

I fell back a step and looked around, needing a bit of distance in case I blew my top like a faulty pressure cooker.

"I *know* you're not accusing me of being a freeloader right now."

Meeting her eyes again, I willed Scarlett to own up to the truth of that week. "We ran up that tab together—on purpose—to stick it to your stupid runaway groom, remember? I didn't *need* your money, Scarlett. I stayed the week because you gave me your whole 'this is supposed to be my honeymoon' sob story."

Scarlett's face matched her name—she was furious. "Are you saying you stayed out of *pity*?"

Of course that wasn't the whole reason I'd stayed, but I wasn't exactly in the mood to shower her with compliments at the moment.

When I'd imagined running into Red again someday—and I had imagined it more often than I cared to admit—this was *definitely* not how things had gone. I'd pictured something more along the lines of falling into the nearest bed and devouring each other for days on end than a shouting match.

"What else was I supposed to do?" I asked. "Leave you to get drunk alone at the bar every night? Those resorts are crawling with hustlers and con artists."

"Yeah—and *you're* one of them." She held up my business card and ripped it in half. "This is probably fake."

I was so mad I could hardly see straight. "Oh, I'm not just a mooch—now I'm a con artist?"

"You must be. Or maybe you're just hanging around with an eighty-nine-year-old woman—who happens to be filthy rich—for fun." Her tone was pure sarcastic disdain.

"As a matter of fact, we do have fun together—something you apparently have forgotten how to do in the past three years. Your grandmother and I are *friends*. She's a bright, charming, talented woman with excellent taste in art."

Scarlett sneered. "And I bet you'd just *love* to get your hands on some of it, wouldn't you?"

This was getting ridiculous. Here I was, overwhelmed to see her, and she was treating me like a criminal.

What had happened to her to make her so hostile and suspicious?

Holding up two hands in a referees' *time out* gesture, I said, "Can I get a twenty here? Why are you treating me like a stranger?"

"You *are* a stranger."

I raised a sardonic brow. "If memory serves, we got to know each other *quite* well."

She flushed deeply. "That's not what I mean, and you know it. We didn't even know each other's names. We spent five days and six nights together three years ago and haven't spoken since."

"And whose fault is that?" I asked.

"Yours. You left while I was sleeping and didn't even bother to say goodbye."

"I had to. I..." My response drifted into silence. I couldn't tell her why I'd had to leave so suddenly that day.

My platoon leader had gotten a call about a hijacked yacht off the coast of Greece. Because we were so close, we were called into action and had to begin pre-deployment prep immediately. I'd basically gone right from her bed into a life-and-death operation.

Immediately after that we'd been deployed to Iraq, and that was where my life had changed forever.

"... I had to work."

"Big dildo emergency?" she asked, clearly disbelieving my excuse.

How could I blame her? That stupid story of Badger's was coming back to bite me in the ass once again.

I supposed at this point, now that I was no longer in active service, I could admit to her that I'd been a SEAL without giving her any details of the actual operation.

But I also remembered she was basically allergic to the idea of getting involved with a military man.

Hell, it didn't even matter. Scarlett was here for a few days and then she'd be out of my life again.

The thought bothered me more than it should have.

We had to put the conversation on pause because the bedroom door opened. Victoria stood there smiling.

"I'm so sorry, Vivi," Scarlett said. "Did we wake you?"

"No dear, my mind did. I remembered something very important—it's the reason I wanted you both here today at the same time."

"What's that?" I asked. "Do you need help with something?"

Victoria smiled at me. "I certainly do. Let's go to my sitting room."

We followed the elderly woman down the hall to the room where she spent most of her time. She'd told me the family in the past had used at least half of the rooms in the enormous mansion, but now that it was just her and the housekeeper living here, she used very little of the space.

The informal parlor—or sitting room—was sunny during the day and cozy at night with the big fireplace at one end lit. She read there, watched TV, exercised, and listened to music in the room.

When we reached it, she went to a table in the corner that held a computer and printer as well as a basket where she kept her correspondence.

Rifling through the basket, she extracted two legal-sized envelopes and offered one each to me and Scarlett.

"What is this?" Scarlett asked.

"Open it and see," Mrs. Hood said.

Scarlett's reading pace must have been about the same as mine because we both gasped simultaneously.

"Power of attorney?" I asked. "Victoria, why?"

"I'm not sure what this means," Scarlett said to her then looked at me with a quizzical glance.

Victoria took a seat in her favorite wing-back recliner chair.

"In case you two haven't noticed, I'm old." She chuckled. "I feel fine, but I'm noticing changes. I move slower, I think slower. My vision is going, and my hearing's not too hot either. I'm not buying any green bananas these days, if you know what I mean."

She chortled at her own joke before going on. "Thanks to the sale of Stuart's company and some smart investments I made in art and collectibles, I have quite a lot in assets. I would like to start finding new homes for all those pretty things. It's time."

Scarlett knelt next to her chair, looking distressed. "But you could live a *lot* longer—another decade, maybe even more."

Victoria stroked her granddaughter's cheek with a gnarled hand. "If I do, it'll be with far fewer possessions... and in a smaller house. This is too much for me, and your priorities change as you get older. It's ridiculous to have cleaners dusting rooms no one ever goes into. A young family should be living here— or an active couple who will *use* the house."

She turned from Scarlett to me. "I know you don't like me talking about it, but it's fair to say that at this age, any day could be my last. I want to see my art collection in loving hands. There are people who've contacted me over the years wondering if I'd like to sell this piece or that."

Looking back at Scarlett, she said, "And I'd like you to find the perfect buyer for the home and some worthy causes to donate my fortune to. It'll be a lot of work, and it'll take time, I'm afraid. But I have no one else to ask."

"Of course," Scarlett said. "I will if you want me to, but..."

"But what dear?"

"I hate the idea of you leaving—especially when I just got you back in my life."

"We'll make the most of the time we have left, shall we?" Victoria asked with an affectionate smile.

Scarlett nodded then went to sit on the sofa, reading through the paperwork. At one point her expression clouded.

"This says Gray and I are *both* to have power of attorney."

Victoria nodded. "That's right. Many hands make light work. It's too much to ask one person to do. Gray knows art, and he knows what I have in my collection. I figured that could be his responsibility."

I nodded to her, swallowing hard.

She went on, pointing at Scarlett now. "You can handle some of the other things like arranging an estate sale for the things that aren't going in the auction. You two can divide the work evenly."

Now Scarlett's eyes came up to meet mine. I knew what she

was thinking before she said it. "Vivi... are you sure you can... trust him?"

I huffed an irritated laugh. "Are you sure you can trust her?"

Victoria slapped one scrawny thigh, looking and sounding thrilled. "This is working already. I trust you *both*, but the fact that you don't trust each other will ensure that my estate is liquidated properly and fairly. Of course you'll be compensated for your efforts."

Both Scarlett and I spoke at the same time, protesting.

"You don't have to do that. I don't want your money," she said.

"It isn't necessary. I don't need it."

Victoria held up a silencing hand. "You *will* be compensated. That's final. I have only one more thing to ask."

"What is it?" Scarlett asked.

"Anything," I said.

"No more of that bickering I heard outside my bedroom door. The two of you are enough to wake the dead when you get going."

The housekeeper came in and announced the visiting nurse had arrived to give Victoria her bath and medications, so Scarlett and I both bid her our goodbyes and left.

As we walked down the front steps toward the driveway, I said, "So, I guess you'll be moving in here."

She nodded. "I have a hotel reservation, but only for two nights. I'm not sure how long this will take, but Vivi asked me to stay here with her, and the hotels around here are incredibly expensive."

"Makes sense then."

"I really didn't expect all this." She looked a little dazed, as if the reality of the situation was just now hitting her—with no gloves on.

"I've got two weeks' vacation time," she said. "If it takes longer than that, maybe I can work remotely?"

"You know... I can handle everything alone," I offered. "I'm already here, and I don't mind."

"No," she blurted. Then in a quieter tone, she said, "No thank you. She's my grandmother, and I should handle it."

"Right. Okay, well I'll come by as often as I can get away from work to help out."

"Don't go out of your way or anything. I mean, I'm sure you're busy," she said.

Ah. She's trying to get rid of me. Not so fast there, Red.

"It's no trouble. I live close by, and my work hours are pretty flexible. So... I guess we'll be seeing a lot of each other."

"I guess so." Scarlett didn't look too jazzed at the prospect. "Hopefully, it'll all go really quickly, and we can both get back to our lives."

A cab pulled into the drive, and she took a step toward it.

"Scarlett."

She twisted back to face me. "What?"

"How *is* your life? You know... after your wedding fell through and all?"

What I *wanted* to ask was if she'd gotten over the broken heart and whether she was dating someone or engaged again, but under the circumstances it seemed kind of crass.

Her expression frosted over. "That's none of your business."

"I'm sorry," I said. "And... I'm sorry I left without saying goodbye. Trust me when I say I didn't *want* to leave—especially not that suddenly."

I probably shouldn't have, but I added, "Especially not when you looked so spectacular with your hair spread out across the pillowcase and the sheets pushed down to your waist."

She flushed a bright red and shook her head as if trying to dislodge bothersome thoughts. "That was a *long* time ago, and it wasn't real life. Anyway, I'm over it."

"You were really upset that I left?" Not sure why that idea pleased me, but it did.

She hesitated before answering. "I was—at first. Because it was rude, that's all. Then I realized what a good thing it was that we *weren't* going to keep in touch. Because that's not who I really am —I'd never done anything that crazy before and haven't since then. I was in a weird place. And I'm a completely different person from the one you met three years ago."

"So am I." And *that* was the absolute truth.

When I'd met her in Greece, I'd been riding high, at the top of my game, loving what I did, loving my team and placing implicit faith in our leader.

Things went downhill pretty quickly after that, and a lot of damage had been done. I'd had to harden my heart to do some of the things that had been required of me on the job, and I'd accrued my share of scar tissue.

But I'd worked through it, fought my way back to health, physically and mentally. I wondered what kind of battle damage Scarlett had suffered over the past few years—and what kind of scars it had left her with.

"So why don't we start over again?" I suggested with a smile and a hand extended toward her. "Gray Lupine, home security specialist and unlikely friend of eccentric old ladies. It's nice to meet you."

She took my hand—reluctantly—and let it go after a brief clasp.

"Scarlett Hood. Prodigal granddaughter. And apparently your new watchdog. And, Gray, I *will* be watching," she warned before getting into the cab and slamming the door shut behind her.

I laughed. "Not if I see you first, little Red."

I'd be watching, too.

TEN

A Good Liar

Scarlett

Well, *that* was a shock.

When I'd flown out here from Minnesota, I'd prepared myself for surprises and possibly the unearthing of some uncomfortable emotions.

But seeing Wolf—I mean Gray—again... *wow.*

When I'd said he looked the same, I hadn't been lying. He'd looked amazing then, and he looked amazing now.

How was it that one week with the man had affected me almost more than the entire two-year relationship I'd had with Bryce?

It was irritating. Especially now that we had to work together.

That was another thing I would never have predicted. I expected to fly here, meet my grandmother, reminisce about the handful of memories we shared, then go back home and maybe have the occasional phone call with her if things went well—or if they didn't, say, "goodbye and good riddance," and try to forget all about her.

She'd obviously had other plans.

I sat at the desk in my hotel room, reading over the document again. Victoria had already signed it. I supposed I didn't *have* to. I could just walk away and say, "no thanks" to the responsibility and whatever compensation came with it.

But if I did that, Gray would take over the job of putting her affairs in order—alone. And I didn't trust him.

Yes, he'd apologized for sneaking out that morning while I'd slept, but his reason didn't hold water. He'd had to work?

Please. He'd already told me the promotional products convention was winding down and that he had some days off for recreation.

While I didn't know my grandmother well, I certainly wasn't going to stand by and do nothing while some smooth-talking con artist "took care of" her affairs.

She needed someone to protect her, to make sure she wasn't taken advantage of.

That someone would have to be me.

The upside was the extended stay would give me a chance to finally get to know her. I already liked her, and I was full of questions about her life and my father. I was excited about filling in some of the blanks my mother's account of their marriage had left.

Speaking of that, I called Mom, telling her about the meeting with Vivi and asking her about the estrangement. She explained the mystery of Vivi's missing letters.

"Your father's family had so much money, they were so powerful. I was afraid when he died, they'd try to take you away from me—and succeed," she said. "Your grandfather, Mr. Hood, never liked me in the first place. I had nothing—I couldn't afford a lawyer. So, we left Florida, and I told no one where we were going. I didn't have my mail forwarded or have any of your school or medical records sent to Minnesota. We started over, and I just hoped they'd never find you."

The story made me sad—for my mom and for all the years I'd missed with my grandmother because of her wrong assumptions and fears.

"I understand," I told Mom. "But I hope you understand that I'd like to have a relationship with her now, if I can."

"Of course. And Scarlett... I love you, honey. Everything I did was because I loved you and didn't want to lose you."

"I know. I love you, too."

* * *

As we spent time together over the next few days, I started learning to love my grandmother again as well.

One particularly beautiful morning, Vivi invited me to take a walk in the gardens at Indigo Point. Her gait was slow, but her memory was amazing.

"Many of the trees on the estate were imported. This is a Blue Atlas Cedar from North Africa. These copper beeches and weeping beech trees are from England."

Reaching one of the flower gardens, she bent down to smell a bloom. "Now these are belladonna lilies. The bulbs were transplanted from Doris Duke's estate—we used to run in the same circles back when we were young. So sad she ended up alone in the end."

She snickered. "Listen to me. I'm in the same boat."

"You're not alone," I assured her. "I'm here now. I'm sorry we missed so many years, but I promise you—you will *not* be alone anymore."

At the moment, I wasn't sure exactly how to keep that promise. Maybe I could find her a paid companion or get the nurse to come and stay full-time.

Vivi smiled and patted my hand. "Thank you, dear. You're just as sweet as you were as a child."

Starting to walk again, she brushed her hand over the tops of the flowers. "I always dreamed of one day seeing great-grandchildren running around on this lawn. Do you have a beau, Scarlett?"

"None that will lead to frolicking great-grandchildren," I said, and we both laughed.

"I had one... several years ago. It didn't work out."

"What happened?"

"He asked me to marry him, we planned a wedding, and he changed his mind. He didn't love me enough, and he left, simple as that. It's no one's fault, really."

She nodded. "A man who doesn't know his own mind isn't much of a catch, anyway. Now Gray... *there's* a man who knows what he wants."

Yeah. Your money.

I didn't voice my suspicions aloud. It was clear Gray had a huge influence on my grandmother, and it would be fruitless to try to convince her the sun didn't shine out of his perfectly sculpted ass.

"Really? And what does he want?" I asked to humor her.

"To create beauty out of chaos."

Not the answer I'd been expecting. "What do you mean?"

"He hasn't had an easy life, dear. But he has an incredible eye for art and beauty. The way he sees the world is remarkable. And he's quite creative himself."

"How so?"

"Gray was a student at Rhode Island School of Design before deciding to switch careers. With all his talent, I'm not sure why he spends his time installing alarm systems and cameras."

"His talent? You've seen his artwork?"

"Some of it," she said. "Did you notice his ink yesterday?"

I choked back a laugh over her up-to-the-moment word choice. "I noticed."

In fact, I was quite familiar with Gray's *ink*, having studied his tattoos up close—and tasted most of them—not that I'd be telling my elderly grandmother about that.

"You're a fan of tattoos?" I asked Victoria.

"I'm a fan of art, all kinds, and his tattoos are pure artistry. He designed them himself, you know."

"Oh. No, I didn't realize."

"He designed the tattoos for all his platoon members when he was a SEAL, you know. Several of them work with him at Viridian—all of them except for their commander, I think."

I stopped walking, my feet feeling like they'd sprouted roots and implanted themselves on the spot. "Gray was a... a Navy SEAL?"

She nodded enthusiastically. "Yes, like your father. Isn't that something?"

"It certainly is." And it wasn't something *good*.

I knew it.

I'd been right about him and his friends at the bar that night.

He lied to me. And I'd bought that stupid tale they'd spun.

He was a *good* liar.

Then it hit me—*that* was why he'd left so suddenly without a look backward at the end of our week together.

He'd probably been called into duty somewhere, thrown himself into some godawful international situation where he could have been killed or maimed for life.

In fact, he probably was. Not physically obviously—he looked very... intact. But mentally, emotionally, he was probably a wreck.

Just like my dad.

And like my mom, I'd been left behind with no idea where he'd gone or how to reach him.

Now I felt even more certain Gray shouldn't be solely responsible for my grandmother's well-being.

A man like him couldn't be counted on. He was capable of divorcing himself from his emotions whenever necessary, of walking away at the drop of a hat.

Now that I thought about it, as a security specialist with Viridian, he probably could have found me at any point if he'd wanted to. And he hadn't.

At least the career in high-profile security made sense now. A lot more sense than the ridiculous promotional sex toy salesman story.

Thank God we *hadn't* exchanged contact information and

kept in touch—or worse, gotten involved seriously. I would have been just another statistic in the left-behind ninety percent.

Whatever poor girl he was dating had my pity—if he had a girlfriend, that was.

"Is Gray seeing anyone?" I asked Victoria in as casual a tone as I could muster.

"I don't think so, dear. But then he doesn't run his social calendar by me. If I had to guess I'd say no. I don't think a girlfriend would approve of how much time he spends with an old 'cougar' like me."

She scratched the air like a cat and cracked up, and I couldn't help but join her infectious laughter.

"These old claws are getting pretty dull now I guess," she said.

"You're enough woman for any man," I assured her.

"So are you, sweetheart. So are you."

ELEVEN

Starving Artist

Gray

After work I went to Victoria's house to start the process of preparing her paintings, sculptures, and other valuable collections for auction.

I was already familiar with them, having created unique security systems for each item. With a few exceptions, I'd already had the pieces appraised for current market value.

Clearly suspicious of my intentions toward her grandmother, Scarlett stayed close, shadowing me as I moved through the mansion.

Not that I minded.

Seeing her again had done something to me. It was like a medic had applied defibrillator patches to my chest or something.

The current had reverberated out from my chest to all my extremities, waking them from the state of numbness they'd been in the past few years.

Even my dick had come out of a coma—I'd awakened several times during the past few nights with a hard-on, fragments of dreams starring Scarlett still in the corners of my half-awake mind.

She followed me into the main gallery at Indigo Point, setting up her laptop on a table in one corner of the room where she could keep an eye on me while she worked.

Watch all you want, darlin'. As if I'm going to stash a Renoir in my jacket and walk out of here.

With Victoria's trusting nature and the unlimited access I'd had to her house these past few months, I could have robbed her a thousand times over.

Of course I wouldn't take so much as a stick of gum from the woman without asking.

For one thing, I wasn't a criminal. For another, I had more money of my own than I could ever spend in a lifetime—or several.

I did like seeing this protective streak in Scarlett, though. It went a long way toward assuring me *she* was here for the right reasons and could be trusted to look out for the family matriarch in her waning years.

Unless she was just looking out for *herself*, which was still a possibility. As Victoria's only living descendant, her granddaughter was in line to inherit a fortune someday.

I didn't want to think the woman I'd spent that unforgettable week with three years ago was capable of being so cold-hearted, but it *had* been three years. I knew all too well how much could change in that span of time.

Walking the perimeter of the room, I made note of each item and prioritized them in order of value for the auction Victoria had asked me to plan.

When I got close to Scarlett's spot, I decided to test the waters.

"Victoria has a pretty sweet collection, huh?" I asked.

Scarlett looked up briefly then back at her laptop screen. "I guess so. I'm not really that into art."

"Why not?"

She lifted her shoulders and let them fall. "I've always thought of it as kind of... snooty."

I barked a laugh. "Snooty? A lot of people would say art is subversive, which is pretty much the opposite of snooty."

"I guess it depends on the art," Scarlett said. "I've never really been able to afford any, so I guess I wouldn't know."

"Well, there's art available at every price level. And some of it's free, like public installations and street art."

"What are you, the Rhode Island Ambassador for the Arts?" she asked.

That set me back on my feet a bit. I needed to tone it down about my favorite subject.

I moderated my voice. "It's an interest of mine. It's one of the things that connected me with Victoria. How's it going with you two?"

Scarlett glanced up from her laptop again. "Great. We're having fun, finding a lot to talk about. I did her video exercise class with her today—completely kicked my butt."

"She's a hoot, isn't she? I told you she was fun."

"She is." Scarlett hesitated before going on. "She says you've been coming by almost every day of the week over the past few months to share a meal, or change the batteries on her remote, or play a game of cards."

"Yeah, she may look like a sweet old lady, but when it comes to Rummy, she's a pirate."

Scarlett gave me an appraising glance that fairly screamed, *Are you a pirate?*

"I still have a hard time believing you could care so much about an old woman you met less than a year ago and aren't related to," she said.

The accusatory words got under my skin like a bee sting.

"I have a hard time believing you could care so little about someone you *are* related to. You've gone twenty years without a word of contact then suddenly want to reconnect? If you're accusing me of trawling for a sugar-momma—or sugar-grandma —you can stop worrying. I don't need the money. Do you?"

Her jaw dropped in apparent horror. "What's that supposed

to mean? I have a job. I'm doing fine. Besides, *you're* the one who invited me to come."

"On her behalf. And you shouldn't have needed an invitation," I said. "You should have been here all along instead of waiting until your wealthy grandmother was practically on her death bed."

Scarlett's eyelids flared. "How dare you. You have no idea about the family dynamics at play here."

"So fill me in."

"Why should I? It's none of your business."

"Victoria thought it was. She mentioned her son struggled with mental illness post-deployment. You said your father was a former Navy SEAL who had CTE, right?"

"You remember that?"

"I remember *alot* about that week," I told her honestly.

Then, just to watch her squirm, I ran my gaze up and down her body. "In fact, I remember every... last... detail."

To my delight, she did squirm, and her face turned the most appealing shade of pink. I flashed back to a vision of Scarlett in bed, underneath me, just after I'd made her come. Again.

She straightened her shoulders and jutted out her little chin.

"I guess you'd know something about battle damage, huh, *Wolf*? Is that your special ops nickname? You and Sharkbait and Gandalf and Wildman and Volt and Badger. You guys were a SEAL squad, huh?"

I closed my eyes for a moment then opened them, meeting her gaze straight on. "Victoria told you."

"Yes, she told me. I guess I know why you didn't. *And* why you didn't have any condoms with logos with you when you supposedly sold them for a living. You guys were in Greece on pre-deployment for an operation, weren't you?"

"Post-op," I said. "I'm sorry. I wanted to tell you the truth, I just couldn't. Besides, you seemed to have something against military guys. I liked you. I wanted to keep talking to you. And then we were having such a good time that week, I didn't want to ruin everything by confessing that I lied. You seemed to have some trust issues."

"Gee, I wonder why." She looked away and tapped a few keys on her laptop. "It doesn't matter. That's all water under the bridge. We don't have to like each other—we just have to work together and be civil for the next few weeks. But since we *are* going to be working together, I should mention... honesty is *very* important to me."

"Okay..." I dragged out the word, my tone expectant.

"So if you're keeping any more big secrets, now's the time to fess up."

A thrill of panic went through my midsection. Which was weird. After all I'd been through, nothing made me panic anymore.

Besides, my secret wasn't the kind she was referring to. It was not something I could share with her, but in the grand scheme of things, it wasn't that big a deal.

"None that pop to mind," I said. "And since we're going to be working together for the next few weeks, I'd also like to make an announcement. I really am sorry about the way our non-honeymoon week ended."

She gave me a half-hearted, "Thank you for saying that."

"I thought about looking you up later... when the operation was over, and I was back in the States. But I felt weird about it since I'd lied to you. Also, I wasn't in the greatest frame of mind for a while. Anyway, I figured you wouldn't want to hear from me. You still seemed pretty hung up on that bozo you were supposed to marry."

"His name is Bryce, and he's not a bozo. He was just confused."

"Oh shit, don't tell me you're back with him?"

"What? No. Of course not. It's just... he's not a bad guy. He just made a mistake by promising to love me forever when he wasn't really sure how he felt."

"Exactly. Bozo."

"What? *You're* so in touch with your feelings?" she challenged. "Oh wait, I remember. Your gut has never steered you wrong."

"I never said that." If I had, it would have been a lie.

My gut had absolutely steered me wrong in the situation in Iraq. And later, when it had told me I had no choice but to testify against my commander. Goodbye military career, hello civilian life.

But I'd made peace with it, and my gut and I were once again on speaking terms. And since rediscovering my love of painting, I'd become completely in touch with my feelings.

At the moment they were pinging all over the room, thanks to Scarlett's close proximity.

"You definitely did. You said it, all cocky and sure of yourself. I remember things about that week, too, you know," Scarlett said.

Stepping even closer, I looked down at her. I was completely invading her personal space—but that's exactly what I meant to do.

Something in me wanted to... *bother* her.

Scarlett made me feel like a middle-schooler who had no idea how to talk to girls but craved their attention and acted out in ridiculous ways to get it.

"Oh yeah?" I asked. "Which things?"

She pushed at my belly, which was at her eye level. "You're disgusting. Get back to work."

Laughing, I went to stand in front of the next painting. It was an original by Inksy. I seriously doubted Victoria wanted to auction *this* off   it had been a gift from a friend.

"What do you think of this one?" I asked over my shoulder. "It's called *Confluence*."

"It's decent, I guess," Scarlett said, making me bark with startled laughter.

"Decent? This painting was just appraised at twenty-five million dollars."

She squinted at it. "Is it worth it though? What makes a painting or sculpture valuable? I mean it's all so subjective. I read about a guy who ate a whole bunch of fruit and then spread his... poopy all over a canvas and called it art. It sold for almost two million dollars."

Her use of the toddler word "poopy" combined with the ridiculous story took the sting out of the insult she'd just hurled at the highly acclaimed painting on the wall.

"You're comparing *Confluence* to 'fruity poopy?'"

"No, I told you I think it's okay." She seemed flustered.

"I feel like I can at least understand that one. Most art makes me feel... inferior," she confessed. "No, that's not the right word. It's... intimidating, I guess. It makes me feel ignorant, like I don't know whether it's good or bad or what I'm supposed to think about it or how it's supposed to make me feel."

"There is no 'supposed to' when it comes to art," I said. "There's no right way to think about it or right way to feel. You think what you think and feel what you feel. That's kind of the whole point. It's created to make you feel *something*—and that something is going to be different for every person."

"For instance, how does looking at this one make you feel?" I gestured to the Inksy, keeping my tone casual, not wanting her to suspect how invested I was in her answer.

Scarlett flushed and looked away, her shoulders tensing. "I don't know."

"Yes, you do. There's no wrong answer. Just say the first thing that comes to mind."

"I don't know... hungry?"

"Hungry?" That one took me by surprise. Though the painting was abstract, it had nothing to do with food.

"I don't mean like hungry for food," she explained. "It makes me feel like... like I *want* something. It's filled with longing... with desire."

For a moment all I could do was stare. My heart was blocking my throat, so speech was impossible.

This woman, who claimed to know nothing about art, had seen directly through the painting—to me.

She'd seen the exact things I'd been feeling when I created it. It was a surreal experience.

Her eyebrows lowered, and she gave me an insecure look. "Is that a stupid answer?"

"No." My hand shot out to grip her arm, but I let it go just as quickly and let my hand fall to my side. "No, not at all. I think you're right. I think that's what the artist was trying to convey. Probably."

"Who's the artist?" she asked.

Again my heart did its level best to suffocate me.

"Inksy."

"Inksy," she repeated. "Just one name?"

I nodded. "His real identity is anonymous. He's an urban street artist. He first started with overnight wall murals in public spaces and smuggling his work into museums as pranks. The publicity increased museum attendance, and that raised Inksy's profile. He's done stealth street pieces and pop-up art installations all over the world, kind of like graffiti but usually more appreciated. I'm surprised you haven't seen anything on the news about it."

"I have now that I think about it. How does everyone know Inksy is a 'he?' Maybe Inksy is female."

"Could be. No one knows for sure." *Except for me.*

Scarlett closed her laptop, fully engaged now. "So how does she—or he—stay anonymous? *Someone* must know who Inksy is."

I held up a finger. "This one I can answer—one of Viridian's specialties is helping celebrity clients maintain their privacy. Inksy probably uses nondisclosure agreements and employs a lot of lawyers."

"*Why* remain anonymous though?" she asked. "Why not take credit for your work? Why paint murals in the middle of the night then sneak away like some kid who's rolled the football coach's yard in toilet paper?"

I chuckled at the mental image. "I think Inksy likes surprising people. Not too long ago, one of his pieces was up on the auction block. It had just sold for five million when it suddenly burst into flame."

Her head jerked in surprise. "Wow. How did that happen?"

"A remote-control incendiary device. He had a back-up painting he sent to the buyer, but it was quite an attention-getter."

"He must be really good at being sneaky," Scarlett said.

"Maybe he just wants to create art without drawing attention to himself."

I stepped back and studied the painting as if I hadn't created every stroke of it myself.

"It's kind of like when people post things online hiding behind a shadow account, or going into a curtained confessional booth, or writing books under a pen name. You can express what you *really* think and feel—be your true self—when no one knows who you are."

"Well, whoever that artist is... he's *really* hungry," Scarlett said.

You have no idea, darlin'.

TWELVE

My Favorite Mistake

Scarlett

How I'd gotten roped into a conversation about art—about *anything* with Gray Lupine was a mystery to me.

I'd fully intended to keep my distance from the man. But he'd basically dared me to catch him stealing from Vivi's collection, and while I highly doubted he'd try anything while being watched, it was a good idea that he be *supervised* while here in her house.

I opened up my laptop again but continued to keep him in my peripheral vision.

He moved about the room so silently I wouldn't have been shocked to learn he *was* a cat burglar.

When he turned his back to me to take notes on the paintings on the opposite wall, I let myself peer over the top of my screen at him.

Gray was no longer a SEAL, but he'd clearly continued working out. His wide back tapered to a lean waist. He was casually dressed today in shorts and a t-shirt which showed off long, strong legs and heavily muscled arms that boasted a few more tattoos than I remembered.

I wondered what the new ones signified. Happy times? Bad memories?

Desperate attempts to cope with the horrors of war?

Whatever they meant, they were devastatingly sexy.

Glancing back over his shoulder, he caught me staring.

"Whatcha looking at?" he teased.

"That sculpture there... in the center of the room," I lied. "What is it?"

"That's a Modigliani. Very few of his pieces are in private ownership today. Most can only be seen in museums."

"You know a lot about art," I begrudgingly admitted.

Clearly, Gray was the right person to help Vivi find new homes for her prized sculptures and paintings, and he seemed to be taking the job very seriously.

He shrugged. "I know a bit. It's a hobby."

"Seems like more than a hobby. Vivi told me you designed your tattoos and those of your squad members," I said. "Why'd you go into security when you left the SEAL teams? Why not become a tattoo artist?"

He laughed as if I'd just told a joke.

"I'm being serious. You're really, really good. You could maybe even make a living with your art."

Gray rolled his lips in then out and gave me a half-smile. "Thanks. As for why I haven't turned it into a full-time gig, first of all... needles."

He faked a silly, dramatic shudder. "And second, I still wanted to help people. I couldn't be a SEAL anymore, but as a home security specialist, I can help make the world a safer place on a small-scale individual level. It's another way of protecting people. Plus, I get to work with my former squad members. Not sure if you remember Wilder? He introduced himself as Wildman the night you met him. He's the one who started Viridian."

"I remember him." A man like Wilder was impossible to forget. "Super-tall, dark-haired athletic guy, right?"

Gray's brows pulled together in a disgruntled looking V.

"Right. He started the company so we could all keep working together as civilians."

"That's cool. So... you *all* retired from the teams then. All at once?"

Gray's furrowed brow creased more deeply. "Pretty much."

"Why?"

While he'd been open and animated discussing Vivi's art collection, he completely shut down. "It's a long, unpleasant story. I should get back to work."

His stony face and cold tone of voice caused me to flinch.

It reminded me of my father when he'd been home between deployments, shutting me out, squashing any kind of close connection that might have attempted to blossom between us, like a boot crushing Spring violets underfoot.

"Fine," I said and went back to my own task of researching non-profits Vivi might want to make endowments to.

Considering her love of art, I was focused on finding some programs that utilized art as therapy for trauma survivors or people with anxiety and depression or opened new doors for disadvantaged kids.

A few minutes later, Gray left the room, muttering a few terse words about something he had to do tonight.

Well, okay then. Clearly, I'd hit on a sore spot when I'd asked about him leaving his service as a SEAL team member.

Now, of course, I was curious. It occurred to me I might be able to get some answers about his past by typing his name into the search engine I'd been using.

Seconds after I did, the screen filled with photos and news articles about an ugly and sensational trial involving Gray and Wilder and the other platoon members I'd known only by their nicknames.

Now his reticence to discuss it made more sense. Apparently, all the guys on the squad had testified against their commander about some incident that had taken place in Iraq several years ago.

From the account of events, it seemed like the SEAL team

members had done the right thing. Loyalty was important, but you couldn't stand by and let an atrocity like that one go unpunished. I mean, the US forces were supposed to be the good guys, right?

The only way that could remain true was to weed out the bad apples and make sure they didn't get a chance to rot the whole barrel.

None of the guys had spoken to the media, but whatever they'd said in their testimony must have been pretty damning. The platoon leader had been convicted.

Scrolling to the bottom of one article, I read some of the public comments then swiftly shut the page down. They were filled with such vitriol—on both sides—I was kind of surprised the computer hadn't caught fire and melted.

It couldn't have been easy for Gray to be in the center of such a firestorm of controversy and public scrutiny. I pressed my fist against my chest, trying to soothe a sudden ache there.

One more piece of evidence that you don't want to get involved with a former SEAL. How much more do you need, girlfriend?

Appealing physique and alluring tattoos aside, Gray Lupine needed to *remain* in the My Favorite Mistake category. In fact, I needed to add him to the Never Again column as well.

Admittedly, he didn't *seem* like a ticking time bomb of suppressed rage or a hollow shell, but still waters sometimes ran deep.

Who knew what lurked beneath that beautiful surface?

THIRTEEN

Welcome Home

Gray

I ran *away.*

Like a rabbit. Or a rodent. Or a three-year-old.

I could hardly believe it myself, but there was no denying that was what had just happened.

Scarlett had asked a simple question. I could have given her a simple answer, something like, "It was just time," or, "Can't be a superhero forever," or some other glib remark then turned the conversation to the beautiful summer weather here in Eastport Bay.

How could a few words from her unnerve me like that? Maybe I wasn't quite as zen as I'd given myself credit for. I had no difficulty making superficial small talk with my clients and the people I saw socially.

For some reason, it was different with Scarlett. Just as I did with her grandmother, I found it impossible to be fake with her.

Maybe it was the scarily accurate way she'd read my painting. Or the way she studied me with those big blue eyes of hers. I could swear I'd actually *felt* them analyzing me before I'd turned around and caught her looking.

Maybe it was just the echo of the time we'd spent together three years ago when she was so vulnerable and emotionally bleeding out. Once I might have been able to be that open, but those days were gone.

That was one of the reasons I protected my Inksy alter-ego so fiercely. I didn't *want* to be seen or known. I'd had enough exposure to last a lifetime during my commanding officer's trial.

Thanks to the *wonders* of modern technology, some of the worst moments of my life were readily available for public entertainment twenty-four-seven, three-sixty-five. Forever.

It was much safer to keep the rest of it, the things that mattered to me—my thoughts and feelings, my art—close to the vest.

Anyway, I hadn't lied to Scarlett about having something I needed to do. Her innocent mention of the inglorious end to my military career triggered something in me—a swell of shame, pride, regret, and unquenched desire that I *needed* to work out.

When I left Victoria's house, I stopped by my studio for some supplies then headed out into the night in search of a canvas.

I didn't usually create street art close to home. The risk of exposure was too great. Normally I'd get in my car and drive three hours south to New York City or an hour north into Boston or hop a plane to some international city where I'd stay a day or two and take in the sights after leaving my own personal stamp on it. I guess you could call me a guerilla-art tourist.

But that wasn't possible tonight. I had to go in early for a few hours of work tomorrow morning before picking up Victoria for our usual Saturday outing.

That would mean another inevitable encounter with Scarlett.

Before I saw her again, I needed to get my head right. Art therapy wasn't just something I recommended to Victoria and the boys I volunteered with at the Ocean State Training School.

It was critical for me as well, probably the only thing that had kept me sane during the years I served as a SEAL and in the aftermath.

Already, just planning the mural I'd paint tonight, I felt

calmer, more centered. I drove from Eastport Bay to Providence, only thirty-five miles away.

Cities were the best place for street art. Somehow, though there were more people living and working there, there seemed to be fewer eyes around after hours—at least none that would care what I was up to enough to call the police.

And there were plenty of spots here that could use a new focal point. I picked a location not far from the freeway near the homeless shelter. Just beyond the shelter's large brick building lay an empty lot containing a single partially demolished cinderblock wall, a remnant from some downtown revitalization project that had begun but stalled along the way.

Perfect.

The people standing in line for services next door would be able to see the mural and so would those driving by on the highway.

Maybe it would give someone a smile, and we could all damn well use one of those right now.

As with many of my street pieces, I would use washable paint. As quickly as I'd created it, the painting would be gone with the next rainstorm—or fire hose, if the powers that be in the city decided to call it vandalism.

Parking a few streets away, I slung my backpack over my shoulder and hoofed it to the empty lot.

The ugly (for now) wall loomed above me, the perfect representation of the dark chaos I felt inside. I checked around first for witnesses, slipped on a paint respirator and my climbing harness, and got to work.

As the image took shape, I moved and breathed, focusing on the blending colors, the shapes and contours, letting my pent-up emotions flow out through the spray can nozzles and create a visual of my mind's interior.

Several hours later, the cans—and my soul—were pleasantly weightless. I used what remained to add a title for the piece

—*Welcome Home*—and stepped back to take in the complete picture I'd created.

It was a mural in four parts that met in the middle. One part portrayed some of the city's more recognizable landmarks. Drivers speeding by would assume that's all it was—a simple welcome message to suburban commuters and visitors.

Below it was an image of Vietnam Vets being booed as they returned from overseas—no doubt some of the homeless center's clients would be able to relate.

In the top right corner, I'd painted a mimic of Salvador Dali's *The Ascension of Christ*. which depicted Jesus rising from the earth into the nucleus of a bright yellow atom.

Finally, the lower right quadrant contained visuals that called to mind cold Mediterranean waters and hot sand and rumpled bedsheets surrounding the shadowy outline of a woman who held her arms aloft in sultry invitation.

Her figure was curvy and lush, her eyelids heavy. Her lips were parted as if she was about to speak or laugh or make some guy very, *very* happy he had a few days off between operations.

Oh yeah—they're gonna turn the firehoses on it all right.

I chuckled, packing up my gear and jogging back to my car. It didn't really matter if my work lasted a few hours or a few days or if they roped it off and built a museum around it. Its purpose had already been served.

I could go back to Eastport Bay and face Scarlett again. Nothing she could say or do would bother me—I'd gotten my troubling desire for her out of my system and onto a canvas.

I only hoped she didn't see a photo of it and recognize herself.

FOURTEEN

A Peek into his Soul

Scarlett

The next day, Gray arrived, saying hello and smiling at me and Vivi as if his strange, abrupt departure from the gallery last night had never happened.

His inconsistent behavior reminded me so much of my dad I felt like an eight-year-old again, unsure whether I wanted to clutch his leg and beg for his attention or run away and hide.

It didn't help that I was sitting on the floor doing a puzzle when he arrived.

Vivi had invited me to help with her current work in progress, an eighteen-thousand-piece behemoth depicting one of Van Gogh's famous Sunflowers paintings. She told me Gray had given it to her last week.

The entire image was comprised of shades of yellow, so it was a challenge to say the least.

While I sat cross-legged on the floor, she sat on the sofa, leaning over the puzzle board which rested atop the large, square ottoman between us.

For some reason Gray stayed in the doorway, leaning against the frame and watching from a distance. When I glanced up at him, he was wearing an odd expression.

He looked... concerned. Or distracted maybe.

"Come and join us, son," Vivi said. "Doing puzzles is the best way to keep your mind sharp and improve your finger dexterity. Your lady friends will appreciate that."

Gray burst into laughter. "Thanks for the tip. I'll keep that in mind in case I ever get one of those."

The unexpected racy remark from my eighty-nine-year-old grandmother seemed to break the invisible tension in the room. Gray strolled inside and made himself a cup of tea. While he didn't join us in puzzling, he took a seat in a chair nearby, observing.

His watchful gaze made me nervous. I had to stop at one point and remove my light cardigan. Then I felt even more self-conscious because all I wore underneath it was a filmy camisole top.

Not that it was risqué. He'd seen me in much less.

Not helping. Don't think about that.

Did *he* ever think about that week we'd spent together? Since I'd arrived here and seen him again, the memories had been flooding my brain, and my senses seemed to be in overdrive.

I was hyperaware of everything about Gray, his slow and steady breathing behind me, the shift of his body as he crossed one long leg over the other at the ankles.

The light scent of his cologne—the same one that had lingered on the t-shirt I'd somehow managed to bring home in my luggage from Greece.

I *might* have placed it, unwashed, on the top of my dresser and created a little shrine around it until the last of the scent had mercifully dissipated. Julianna had tactfully neglected to mention it, and I tried my best not to think of it now.

"Looking good," he drawled.

His bemused tone made me glance back sharply. Oh, he was looking at the puzzle.

What a mess I am.

Leaning forward with his elbows resting on his knees, Gray smiled. "I'd say you'll finish that in another, oh, five years or so?"

Vivi swatted the air. "I'll have it done in no time now that I have Scarlett's help. She's a master dissectologist like me."

"Dissectologist?" It sounded like someone who cut up small amphibians for a living, which I'd never be able to do. I'd literally vomited on frog dissection day in middle school.

"It means someone who enjoys assembling jigsaw puzzles," she explained. "You got my genes for sure."

"Well, you two certainly are a lot alike," Gray said. I looked up and caught him in a full smile that wrinkled the corners of his eyes and stole my breath.

For a moment we held fervent eye contact. Something instinctive and alive expanded in my chest.

"Same birthday, same laugh, same sky-blue eyes, ..." he said. "... both stone-cold foxes."

Happy, warm feeling ruined.

In spite of Vivi's assurances of what a great guy Gray was, he was still a player, still *so* smooth with the lines. No doubt he and the members of his SEAL team had stolen many a heart and collected innumerable bedpost notches while in between operations over the years.

"I'll bet you say that to all the girls—in *all* the resorts," I added with a sneer.

Perhaps sensing a brewing storm, Victoria chirped, "So where are you taking us for our outing today, Gray?"

"Us?" When Vivi had told me Gray usually took her out on Saturday afternoons, I'd assumed it would be just the two of them going today.

"Yes, dear. I want you to come along. It'll be fun. We always have a good time—Gray surprises me every week with something new to see and do."

While I wanted to see some of Rhode Island and keep an eye on Vivi, I did *not* relish the idea of being the third wheel on a "date" that included Gray. Especially not after his remarks today.

"If I tell you, it'll ruin the surprise," Gray said. "And don't even try to guess. You'll never get it. But you're going to love it. *Both* of you."

"Sure," I said, unfolding my legs and standing. "Why not?"

There were myriad answers to that question, but I was ignoring them all.

Gray and I helped Vivi to the elevator then out the front door to where his car waited in the circular drive. It was a new-looking Range Rover.

"*Nice*," I said. "Security work pays more than I thought."

Gray chuckled. "I like driving, so investing in a nice car was worth it for me."

He opened the door for me and then for Vivi, helping her into the front seat where she could see the scenery as we traveled.

As we made our way down Oceanside Avenue, she pointed out various houses.

"That's where Sullivan Reece lives—he was the heavyweight boxing champion of the world, but he retired not long ago to spend more time with his young family."

Indicating an enormous Italianate stone mansion, she said, "That's the home of Jack R. R. Bestia, the author. He writes those dragon books they made into a TV show."

I nodded. "I've read them."

"His brother Hunter used to live in this next one with some of his friends and co-workers—the young men who created that Chipp company, something to do with computers. They call that place the Billionaire Bachelor House. Several of the boys have gotten married now and moved out, but I think a few still live there."

"And this one is the summer home of the Wessex family—the prince of Aubernesse and his wife and three children," she said. "Cinda Wessex grew up here in Eastport Bay. I think she was his maid before they got married," Vivi said.

"*That* sounds like an interesting story." I had Hollywood rom com visuals running through my mind, wondering if the princess of Aubernesse looked more like Jennifer Lopez or Amy Adams.

"Gray, your friend Wilder lives around here doesn't he, with that cute little singer he married?"

Gray, who'd been quiet as he drove, said, "He moved into her house after they married. They live on Atlantic, not too far from here. I'll drive you by their house and point it out sometime."

"You certainly have a lot of famous neighbors," I said.

"That's Eastport Bay for you," Vivi said. "It used to be all old-money families dating back to the Gilded Age. Then word got out about the beautiful coastline and mild summer weather, and all the celebrities and CEO's started moving in. It's good to have fresh blood—keeps things interesting."

Speaking of interesting, Gray drove us through Eastport Bay's downtown, along the waterfront main street with its yacht-filled harbor and quaint shops and restaurants. The Colonial-era village looked like something out of a storybook.

"This is charming," I said.

"You won't find anything like *this* in Minnesota," Gray said, meeting my gaze in the rearview mirror.

I squirmed to stifle the tingly sensation that filled me, and my eyes flickered away to the view outside the window.

We left the bustling tourist-filled area and drove into a more industrial looking section of town. Gray parked outside what appeared to be a warehouse.

"This is it?" I asked.

"Yep. We're here."

As I followed him and Vivi toward the nondescript building, I couldn't imagine what kind of "fun" we could possibly find in a place like this. Once we rounded the corner, the answer became clear.

The side of the warehouse had been painted a royal blue and decorated with large, bright yellow flowers. Near the entrance was parked an antique truck that had also been painted yellow.

Above it, a sign read, "The Original Immersive Van Gogh Exhibit."

Vivi picked up her pace, hurrying toward the entrance. "I've heard about this! It's like being inside his paintings, isn't it? How do they do it?"

Gray smiled. "You'll see. It's a digital presentation of his works throughout his career, but it's all around you, on every wall, and it's always changing. The soundtrack is phenomenal. I'm excited to experience it again—once is definitely not enough when something is really good."

For some reason he shot a glance at me just then. And for no reason at all, I flushed with heat.

The immersive exhibit was all in one large high-ceilinged space. People sat on the floor on cushions so they could turn to observe the walls in each direction.

There were also a few two-person benches, and that's where I took Vivi, sitting beside her. Gray sat on the floor in front of us just as a bloom of color raced across the floor and up the walls.

The projected visuals were almost overwhelming. Beautiful, shocking, fascinating, they showed some of Vincent Van Gogh's most famous paintings being created stroke by emphatic digital stroke.

Some of the paintings were split into their individual elements then combined again. Fields of grasses and flowers seemed to grow up from the cement floor, and fantastical heavenly bodies danced in whorls and bursts across a midnight blue sky.

All the while, the musical soundtrack shifted from haunting to dreamlike to pensive and back to tranquilizing. The total experience was almost impossible to describe.

One thing it *wasn't*, was "snooty."

By the end of the hour-long exhibit, I felt almost like I'd met the artist, who'd died unknown and virtually penniless a hundred years before I was even born.

We walked out into the disconcertingly bright day, blinking against the late afternoon sun.

"That was marvelous," Vivi declared. "What did you think, Scarlett? A bit better than a puzzle, wasn't it?"

I nodded. "It was incredible. It was almost like... being *inside* of someone else. Inside their mind and heart."

"That's what the best art does," Gray said. "It gives you a window into someone else's soul."

Once again, my eyes wandered to his arms, to his intriguing new tattoos. One was a handsome wolf with piercing green eyes— that one was pretty self-explanatory.

The stories behind the others were more mysterious. I wanted to ask about them, to get a peek into *his* soul, but I resisted.

I was here to help Vivi. When that was done, I'd go back to my life, and he'd go back to his.

While I was here in Eastport Bay, I needed to be able to work with him and be civil, but that was it.

There would be no point in getting close to him again.

FIFTEEN

No One in my Life

Scarlett

From the exhibit, we took a fifteen-minute drive to the next town over, Middletown.

Gray turned off the main street onto a long road dotted with farmhouses and the occasional pocket neighborhood. Eventually he took a left onto a small lane marked by a tall, artificial sunflower.

"We're going to a farm?" I guessed.

He nodded. "A special one—in keeping with today's theme."

The country lane led us past a grove of tall fir trees. Once we passed them, a small building came into view.

And on either side of the road, fields of sunflowers stretched as far as I could see. It was like the sun had fallen from the sky and splattered all over the ground.

"It's beautiful," Vivi said. "It's like his paintings."

"I thought you'd like it. Van Gogh's inspiration—the Rhode Island edition." Gray pulled into a parking spot in the gravel lot and turned off the car.

There had to be thousands of flowers—it looked like several football fields' worth.

We got out and walked into one of the fields, surrounded by

the shoulder-height leafy green plants and their enormous, golden heads.

Their pleasant, light scent was more earthy than sweet. I walked along, touching their leaves lightly. It made me a little sad to know that Minnesota had at least a couple of sunflower festivals I'd never bothered to attend.

I thought about Julianna's advice to me—*go see something new, do some things you've never done*—and felt a grudging sense of gratitude toward Gray for dragging me out of the rut I'd created for myself and taking off my blinders to simple pleasures like this one.

This was an *experience.*

The flowers on the next row must have been planted earlier because their backs were brown instead of green and some of the petals had begun to dry out and fall off.

Gray stepped up to one of them. "These are perfect for eating. You can pull out the seeds and pop them into your mouth whole or crack the shell first and just eat the insides."

He demonstrated, tugging a handful of seeds from the head of one plant and breaking open their thin shells.

"The seeds of these flowers are small because they're being grown for oil production instead of snacking, but they're still tasty." He offered the shelled seeds to Vivi and then to me before eating some himself.

I chewed mine, enjoying the nutty, mild flavor and tender texture. "I've never had sunflower seeds that weren't roasted and salted and sealed into a plastic bag. These are good just the way they are."

"Aren't they?" he asked. "The petals are also edible. They're good in salads."

Vivi chewed her seeds and reached up to the sunflower head to pluck a few more for herself. "I didn't know that. See, you *can* still teach an old dog new tricks."

Gray pulled out his phone and took some photos of her while she harvested.

"How do *you* know all this?" I asked, half-suspecting Gray was full of bs, particularly about eating sunflower petals.

"I've been on some long stakeouts during operations," he explained, clicking a few more angles. "Did a lot of reading. And I figured it would be useful to learn about which plants are edible and which aren't."

Then he turned the camera to me. "Smile."

Feeling self-conscious—I hated pictures of myself—I scrunched my nose and made a silly face. Then Gray encouraged Vivi and me to pose for a few pictures together.

"What a marvelous idea," she said. "We can put filters on ourselves, Scarlett, and look like cats with huge eyes."

Now there was an idea. At least surrounded by bright yellow blooms no one would be looking at me in the photos. I managed a few smiles for my grandmother's sake.

We spent another half hour walking through the field, randomly selecting seeds to crack open and eat.

"Well, this whets my appetite. Who's hungry?" Vivi asked.

"I am," Gray said, "and these little seeds aren't getting the job done."

"I could definitely eat."

Vivi clapped. "I know—let's go to the Cliffhouse. My treat. I want Scarlett to see the view there."

"Cliffhouse it is," Gray said.

To get there we drove back into Eastport Bay then took a winding seaside drive that hugged the rocky coastline and offered breathtaking vistas of the Atlantic Ocean. In some places the outcroppings of dark shale and slate gave way to inlets and sandy coves, and beyond it all stretched the majestic gray-blue water.

We took a right onto a small lane that led past a series of tiny beach cottages, a beautiful private harbor, and then atop a gentle hill, the Cliffhouse itself.

It was a beautiful historic mansion that had been turned into an inn and restaurant. Behind it, the hillside sloped down to the water and offered an amazing view of the bay and the open Atlantic.

White Adirondack chairs covered the grassy lawn. Nearly all of them were filled with well-dressed people holding cocktails as they awaited their dinner reservations at the outdoor tables or perhaps they were just preparing to toast the approaching sunset.

Already the sun was sliding lower in the sky, causing a long suspension bridge in the distance to gleam like a silver crown against the blue of the water.

"Wow," I breathed. This place was breathtaking.

Vivi smiled and took my hand. "This is the Eastport Bay I always wished I could show you. I want you to fall in love with my home—and consider it your home away from home."

"It's lovely. Should we try to find some empty chairs, or do you want to put our names on the wait list for a table?"

She gave me a wink. "We'll let Gray take care of it."

He'd stepped away from us toward the outdoor host stand and was smiling and talking to the young woman who worked there. Like every other woman in his vicinity, she appeared to be dazzled by his looks.

After a short conversation, they shook hands, and he returned to us.

"They can seat us in about fifteen or twenty minutes," he said. "They're going to pull three chairs together for us on the lawn while we wait. I've already ordered us some sparkling waters."

He shot me a mischievous grin. "Unless you'd prefer an Ouzo lemonade, Scarlett?"

I mouthed the words *ha ha* at him and narrowed my eyes. "Sparkling water sounds perfect."

We followed a young hostess to our chairs and sat facing the water. Sailboats passed by so close I was able to make out the faces of those aboard, and the breeze carried the scents of the ocean and the plentiful beach roses that bordered the inn's property.

As the sun set, I looked over at my grandmother. The waning

light bathed her face in soft, peachy color, making her look much younger, almost like she had when I'd last seen her as a child.

I had a sudden memory of the two of us walking on the beach in Florida, laughing and chasing tiny sea crabs along the wet sand.

Then I looked over at Gray, and I wished *I* could take a photo of him. The sunset absolutely *loved* his face.

The color-changing light from the day's last rays sent me back to all those evenings we spent together on the Mykonos beaches, milking every drop of beauty the island's days had to offer.

Those had been some of the happiest days of my life, in spite of the odd timing.

Today had been a good one, too. I had, as Julianna had urged me to do, seen things I'd never seen before.

I couldn't help but be a little jealous that Vivi got to spend every Saturday afternoon with someone who went out of his way to surprise her, who spent time and effort trying to delight and please her.

There was no one in my life who would do that for me.

I also thought how unbelievably sexy it was that Gray had chosen an unusual art exhibit and a walk in a majestic field of blooms as the day's activities instead of something mundane like a movie or bowling.

No one in my life would do that either.

That was when I truly *understood* what Julianna kept saying to me about Kevin and Henry. No offense to them personally— they were nice guys.

But they didn't thrill me like this. They didn't even excite me a little bit.

Gray suddenly looked away from the gorgeous painted sky, catching me in my perusal of his even more gorgeous face.

He smiled. "Beautiful, huh? Eat your heart out, Van Gogh."

My pulse thumped in my ears, giving the surreal moment a soundtrack. All I could do was nod.

One of the hostesses walked over to where we were seated to tell us our table was ready. With Gray on one side of Vivi and me on the other, we made our way slowly up the hill toward the dining patio.

When we reached it, Vivi dug through her purse and withdrew her phone. "Oh good. Stephanie is here to pick me up."

"What?" Gray and I said simultaneously.

She smiled a not-so-innocent smile. "I'm feeling a little tired after such an active day and not all that hungry anymore. I texted Stephanie and asked her to come pick me up. She and I will have a chicken pie together in the kitchen."

"You should have told me you were tired. I would have driven you home," Gray protested.

Now Vivi's smile turned absolutely naughty.

"That's why I didn't tell you. Your table is waiting. You and Scarlett stay and enjoy a nice dinner for *two*."

SIXTEEN

Dinner for Two

Gray

Victoria turned to her granddaughter. "Gray will walk me to the car. Don't rush home because I'll be going to bed early. I'll see you in the morning, dear."

That crafty little sneak.

She'd planned her escape before we even got here. In fact, she'd probably planned it before either Scarlett or I woke up today.

"Okay, if you're sure." Scarlett gave her grandmother a bewildered look and a kiss on the cheek then followed the hostess to our table.

I joined her a few minutes later after helping Victoria into the housekeeper's car.

"The diabolical matchmaker of Eastport Bay is safely on her way home where she will no doubt spend the evening concocting *new* ways to throw us together."

Scarlett looked down then gave me a reticent smile. "You think that's what she's doing?"

"I know that's what she's doing. She's been telling me what a 'brilliant, beautiful, *darling* girl' you are almost non-stop since you got here."

Scarlett giggled. "She's been singing your praises as well."

"She's definitely up to something."

I couldn't say I was disappointed in the turn of events. I'd been sorely mistaken last night in my belief that painting Scarlett into the mural had purged my desire for her.

The instant I'd seen her this morning, it came roaring back.

It was strange, I'd been out with many beautiful women—some of them technically more beautiful than Scarlett. But no one made me feel the way she did.

I wasn't sure if it was because our romantic interlude had occurred before the Iraq incident and its horrible aftermath or if it was simply an effect of her unique chemical makeup and the way it interacted with mine, but this woman *did it* for me.

It was kind of a scary feeling to be so powerless before another person.

Completely unaware of the train of my thoughts, she smiled at me over the top of her menu. "Know what you want?"

Yes. You.

"I think I'm going to go with the citrus and beet salad and the grilled flatiron steak. You?"

"I can't decide between the baked sole and the lobster roll," she said. "The crispy chicken looks good, too."

"You really can't go wrong. The Cliffhouse is one of the best restaurants in Eastport Bay and a personal favorite of mine. The guys from Viridian come here together to celebrate whenever we score a big new contract. You should check out Nooky's too—another Eastport Bay tradition."

"Nooky's?" She wrinkled her nose and giggled. "Is that a strip club?"

I laughed out loud. "I guess it sounds like one. No, I'm not urging you to try the 'legs and eggs' special. Nooky's is a twenty-four-hour diner. The guy who founded it was named William Nookson. I'm guessing Nooky was his nickname."

"Was he a SEAL, too?" she asked. "Eastport Bay seems to be crawling with them."

"Not that I know of. Anyway, he made a hell of a chocolate cream pie. I'd eat a whole one without stopping—couldn't help myself. His daughter Pam took over the business when he retired. Now they serve at least ten kinds of pie every day of the week."

The waiter came and took our orders then disappeared again, leaving us in relative privacy.

Scarlett took a sip from her water glass. "Do you miss it?"

"The chocolate cream pie?"

"No silly. Being a SEAL."

"Sometimes," I admitted.

"Regular life must seem pretty quiet after all the things you've seen and done, all the places you've been and people you've met."

"It does, but that's not a bad thing," I said. "I've never seen anywhere more beautiful than this place." I swept my hand toward the ocean view.

"And most of the people I met during those years were in and out of my life pretty quickly," I said. "Some of them I prayed never to see again—present company excluded."

Scarlett blushed and looked away, letting her eyes drift along the coastline. "It *is* beautiful here. Even the trees and shrubs and flowers are different than they are in Minnesota."

"What's your favorite flower?" I asked.

"Why?"

"Just curious. Can't a guy be curious?"

"Poppies," she answered.

"I wish I'd sent you some after Mykonos. Just to say thank you for an amazing week. Or maybe I should have cut off my ear and mailed it to you," I joked, referencing the famous account of Van Gogh cutting off his ear and sending it as a gift to a woman he was smitten with.

Scarlett shook her head, dismissing the thought. "You didn't owe me anything. We were *both* there that week—and I *was* the one who insisted on no names. I completely understand why you left suddenly without a goodbye."

"Still... I wish we hadn't lost touch."

Her expression clouded. "Gray—nothing's going to happen here. You know that, right?"

"Why not? I mean, you don't still think I'm some kind of con artist out to swindle your grandma, do you?"

"No, but—"

"You liked me once," I said. "You could like me again."

She chuckled, shaking her head. "There's no point."

I disagreed, but I wasn't going to get into all the reasons why. It was too soon to let her see the intensity of my interest in her. Hell, it would probably terrify her.

"Why does there have to be a point?" I asked. "We could just have fun together."

Scarlett's phone buzzed on the tabletop. Though the screen was upside down from my position, I could still read the name.

Bryce.

She snatched up the device and pushed away from the table. "Excuse me. I'll be right back."

I swallowed down a surge of bitterness and shoved my hair out of my eyes as I watched her stroll the Cliffhouse lawn, just out of earshot, talking to her former fiancé.

She even laughed a couple of times.

When she returned to the table, she tucked her phone into her purse, looking sheepish. "Sorry about that. It was work."

"I saw the screen, Scarlett. It was Bryce, your former fiancé—unless you know some other tool with that name. Why does he have your number?"

"Because we *work* together," she said. "At my stepfather's company."

My head snapped back in shock. "You work with your ex-fiancé every day? What's *that* like?"

"It's fine." She looked down at the tabletop, smoothed her napkin in her lap. "I mean, just after the canceled wedding it was a bit awkward, but we're both grownups. My stepdad David offered to fire him, but Bryce is a good robotics technician. They're hard to find in Anoka. Plus, I didn't want David to get sued or something. I don't think you can legally fire someone for breaking your stepdaughter's heart."

"Why would he stay, though?" I asked, baffled. "And why is he calling? I thought you had some time off."

She shrugged, tilting her head in a defiant way. "We talk sometimes. He wants to start dating each other again. It's no big deal. I'm not sure why *you'd* even care. You have no right to say anything about the men I talk to."

Men. So she *was* dating—maybe several people. She was right —I had zero right to feel possessive of her.

But I did.

"I think I have a right—when it comes to this one. I was *there*, you know," I said. "I saw what kind of shape you were in after he did what he did. I hope you're not thinking of giving him a second chance."

That defiant little chin rose higher. "You don't believe in second chances?"

"Hell yes, I do—for some people. Not for him."

"You don't understand," she said.

"What's there to understand? He's a selfish prick. He's a chicken-shit who didn't man up when it was time to honor his promise to you. Now he wants to start hooking up again with no commitment. I can see why *he'd* want to, but what could you possibly see in him at this point?"

"Well... he still loves me for one thing."

I attempted to argue, but she held up her hand in a gesture to let her continue. So I did.

"He says he loves me and that he's sorry. And you have *no* idea what my life is like back in Minnesota. I love my stepdad, but I hate my job. It's boring. And the guys I've been going out with are boring."

"So why don't you change it? Get a more interesting job." I probably shouldn't have said it, but I added, "And clearly, you need to find a more interesting man to spend time with."

My hint went right over her head. "That's easier said than

done. My stepfather depends on me. How can I leave my job there? He's been so good to me, and no one else knows the company's books like I do. He trusts me."

The waiter returned with our salads, and we pushed pause on the conversation.

When he left, Scarlett said, "Maddie says I should just *do* it, look for my own replacement and train them then tell David I'm leaving. She says ultimately it'll be better for him to have someone in the position who actually *wants* to be there."

"I liked your sister. Sounds like good advice."

"Maybe. She makes everything sound so easy. She and my roommate Julianna keep pushing me to take more chances."

"Also good advice." Gathering my courage, I said, "Why don't you take another chance on me?"

Scarlett blinked several times, setting down her salad fork. "Another chance to what—dazzle me in bed?"

A pleasurable tingling sensation started at the top of my head then zipped down my neck and spine to my dick.

"You were dazzled?"

She rolled her eyes. "You know what I mean. What's the point of getting involved, even if you like me and I like you? I have to go home soon. There's no chance of this going anywhere—just like there was no chance before."

"Wait—you *like* me? I thought you hated me."

"I don't hate you," she admitted. "Maybe I did before, but it was only because I liked you so much first. And then you left without saying goodbye. Anyway, it doesn't matter. I've vowed never to have another fling."

"It was that bad, huh?" I asked, my erection deflating a bit.

"No," She hesitated then, looking embarrassed, lowered her voice. "Actually... it was that *good*."

My hard-on returned, no harm no foul, no questions asked. *We're back in business, boys.*

And then she finished her thought. "But I'm not into casual sex."

"We could have formal sex. I'll wear a tux," I offered.

Scarlett laughed and shook her head. "You're bad."

"I hear what you're saying, and I respect that," I told her. "So let's have a sex-less fling."

She quirked her head to the side. "Is that a thing?"

"It is now. We'll be the pioneers of the no-sex fling. We can hang out, have fun while you're in town—no hanky panky and no strings attached."

"We tried that before. It got pretty stringy," she said.

"We'll do better this time. It's hard not to get... 'stringy' in a hotel room on the beach in Greece. But this time you've got an entire mansion to roam around in, and I've got my own house to go back to, so it'll work."

"Where do you live?" she asked.

"I've got a townhouse in the harbor area, overlooking the water. It's nice. Not a huge place, but it's all I need."

"Sounds nice. I'd like to see it sometime."

I broke eye contact, reaching for a piece of warm ciabatta and dipping it in the small olive oil dish. I could *not* let her see my place. Not if I wanted her to buy into this plan.

"Sure. I'll give you a tour sometime. Not today, though—it's a mess."

She smiled, settling back in her chair and studying me with her fingers tented beneath her chin.

"A sex-free fling, huh? You really think we could do that?"

My dick, which was feeling jerked around at this point—and not in the *good* way—wasn't happy with me, but I ignored it and gave her a reassuring smile. I'd take any time with Scarlett I could get—in or out of the sheets.

Though she would *look fantastic rolling around in the 600 thread-count ones on my bed.*

My fingers clenched the tops of my thighs under the table.

"Absolutely," I said. "No problem. As easy as Nooky's chocolate cream pie."

"I thought you said you couldn't stop yourself from eating that?" Scarlett challenged.

"Oh. Right. Let me amend that to 'as easy as boiled okra.' Now *that*, I can resist."

Scarlett was definitely not okra.

She was the chocolatey-ist chocolate cream pie with chocolate sauce in a chocolate crust with shaved chocolate sprinkled on top.

"I'll think about it," she said. "In the meantime, I think I'll look at a dessert menu. You're making me hungry again."

Tell me about it.

SEVENTEEN

Rock Star

Scarlett

Vivi had told me she meant to turn in early, but she was still awake when I got back to the mansion.

I peeked into the open door of her sitting room before going to my own room to shower and get ready for bed. She saw me from the corner of her eye and turned her head.

"Scarlett. Come quickly. Come look at this on the late news. It's so exciting."

"What is it?"

The scene on her television featured a young reporter doing a live report from a dark street in Providence, the state capital.

Vivi turned up the volume.

"There is massive excitement within the art world tonight as the anonymous street artist known only as 'Inksy' appears to have struck here in Providence."

The young woman walked as she talked while the camera followed her. "City officials say normally works of graffiti are quickly painted over to deter vandalism to public and private property, but faculty at RISD and the Brown University Department of Fine Art persuaded them to wait while experts are called in to try to determine whether this piece, which appeared sometime during the night last night, is indeed a genuine Inksy."

As the reporter continued to speak, the photographer zoomed the camera out to show the entirety of the wall behind her.

The mural painted on it was colorful and interesting and certainly bore a resemblance to the style of the painting Vivi had in her gallery.

"Can you believe he was right here in Rhode Island?" my grandmother said.

Her hands were clasped below her chin as she watched the report. "I wish they'd show the mural up close."

The videographer did zoom in a little closer, but only on one part of it. It featured a stylized cityscape. The camera panned over and revealed another section of the mural, which looked like a brighter, more modern version of a Salvador Dali painting I'd seen somewhere.

Though I was the farthest thing from an art expert, I suspected the mural was a genuine Inksy. Because unlike most art, it made me *feel* something.

I wouldn't have been able to explain it if I tried, but for whatever reason, the piece spoke to me. About thirty seconds later, the report ended.

"Oh, we have to call Gray," Vivi said. "I wonder if he was watching?"

She held her phone out to me. "Would you dial it for me, dear? I can't see the screen that well at night."

With a knowing grin, I took the phone and searched her contacts for Gray's name, tapping it. He answered after one ring.

"Victoria? Everything okay?"

"It's Scarlett. She wanted to talk to you."

"Wait..."

The sudden pounding of my heart in my ears threatened to drown out his voice. "What?"

"How are you?"

"I'm the same as I was half an hour ago—very, very full. I should not have had the ice cream."

"Yes, you should have. The next few weeks are supposed to be all about fun, and dessert is fun." He hesitated before asking, "Have you thought about it?"

"What?"

"You know... the fling."

The pounding returned, louder and faster.

"Vivi and I were just watching the news." My voice sounded unnaturally high. "She's right here."

"The news?"

"Hold on. I'm handing the phone to Victoria. Good night, Gray."

"Wait—Scarlett..." I didn't hear whatever he said next because I'd already handed the phone off to Vivi.

They spoke for a few minutes, and she hung up.

"He says he didn't see the report, but he doubts it's real," she told me. "Supposedly Inksy is European. What would he be doing in Rhode Island?"

"Maybe he's here on vacation?" I suggested. "While we were at the Van Gogh exhibit and at Cliffhouse, I heard accents and languages from all over the world."

"That's possible," she said. "I'll have to check his Insta profile page and see if Inksy takes credit for it."

I laughed as my eighty-nine-year-old grandma scrolled Instagram.

Excitement over the mysterious mural grew as the days went by, and Vivi kept me apprised of the latest news reports. The city of Providence had assigned a twenty-four-hour police detail to protect it from vandalism, and Inksy experts were flying in from London to authenticate it.

There was talk of building a temporary shelter around it on the empty lot to protect the piece from the elements, should it turn out to be the real thing.

I thought it was much ado about nothing. I mean, yes, it was good, but it was just street art, after all.

One afternoon later that week, it was windy and overcast and a little too cool to sit out on the loggia, so Vivi and I went back to the sitting room to work on her puzzle some more. She turned on Action News 3's early newscast.

The news anchors were talking about, what else, the Inksy mural. It had been authenticated as genuine. They tossed to a reporter for another live report.

This time the young woman was surrounded by a crowd pushing at the ropes that cordoned off the wall.

She interviewed several people, including art students and some collectors who were practically frothing at the mouth in their enthusiasm about the mural and what a rare and special opportunity it was to see the artist's work with their own eyes.

"Apparently this Inksy guy—or woman—is a really big deal," I said to Vivi.

She beamed. "He is. I read in today's paper that collectors from around the world are competing to have the wall removed and shipped to them overseas. They're willing to pay tens of millions for it."

"Wow. That's so crazy. Where's the article?"

"Over on the table next to the tea service. I saved it for you."

"Thanks." I got up and retrieved the newspaper. A small photo of the mural was featured on the front page with the promise of more photos and an article in the Arts section. I turned to it and gasped.

There was a large, color photo of the full mural along with several others highlighting its individual sections. I recognized the Salvador Dali simulation and the cityscape from the TV report I'd seen, but there were two more sections I hadn't seen before.

One featured soldiers returning from war to an unfriendly reception. Its mood, naturally, was dark and mournful.

The other segment had a completely different feel. It was brighter and filled with vibrant color. There was the turquoise of the ocean, azure skies, pink sand like the beach I'd marveled over in Crete, and creamy white bedsheets.

In the center of the bed was a woman. A very curvy, sexy woman. She was mostly in shadow, but it was pretty obvious what was going on.

She was tempting someone to join her in bed.

Suddenly I was blazing hot as a spark of recognition set my brain and body on fire. The woman... did she look like... no.

"Vivi, did you look at these pictures?" I took the paper to her and lay it atop the puzzle.

"I did. They're quite something, aren't they?" she responded.

"Did anything about them look familiar to you?" I asked.

"Well, I recognized the State House of course and the Superman building downtown. And there's Waterfire lighting up the rivers."

"What about the woman in this section?" I tapped a finger on the mural featuring the sea and sky and the sexy silhouette. "Does she look familiar to you at all?"

Vivi leaned forward, studying the newspaper photo. "I can't say that she does. She's quite a saucy siren, isn't she?"

For some reason, I felt embarrassed, like I'd been spotted in public in my underwear. "I guess so. I wonder who she is?"

She chortled. "Inksy's dream girl—that's who she is. Maybe if those reporters figure out *her* identity, they'll finally figure out who he is."

I squinted at the photo a little longer. The grainy nature of the newsprint made it impossible to make out small details. I wanted to see the mural in person.

Reading the article that accompanied the photos, I learned the journalist had spent some time mapping out Inksy's street art pieces across the United States and trying to match them to known sightings of various artists with similar styles.

None of them seemed to be exact matches.

The street art had popped up in various locations, mostly along the coasts, but there'd been a concentration of them along the East Coast. With this information in hand, the reporter specu-lated Inksy might actually be a New England resident or own a vacation home here.

There were several quotes attributed to RISD art students, Brown students, and Providence residents, all of them excited at the idea that Inksy might have walked by them on the street at some point.

"It's like he's a rock star or something," I mused aloud.

Vivi laughed. "To people in the art world, he is."

* * *

The next day, Gray came by for his usual Saturday outing with Vivi.

It had been several days since either of us had seen him. He'd had an out-of-state job and had only returned to Eastport Bay last night.

It was still cool and cloudy—not exactly a great beach day. I suggested he take her for a drive to Providence, hoping of course to be invited along.

I also hoped once we were there we could drive by and get a look at the Inksy mural in person.

"I'm not sure she'd be up for such a long drive," he began, but Vivi cut him off.

"Of course I would. I'd love it. Just give me a few minutes to get ready. Scarlett, you change, too. You're coming along, and we might want to have dinner in Providence while we're there. They have some fine restaurants in the city."

"Great," Gray said, but he didn't look happy about it.

EIGHTEEN

Wabi-Sabi

Gray

Damn. I didn't mind driving to Providence, but I'd sort of been hoping to keep it local today so I could get in my weekly "date" with Vivi and still have time left over to spend alone with Scarlett.

Not seeing her these past few days had been surprisingly hard. In fact, it had sucked.

What am I going to do when she leaves for good?

I shouldn't consider that awful eventuality right now. I needed to focus on the time I did have with her.

Since she'd come back into my life, I'd felt more, well, *alive*, than I had in years.

Seeing her today, my heart raced like a kid about to enter the gates of an amusement park. The prospect of spending all afternoon and evening with Scarlett was tantalizing, even if we *didn't* get to be alone.

"I'll be right back," she said to Victoria and me and went to dress for dinner.

"Have you seen the papers this week?" Victoria asked casually.

"No, I didn't get a chance to look at them since I was out of town."

"You should. Everyone's going crazy over the Inksy mural." She gave me a funny look. "Have *you* seen it?"

"You mean in person?" A muscle in my cheek twitched. "Like I said, I've been out of town."

Victoria waved the newspaper at me until I took it from her. "It's quite something. There's a hot gal on that wall who looks just like Scarlett."

Giving the photo a cursory glance, I said, "Hmm, I don't really see the resemblance."

Scarlett returned to the parlor, and I dropped the incriminating paper to the table beside me. Victoria stayed seated.

She hadn't yet changed out of her teal velour track suit as she'd said she planned to.

Scarlett seemed surprised. "Vivi, you're not changed yet? You don't have to—you look great in that."

Victoria smiled. "You know what? Looking out the window, I've changed my mind. The dampness doesn't agree with these old bones."

To prove her point, she pulled a knit blanket around her and propped her feet up on the ottoman.

"I think I'll just stay here and be cozy today. Why don't the two of you drive into Providence? I texted Stephanie and asked her to make dinner reservations at Bacaro. Gray, you can show Scarlett the city then take her to see the Inksy wall before you have dinner."

I smirked, realizing what was going on. We'd been played again. Victoria had never intended to go to Providence with us. It was another setup.

I was fine with it—at least the dinner reservation part. The city tour as well.

Not so much the mural field trip.

It would be too weird to go look at a painting I'd done of Scarlett—*with* Scarlett.

I was nobody's idea of an actor. How would I manage to act "innocent" with her sitting right beside me?

"Okay then, ready to go?" I asked her. Maybe we'd just happen to "run out of time" to go see it once we were in the city.

She nodded. "Yes. Are you sure you don't want to go, Vivi?"

Victoria assured her she was happy right where she was, and Scarlett kissed her grandmother's cheek before we left.

On the way to Providence, we chatted about her week and my work trip. It had taken me to Los Angeles where I'd worked on the security system for a movie star who'd just bought and renovated the estate of an older movie star.

When we reached the city, I drove her around the East Side, showing her the Brown University campus, the first Baptist Church to exist in America, the State House, and the home where Edgar Allen Poe had stayed when he came to Providence in 1848 to court a wealthy widow. The alcoholic writer had purportedly died of a broken heart less than a year after the woman broke their engagement.

I tried to extend the tour, but Scarlett noticed the time. "Could we go see the Inksy wall now?" she asked.

"The crowds will be thinner later on. I'm afraid we might not even be able to see it right now."

"What if it's too dark after dinner?" she worried. "Especially with as cloudy as it is today."

My hands started to sweat. "They've got portable spotlights. I really think we should just head to the restaurant. It's getting pretty close to our seating time."

"We don't have to stay at the wall long. I just want a peek." She gave me big puppy dog eyes and formed those tempting lips into a pout.

Damn, she was cute. It was hard not to give in. But if Victoria had noticed the resemblance to Scarlett surely she'd notice the resemblance to herself?

I'd be busted, and I was *not* ready to out myself as Inksy. I also wasn't sure I wanted to reveal that much of myself to Scarlett. I put every bit of my raw emotion into my work.

Letting her look at it—knowing it was me who'd created it—would be like inviting her to read my private journals.

"I don't know if it's smart," I said. "There's a pretty high demand for tables there on the weekend. If we're late, they might give ours away. The other decent restaurants in the city will be packed as well. And I'm starved."

Her hopeful expression wilted. "Okay. But promise we'll go after dinner? I really want to see it."

I promised, let out a breath of relief, and drove to the restaurant. Hopefully during dinner I'd manage to come up with another brilliant evasion tactic.

* * *

Bacaro was located on the waterfront in Downtown Providence, one of the city's most romantic restaurants.

Housed in a historic brick building overlooking the river, the contemporary Italian eatery offered a split-dining concept. The main dining room was on the second floor, but I thought the first floor was more fun.

It was an enoteca (wine bar) with salumeria and cicchetheria (tapas bar.) Diners could enjoy sharing Venetian tapas as well as boards of cheeses, olives, and salumi (Italian cured meats.)

Once we were seated, our waiter brought us drinks and pencils with a pad of paper to check off our selections from a long list of options. He informed us we could always order more if we wanted it.

"I don't recognize half the things on here," Scarlett confessed, but I could tell she liked the atmosphere.

Though it was gloomy outside, the interior of the place was filled with warm light and mouth-watering smells.

"Don't worry about it. We'll order several things, try them, and see what you like. We can get more of whatever appeals to you or just keep trying new things all night."

We started with a grilled prosciutto pizza and some crostini with olive tapenade. Then we pored over the extensive lists of cheeses, all of which were served with house spiced nuts and homemade jams.

Reading down the pad, we checked off our selections, adding the assorted olives, and deciding to try the speck, a sweet smoked ham from the Italian Alps as well as the New England Charcuterie Wild Boar Sausage.

The items came out in separate batches, which was perfect as it dragged out the dining experience. I *wanted* it to last—for many reasons.

When the meal ended and I couldn't persuade Scarlett to have a second dessert or another cup of tea, we finally left the restaurant. The bad news was I hadn't thought of a great excuse to avoid taking her for an in-person viewing of the wall.

The good news? It was raining.

Thank you, God.

"Oh wow, it's really coming down." Scarlett ducked back inside, and I followed her.

"I didn't check the forecast," she said. "I should have brought an umbrella."

"I've got one in my car. Tell you what, I'll run out to the valet stand and give him my ticket. When the car gets here, I'll grab the umbrella and come get you."

"But then you'll get all wet."

I grinned at her. "I'm an ex-Frogman, remember? I've spent half my life wet. Be right back."

If I'd had my SEALs wetsuit, it would have been perfect. Getting drenched in my street clothes *wasn't* actually all that pleasant. But I was grateful for every single raindrop.

Because with each one that fell, a little more of the mural would wash away. If I drove slowly enough, it might be a total ruin by the time Scarlett and I got there.

I walked her out to the car, keeping her as dry as possible—which didn't turn out to be very dry at all since the wind was blowing the rain sideways.

Running around to the driver's side and sliding in, I asked, "Want to just head home? Since we're soaked? Are you cold? I'm cold."

Scarlett wasn't going for it.

"Not unless you can't stand to be a little damp for a few extra minutes, Mr. Frogman," she teased. "We can turn on the heater. I *really* want to go see the mural, Gray."

I drew in a deep breath. *Please let it be gone. Please.* "Well, how can I say no when you've challenged my manhood and mental toughness?"

She laughed. But when we pulled up to the location of the wall, her happy expression disappeared.

"What happened to it?" She sounded truly distressed.

The spotlights were still on, but there was no crowd. Because there was nothing left to see. Where the lights illuminated the old, battered wall, there was nothing left but streaks of muddled color.

Yes. I did a mental fist pump and end zone dance.

"Oh no." Scarlett sounded like she was on the verge of crying. "We missed it. I can't believe we missed it. How could it just be gone?"

"Washable paint?" I tried to make it sound like a wild guess.

"Why would a great artist use paint that would just wash away?"

"Who knows? Maybe it's *wabi-sabi*."

"What's that?"

"It's a Japanese concept," I said. "It's the idea that things can be even more beautiful *because* they don't last. Their impermanence makes them more precious. Like a sunset, for instance. Or a snowflake. Or the bloom on a poppy. It doesn't last very long, and so you love and appreciate it with more intensity than you would if you had all the time in the world."

"I'm beginning to think Inksy isn't just sneaky—he's a tease." Her pretty face pulled into a disgruntled frown.

"But you think he's a great artist?"

"Yes. Everyone does."

Inside I had a good laugh. "Not everyone."

I'd read plenty of harsh commentary of my work. Some critics had called it "silly and overrated," or "meaningless explosions of random energy."

It was best to *avoid* reading that sort of stuff, but when it did occasionally slip onto my radar screen, I just told myself, "Not my audience. I'm painting for myself and those who *do* get me."

"Well, I think he's brilliant. Or she." Scarlett put a hand on each of her cheeks and rested her chin in the cradle of them. "I can't believe a real Inksy was *this close*, and I missed it."

Taking in her crestfallen expression, I had a flash of regret. "I'm sorry. We should have come before dinner."

"It's okay. You didn't know."

Her instant forgiveness made me feel even guiltier. Not only had I known it was likely to wash away I'd been actively hoping for it.

"Why was it so important to you to see it?"

She shook her head. "You'll think it's stupid."

"No. I promise I won't." Never had a truer statement been uttered. I was dying to know why she was so interested in my work.

Turning her head toward the window so I couldn't see her face, she said, "I just... I saw something in the newspaper's picture of the mural. It reminded me of... of..."

"Of?" I prompted. "What did it remind you of, Scarlett?"

She shook her head again as if unwilling to answer, but then she did. "It reminded me of our time together—on Mykonos and Crete. And when I looked at it, it was sort of like I could recapture that feeling."

Well, damn. Now I was sorry the rain had washed it away.

"And the woman in it... she reminded me a little of... me. Of the woman I was that week."

She spoke quickly, apologetically, adding, "I know that's silly. The painting *wasn't* me, but still, it made me realize I'd sort of forgotten about that girl from three years ago, about what it felt like to be that free and happy."

"I'm sorry," I said again.

The remorse was nearly overwhelming now. I wanted to do something to make up for it, to make her feel better.

Hell, if she wanted to see paintings of herself, all she had to do was walk into my townhouse.

It was inundated with them. There were paintings of her on practically every wall. Painting Scarlett had been the only way I could exorcise the lingering desire I'd had for her after the week we'd spent together.

And there had been a *lot* of desire.

Of course I couldn't tell her about that.

"I could draw you," I said quietly.

She turned to me. "What?"

"You liked the work I did on the tattoo designs. I draw them on a sketch pad first. I could draw you... if you want me to."

"Do *you* want to?"

"Yes," I confessed.

She was quiet a few seconds then said, "I hate photos of myself, but a drawing... I think I might like that. Where? At your house?"

"No," I practically shouted. "I mean, it needs to be cleaned up before you come over. We can do it at the mansion."

"When?"

"Tonight, if you'd like to."

"Okay then," she said. "Yes, I'd like for you to draw me."

I nodded. "Great. There's only one condition."

"What is it?" Scarlett asked. She looked intrigued and a little nervous.

"You have to be naked."

NINETEEN

Scarlett at the Fountain

Scarlett

My body went rigid as an artic wind flash froze my insides.

"No. I can't. Why do I have to be naked?"

"Why not? It's not like I haven't seen you naked, Scarlett."

"But... you said you wanted a *no-sex* fling."

"No, I *agreed* to a no-sex fling because it was the best and only offer I was going to get. And this wouldn't be breaking the rules. I said I wanted to *draw* you naked, not *get* you naked. There's a difference."

"Why do you want to draw me like that?" I asked. "If we're not going to have sex?"

"Because that's how I see you. I mean, of course I'm looking at you right now with your clothes on," he clarified. "But if I'm going to *see you* see you, capture your essence as an artist, you're going to have to take off your clothes. The sketch won't be lewd or anything. And I won't lay a finger on you, I promise."

The memory of what he'd done to me with his fingers thawed me instantly. In fact, adrenaline fired throughout my body in jets, making me warm and a little dizzy.

And a lot turned on.

Was I actually thinking of doing it? *This is crazy.*

"I don't know. I'm afraid it would be…"

"Fun? Adventurous? Exciting?" Gray repeated the words he'd said to me on the day of my canceled wedding when he'd been trying to persuade me to stay in Greece and spend my non-honeymoon week with him.

That had felt like a crazy decision at the time, and it had turned out to be the best week of my life.

"Okay," I blurted before I could chicken out. "Let's do it."

Gray grinned that delicious wolfy grin of his. "Great. I'll stop by my house on the way and pick up my pencils and pad."

For the rest of the ride home, I could barely sit still. When he ran into his townhouse to grab his art supplies, I came very close to chickening out.

I considered asking him to just drop me off at the front door of Vivi's house. Or calling a car service and escaping without a goodbye, sending him a cowardly *I changed my mind, see you never* text.

But I didn't. When Gray came back to the car, I was still sitting there on the passenger side.

He deposited his supplies in the back seat and got in behind the wheel. When he looked over at me, his eyes almost gleamed in the dark.

"You okay? Am I going to be drawing a pair of cold feet instead?" he asked with a grin.

I shook my head in rapid, tight jerks, stuffing my shaking hands beneath my legs. "No. But I am cold. I think all my blood's deserted my extremities and headed for my nervous stomach."

He chuckled. "That's how I used to feel before an operation. It's not bad to feel nerves, you know. That's your body's way of preparing for something extraordinary to happen."

Extraordinary. Yes. That was a good word for it.

Every time I was with Gray, no matter where we were or what we were doing, it felt like an extraordinary experience.

This was what had been missing from my life back at home. There was no one like him anywhere. No one who thought like he did, talked like he did, *looked* like he did—or looked at *me* like he did.

When we got back to the mansion, he stayed downstairs while I ran up to my room to put on my cozy hooded robe—and nothing else.

As I tiptoed back down the hallway toward the main staircase, I stopped outside both Vivi's bedroom door and her sitting room, listening and verifying that she was indeed in bed for the night.

I took the staircase instead of the elevator—the old contraption was noisy, dating back to the construction of the house in the 1920's.

Once on the main floor, I turned and crept over to the left side of the grand hall where one of the staircase supports formed a curved alcove.

Tucked beneath it was one of my favorite features of the mansion, a small fountain and reflecting pool.

If I'd come here for visits as a child—and I *so* wished that I had —I would have loved this little hideaway.

The arched ceiling of the space was decorated with ornately carved stonework, and the fountain itself was shaped like a large scallop with fantastical sea creatures perched on its sides. Full green plants flanked the fountain and contained tiny twinkle lights.

The overall impression was that of an indoor secret garden or a fairy pool.

The alcove featured two small marble benches meant for sitting and meditating while one watched the streaming water. Gray sat on one of them, sharpening a drawing pencil.

He looked up when I arrived. "Hey. Ready to be immortalized in charcoal? *Scarlett at the Fountain*, by Gray Lupine."

I pointed at him, the sleeve of my oversized red robe obscuring all but the tips of my fingers.

"This had better not show up online anywhere. When it's finished, you're going to hand me the one and only copy. Tonight —before you leave."

He laughed and tapped his temple. "Don't worry. The only copy will exist in my mind. I have no intention of sharing you with *anyone*."

A shiver passed through me, though the atmosphere was pleasantly warm.

The water from the fountain was heated, and the curved overhang trapped the humid warmth, making the alcove feel a bit like a sauna.

"Where should I sit? Or did you want me to stand?"

Now that we were *doing* this and not just talking about it, my nerves were coming back full-force. I was trembling all over.

He used the tip of his pencil to point. "On the edge of the fountain there. The light is perfect. Oh—and you can keep your robe on. For now."

I nodded and hurried to the fountain, sitting on its low, wide ledge.

"Okay, turn to the side so your legs are stretched out," Gray instructed. "Yeah, like that. Perfect. Okay, you comfortable?"

Again, I nodded. It wasn't a complete lie.

Though the robe had fallen open below the knee to expose my bare legs and feet, my position felt fine. I couldn't say I was exactly *comfortable*, though.

It was impossible to be with Gray's intense gaze focused on me like this. He looked down at his pad, sketched some lines, looked back up at me—at my legs to be exact.

Oh, that must have been why he said I could leave my robe on for now. He was starting with the parts that were uncovered.

Whether it was his usual process, or he'd amended it to help me acclimate, I couldn't say, but either way I was grateful.

And I did acclimate to it, believe it or not. As the minutes passed, the sound of the rushing water and the soft *scritch scritch* of his pencil, the feel of the pseudo-tropical air, and the lateness of the hour combined to ease me into a state of almost trance-like relaxation.

I watched Gray's hand, the subtle play of powerful muscle

and tendon moving under smooth skin as he translated his vision of me from optic nerve to paper.

And I flashed back to what those hands had done to me during our fleeting but never-forgotten time together.

No wonder his fingers had been so skillful and delicate as they'd opened me, toyed with me, nudging me ever closer to ecstasy time and time again.

He didn't speak but focused on his work, every now and then looking up and making a small hand gesture to indicate that he wanted me to shift position a little. I could tell when he moved from drawing my legs and feet to my face, because when he looked up at me, his eyes would connect with mine ever so briefly before skating away to study my ear or chin or hair.

Finally, he murmured, "Open your robe, Scarlett."

My heartrate skyrocketed as heat bloomed between my legs. But I obeyed, moving slowly as if this was a dream and not the totally uncharacteristic real-life decision I'd made an hour ago.

I unfastened the belt and started to slide the robe from my shoulders and arms.

"Leave the hood on," Gray instructed. "Just let it gape open. Good—like that."

Exposed to the slightly cooler air, my nipples tightened.

Gray's only reaction was a sharp intake of breath. Without a word, he went back to work, alternating between looking at his pad and peering over it at me.

What was he thinking? As for me, I was pinging back and forth between utter disbelief that this was happening and feeling more present and awake than I'd felt since... well since we'd been together those few short days in Greece.

Maybe this was what he'd meant by *wabi-sabi*. Once again, our time together would be short-lived—and maybe that's what made being with him so special.

It couldn't last therefore it possessed an almost magical beauty. He was my sunset, my snowflake, my poppy bloom—

transitory and exquisite, to be appreciated for a moment before it vanished forever.

That was when I decided.

"Gray," I said, the echo of my voice in the small space surprising me.

He looked up. "Yeah?"

"Let's have a fling."

He smiled. "That's what we're doing, isn't it?"

I shook my head, returning his smile and struggling for breath. "Not the no-sex kind, the with-sex kind. Just while I'm here, and then when I leave, it's over."

His eyelids flared, and his chest rose and fell in a quick inhale. "Are you sure that's what you want?"

I nodded, feeling like my heart was going to leap from my body and take a swim in the fountain.

Immediately Gray set his drawing pad and pencil aside and crossed the small distance between us.

Reaching for my hand, he pulled me to my feet then crushed me to his body, taking my mouth in a savage—and absolutely mind-blowing—kiss.

TWENTY

More than a Fling

Gray

Finally.

Thank *fuck* she'd changed her mind. I'd regretted my promise not to lay a finger on her the minute she'd appeared in that fluffy red robe with her red-polished toenails peeking from beneath.

When she'd reclined on the fountain and it had split to reveal her legs, I'd had to bite the inside of my cheek.

And every minute since she'd dropped the robe entirely, it had been hard-on city. Usually that was a *nice* place to be, but when there's no chance of it leading anywhere, it's just annoying.

If you don't believe me, you try going months without any action then sit and study a dazzling woman you're crazy about for an hour while you process your feelings and *rampant* sexual thoughts about her, converting them into an image on paper.

She felt incredible in my arms, under my hungry fingertips, and she tasted amazing.

Having her pressed naked against me after all the years of imagining that very thing was almost too much to take. I wanted to touch her and taste her everywhere all at once.

What I *really* wanted was to pick her up and carry her upstairs to one of the forty or so bedrooms in this place, but that might scare her. I needed to wait until she asked me to take her to bed. Better yet till she begged me.

Oh shit, that image was so fucking hot—Scarlett begging me to take her, to fuck her again and again.

I ran my hands over her back and waist to her hips and down to her enticing round ass. She moved against me, squirming to get closer as she consumed my mouth.

"Touch me, Gray," she whispered. "Touch me."

As if I needed any encouragement.

The sound of her sweet voice inflamed me, though, and I reached for her breasts, cupping them, prodding the tips with my thumbs until they were hard and begging for my mouth.

Lowering my head, I took one sweet tip into my mouth, swirling my tongue around it, sucking and flicking before moving to the other side.

Scarlett's moans filled the warm, dimly lit alcove, vibrating through the small space and ramping me up to an even higher pitch. Her skin was so soft under my hands, even softer than I'd remembered.

And she was just as responsive. One of my favorite things about making love with her three years ago was how much she fucking *loved* being touched by me and how unafraid she was to let it show.

The sexy sounds she made, the way she moved, the scent of her skin—all of it was driving me mad and tempting me to tear off my own clothes and take her right here up against the marble wall.

That might not be so comfortable for her, though. Instead, I whispered, "Come with me," and led her to the small bench I'd been sitting on as I sketched.

Urging her to sit, I got on my knees in front of her and pushed hers apart.

The change in position must have given her a minute to think because she suddenly acted shy. She put her hands down, covering herself.

I gripped each of her wrists, prying them away from her center and pinning them to her sides.

"Gray," she whispered. "We shouldn't. What if the housekeeper is still awake? What if—"

I cut her off, smiling up at her. "Tell you what, you keep on thinking of all the what-ifs, and I'll be down here doing what I do best."

"Gray," she protested.

But then my mouth made first contact, and she had nothing else to say.

Nothing except some very sexy moans. Lust ignited me as I buried my face between her thighs. I kissed and licked and sucked at her sweet center, gripping her hips as she undulated beneath my steady assault.

Scarlett was no longer bashful. She clenched her fingers in my hair, riding my tongue, pleading for more in soft, desperate pants.

Yes. I was going to make this woman come so hard she'd follow me around begging for it every day. And I would give it to her—gladly.

A godawful metallic screech made Scarlett jump and caused me to reluctantly lift my head. She pushed at me, squirming to get out of my grasp.

"The elevator," she whisper-shouted. "Someone's coming."

I chuckled. "That old thing's so slow I can make you come twice before it gets here."

There was another clang, and she jerked again. "Move. Let me up," she demanded.

I rocked backward, rising to my feet. Scarlett darted off the bench to the fountain, grabbed her robe from the ledge, and skittered away, out of the alcove and toward the staircase.

"Scarlett," I called after her. I was tingling all over and could still taste her.

"Shhhh," she said. "Be quiet. Go home. I'll see you tomorrow."

The last thing I saw was her adorable ass as it disappeared at the top of the stairs.

Well, okay then. To be continued.

Still hard and feeling like I'd had four back-to-back Venti Nitro Cold Brews, I packed away my pencils and picked up the drawing pad, preparing to close it before stashing it in my bag.

Instead, I took a minute to study it. The light really was low in here. I liked what I'd done, but I wanted a better look. I'd take it home and live with it for a few days before I decided how I really felt about my work on it.

Shit. I'd promised Scarlett to give this to her tonight. I didn't want to invite her to distrust me.

Ripping the sheet from the pad, I signed my name to the bottom and prepared to take it upstairs to her room. First, I snapped a picture of it with my phone so I could look at it later at home.

I was the artist after all, and this was one creation I intended to enjoy fully.

As for the *subject* of my drawing... I intended to enjoy her as often as she'd let me.

I'd never met anyone like Scarlett Hood, and it wasn't enough anymore to just capture her likeness on paper or canvas or cinder block wall. I wanted *more* than a fling.

For now, I'd take what I could get.

But one thing had become crystal clear in the past few days... I wouldn't be satisfied until I'd captured *her*.

TWENTY-ONE

Pluff Walk

Scarlett

Whew that was close.

What had I been *thinking*, engaging in foreplay at the fairy fountain in my grandma's house?

I *hadn't* been thinking. I'd been feeling. I'd succumbed to the magical sex-pull Gray Lupine exuded like some kind of super magnet.

What was it about this guy that made me lose all semblance of common sense? It happened before in Greece, and now it was happening again.

It was stupid. I knew it was. All the reasons I'd given Gray that we couldn't do this were still true.

-I was leaving soon.

-He was an undoubtedly damaged former SEAL who didn't see a therapist or take meds.

-I couldn't—could *not*—end up with a man like my dad.

Running through that mental list reminded me I really *should* do everything in my power to resist Gray.

Tomorrow I would tell him it had been a mistake, that we needed to go back to no-sex fling status or just abandon the fling idea altogether.

Behind me, there was a soft, shushing sound. At first I thought I was hearing a mouse. But then I saw it.

Someone had pushed a sheet of paper under the door.

I walked over to it and picked it up.

It was the drawing.

The sight of myself depicted there in charcoal by Gray's hand was nothing less than mind-altering.

I look good.

I'd never thought of myself as particularly pretty or sexy. It was clear that Gray saw me that way.

Pride and pleasure swelled inside my chest. Other parts of me were becoming swollen again as well.

Though the sketch was in black and white—except for the red pencil he'd used for my hooded robe—he seemed to have captured the flush of my skin, the shine of my hair, the curves of my calves and hips and breasts.

There was emotion in this drawing. There was desire. There was *lust*—his for me and mine for him. It was emanating from the page in waves.

If I could have gone home—right then—and not had to see him again, hear his voice, smell his mind-scrambling scent, then *maybe* I could have pulled it off.

But while I was in the same town with him—in the same *state* even—I simply wasn't going to be able to resist him.

So considering the inevitability of it all, here was how it was going to go—we were going to have the flingiest fling anyone had ever flung, and *then* I would go back home and be a sensible person again.

* * *

When Gray arrived at the mansion the next evening, he worked on Vivi's art collection stuff for a while then the three of us had dinner in the kitchen with Stephanie.

Afterward, Vivi said, "I'm going to watch my shows now. Why don't you two take a nice walk?"

She was just plain *obvious* about it now, pushing Gray and me together as hard as she could.

"That's a good idea." Gray stood from the table and looked at me. "Want to?"

"The sun's already set. It's dark out," I said.

He gave me a slow, devastating grin. "I'm not afraid of the dark. Are you little Red Riding Hood?"

Mortified by his reference to my red robe, I shot him a warning look and giggled. "No, I guess not."

"We'll walk on the Bluff Walk," he said. "Just the paved part. It's nice and wide and smooth, and the moon is pretty bright tonight."

We said goodnight to Vivi and left the house, crossing the vast back lawn of the estate and unlocking the gate that led directly onto the oceanfront walking trail. I was glad I'd grabbed a light sweater because the ocean breeze cooled the summer temperature considerably.

I'd explored parts of the Cliff Walk during the day. The three-and-a-half-mile National Recreation Trail ran along the top of the bluff where Eastport Bay's famous Oceanview Avenue mansions sat looking out over First Beach and the open Atlantic Ocean.

The walk offered a breathtaking view of the water on one side and on the other, the back side of the mansions, those owned by the historical society and open for tours as well as some of the private homes.

Many of the private homeowners had planted tall hedge shrubs for privacy, so those properties were harder to see.

During the day, the Bluff Walk was crowded with tourists. Tonight, it was deserted. Though the sound of the ocean's movement was a steady pulse, I could still hear our footfalls. A giddy sense of freedom and anticipation swept over me.

As a kid in Florida, I'd always loved taking walks at night. It was a little tougher in Minnesota where the weather prevented it during most of the year—unless you enjoyed bundling up and feeling like a marshmallow waddling down the street.

Being outside in the dark had always seemed a little… illicit. Tonight, it probably was.

"Are we even supposed to be on the Bluff Walk at night?" I asked.

"Technically it's open sunrise to sunset. Are you afraid there are cops lying in wait behind the rocks to jump out and arrest us?" he teased.

"I guess you're right." I smiled and took the hand he offered. Once again, Gray was leading me into adventure and excitement, which seemed to be his specialty.

As we walked, I was conscious of the feel of his fingers intertwined with mine. Strong, warm, gentle in spite of their rough texture.

It was such a simple thing, holding hands. I did it with my mom, my grandmother, my niece Trina. But this was something completely different.

With Gray, holding hands felt… intimate, like a precursor to something even *more* intimate.

And I liked it.

He'd been right about the moon. It was full and bright and looked enormous. The stars were also clearly visible in the inky dark sky.

As we walked along, the trail inclined and declined, sometimes dipping low enough the ocean spray threatened to soak us when the waves crashed against the dark rocks.

"So… what did you think of the drawing?" he asked.

Instantly my belly boiled like a pot of anxiety noodle soup.

"I liked it very much. Actually, I loved it. It's… beautiful."

He squeezed my hand. "You're beautiful."

"Gray…"

"I'm serious. I'm not handing you a line. From the minute I laid eyes on you in Greece I thought you were the most beautiful woman I'd ever seen. You're even more beautiful now. I'd like to draw you again."

He paused before adding. "There are some other parts of last night I'd like to repeat as well."

I stopped walking. Gray turned toward me and wrapped his arms around me, pulling me close. Dropping his head so that our faces were only inches apart, he asked, "So are we doing this? Is this what you want?"

I nodded, my breaths rapid and light. "Yes. I do. I want you."

Gray smiled then looked up and past me toward the property of the estate behind me.

"I have an idea. Come with me."

He took my hand and tugged me toward the low rock wall that bordered the path in this section. Atop it was a decorative black iron fence—not too tall, but not a cinch to climb either.

"What are you doing?" I hissed, though no one was around to hear us, and even if they had been, the waves would have drowned the sound of our whispers.

He didn't answer but stepped up onto the stone wall, reaching back to offer me a hand up. I hesitated but took it. Gray pulled me up beside him with ease.

Now we both stood on the top ledge of the stone wall, the iron fence at our bellies. Clearly he meant for our next move to be climbing over it.

"Isn't this private property?" I asked.

"It's one of the homes owned by the Eastport Bay Preservation Society. No one's here right now."

"Won't there be guards?"

One of his shoulders lifted then fell. "Maybe. Up at the main house. But that's two hundred yards away, and we're not going there."

"Where are we going?"

He grinned. "You'll see."

TWENTY-TWO

Starry Night

Scarlett

Grabbing the top of the iron fence, Gray hoisted himself up and over it in one move. Then he reached over and put his hands under my arms.

"Ready? One, two, three... jump,"

I had no time to think, just followed his instructions. Before I knew it, I was over the fence and standing in front of Gray.

"Not bad," he said. "You'd make a decent special ops soldier."

I rolled my eyes. "I'd make a terrible jail inmate, though. I'm kind of scared. What are we doing here?"

"Don't worry. We're not gonna get caught." He grabbed my hand and started jogging.

Now that we were on this side of the incline, I saw his target —a large, round, glassed-in gazebo. It was spectacular, with white columns supporting a segmented dome-shaped glass roof and French doors on every side.

They were all closed, naturally, but I could picture this little oasis during the estate's heyday in the 1920's. There would have been a harpist or maybe a string quartet playing inside, perhaps an afternoon ladies' card game or a candlelit dinner for two, the open doors providing a cooling breeze on hot days.

When we reached it, Gray tried one of the doors. It opened easily, and he gestured for me to go in.

I was surprised to find the interior warm, almost hot. He answered my unspoken question.

"The glass ceiling and walls create a greenhouse effect. The stone flooring holds onto the day's trapped heat for a few hours. Late at night, it would probably get cold, but the sun hasn't been down that long."

I strolled the small, circular space, taking in the panoramic view, padded window seats, and the two large, padded chaise loungers in the center. My stomach felt a little flurry of movement as I imagined stretching one of them out to its full, flat position.

"How did you know about this place?"

"I toured the mansion a couple years ago when my mom came to town," Gray said. "The society lady who lived on the estate when the place was first built used to hold tea parties out here—and sometimes torrid affairs with her many lovers."

With a wink, he added, "Don't worry, they've changed out the furniture since then."

With a few efficient moves, Gray had both the loungers flattened and pushed together, forming a makeshift double bed.

"I thought we could lie down and look up at the stars," he said by way of explanation. I liked that he didn't automatically assume we were going to have sex.

It made me *want* to have sex with him. More than I already did.

I nodded and sat on the edge of one lounge chair then scooted back and stretched out. Gray stretched out on the chair beside me, lying close with his shoulder touching mine.

Both of us looked up at the stars clearly visible through the glass ceiling.

"It's almost like a painting, isn't it?" he asked. "Though not even Van Gogh could really capture it."

Van Gogh's famous masterpiece, *Starry Night*, was one of the most recognized and beloved art works in the world, but it was far from a peaceful scene.

Instead, his rendering of the night sky was an almost frenetic representation of light and motion and energy. It made me think of something Vivi had said about Gray.

I turned my head toward him and touched his hand lightly. "Gray?"

He grabbed my hand, entwining our fingers. "Hmmm?"

"Vivi told me something about you recently."

Gray's grip tightened. "What was it?"

"She said you wanted to 'make beauty out of chaos.' What does that mean? Does it have something to do with your time as a SEAL?"

He didn't look at me but kept staring at the stars.

"I don't remember saying that to her."

"But that is what you want, isn't it? Is that what your tattoo designs are? Taking something painful and making it beautiful?"

I watched his profile, the thoughts moving over his face in rapid succession. Surprise. Reluctance. Fear?

"I don't really talk about that stuff."

My heart sank. I wanted him to be open with me, to show me his real self. If we were going to do this thing, get naked with each other physically, I wanted to get naked emotionally as well.

Maybe that wasn't very fling-y, but I already knew I was terrible at casual sex. I didn't want it to be like last time where we'd shared our bodies for a week and then parted, still strangers.

"You said before that your gut had never steered you wrong. Listen to it now," I urged. "Isn't it telling you that you can trust me?"

He huffed a small laugh. "Yes, but honestly... I sort of lost faith in my gut somewhere along the way."

I pushed up onto one elbow and studied his face. "Why?"

Once again, his expression shuttered. He wasn't going to talk to me. I rolled onto my back, swallowing the lump that had formed there.

For a few minutes we lay there, side by side, listening to the waves crash. Then Gray spoke. His voice was quiet, more serious than I'd ever heard him sound.

"The first time we met, you brought up the statistic that ninety percent of Navy SEALS' marriages end in divorce."

"I remember—shocking, I know, considering my blood alcohol level at the time."

"There are some obvious reasons—you can be deployed for eight or nine months at a time, and the spouse at home has no idea where the soldier is or when he'll be back," he said. "That's stressful. But I think it's more than that. When they're home, there's a lot of PTSD and sleep problems. There are injuries with some lingering effects. Some of my buddies talk about problems with alcohol and anger issues. Some say they feel emotionally numb."

None of this was a surprise to me. I'd lived with it daily until my dad had moved out and disappeared from my life.

These were all the reasons that had scared me away from dating guys in the military in the first place.

"Have you dealt with any of that?" I asked, assuming that was what he was leading up to.

"I've been pretty lucky, actually," he said. "I didn't sustain any major injuries during training or operations, so physically I've been fine. The hardest part for me was some of the things I've seen... and some of the things I had to do."

"Is that why you quit? Because you couldn't do it anymore?"

He squinted at the night sky, obviously not wanting to talk about it, but he did anyway.

"Nah, I probably would have stayed on the teams forever—or at least until I couldn't walk anymore from knee damage. I testified against my commander in a court martial. All of us did—all the guys in our squad. After something like that, you're not exactly welcome on the teams anymore. He was found guilty, but no matter what, some guys are gonna question whether you've really got their back, thinking maybe you're looking over *their* shoulder with an eye toward reporting whatever they're doing to a superior."

"So why did you testify?"

"I didn't see any other choice. None of us did. You have to do a lot of things on missions you'd rather not do. War isn't pretty. But our leader—Gandalf—was out of control. He used to be a kind of hero to me, you know? He was a badass, but also smart. But he changed. I don't know if he had CTE from too many blast concussions or if he just got numb to the killing after a while, but he was toxic. Scary. I mean, some of the stuff I saw him do in Iraq was fucking evil."

He drew a deep breath and let out a shaky exhale.

"And it was illegal, a violation of U.S. military rules and practices. I mean at what point do you cross the line from soldier to serial killer? It was disturbing. We all talked about it, wondered if we should say something, do something. During our last operation, he was like a robot or something—he didn't care *who* he killed. None of us wanted to turn him in, but it had to stop. So, every member of our squad broke the code of silence and testified against him. I thought I was doing the right thing. Sometimes I still wonder if my gut steered me wrong."

He looked away, anger and shame coloring his face.

"I read about the trial online. You did do the right thing."

He seemed to be irritated by my sympathetic tone. "It doesn't always feel that way. I lost my SEAL career. And a lot of people took his side, refusing to believe a platoon leader could ever do anything wrong. He lied, he called it a 'mutiny,' said we just wanted to take him down because we didn't like his 'leadership style.' SEALs are supposed to be all about honor and integrity. That's what the Trident badge stands for. In this case honor required turning on one of our own. It was the hardest thing I ever had to do. The stuff people printed and posted about us afterward didn't help."

"And you don't think it still affects you?" I asked.

"If you're asking whether I'm fucked up in the head, the

answer is no. I mean, I've dealt with my fair share of fallout, but I found ways to deal with it."

"Like what?"

He darted a look at me then looked away again. "I saw a therapist for a while. My art helps. And I try to help other people when I can."

"There are a few residual effects," he admitted. "I lost faith in my gut. The first time I met you, it was telling me—screaming actually—for me to go for it. With everything I had. I knew something important was happening. But then we were deployed for a hostage rescue. Right after that my team went to Iraq, and everything changed."

"The stuff in Iraq and the trial made you lose faith in yourself?"

He nodded. "In my judgement. For a while after that, I thought my gut was an idiot or a liar."

Gray swallowed hard, finally meeting my eyes again. He rolled to his side, facing me and softly brushing my hair back from my face with one hand.

"But it was right about *you*. I know that now. I made a mistake, Scarlett, not tracking you down years ago. I wish I had. I wish I'd found you sooner."

"I don't."

His head jerked back. Clearly, I'd surprised him. "You don't?"

"No."

Now it was my turn to be honest. Gray had been brave enough to tell me about his painful experiences, and he deserved openness from me in return.

"If you'd found me sooner—if you *had* reached out, there wouldn't have been anything worth finding. I was a mess."

"Well, you were a *little* bit of a mess when I met you in Greece." He held up one hand with his thumb and first finger a couple inches apart.

I laughed. "Tell me about it. It got worse, believe it or not. I told you my dad was a SEAL?"

"Yeah, which is why you hated me on sight."

"I did *not* hate you. I was scared of you. Because you were so attractive, and I didn't want to be attracted to a SEAL."

"I remember. It must have been pretty bad at home to leave you with such an aversion to all military guys."

"It was. My dad was apparently a great guy once upon a time —at least according to what Vivi has told me about him and what my mom says about when they were first married. But he had CTE from his time in the service. It was so bad he had to retire early. When he came home, he had a lot of mood swings and depression. The memory problems were really bad, and that made him frustrated and angry."

"Was he ever violent?"

"Sometimes, when he was really disoriented and agitated. He didn't hit us, but he scared us by punching through walls, throwing things and breaking them. I know he didn't want to hurt us. Finally, he just left. He died alone a couple years later. I think he felt like he was doing us a favor by leaving. Who knows? Maybe he was. All I remember is I felt like he'd deserted me. And then Bryce deserted me, which sort of ripped the scab off all the wounds I *thought* had healed from my dad. I wasn't in a good place for a long time after that."

"I might have been able to *help* you get to a good place," Gray said. "I seemed to be able to take your mind off things a bit in Greece."

I laughed at his naughty expression. "You did *that* for sure. But you can't heal from emotional trauma if you're hiding from your emotions. Which was what I was doing by spending time with you that week. And I kept doing that for a long time afterward."

"What does that mean exactly? Did you go around sleeping with every promotional condom salesman you met?"

He sounded jealous.

"No, actually, I did the opposite," I told him. "I haven't slept with anyone since then."

His eyes went wide. "Really?"

I nodded. "Really. That week showed me I was no good at casual sex."

"Actually, you were amazing at it." He stroked my cheek with the backs of his fingers.

I flicked them away. "You know what I mean. After spending the week with you, I realized sex meant *too* much to me. I got so attached to you—it took me forever to get over you. Your memory haunted me. It was unnatural."

Gray's eyes softened. "It's the most natural thing in the world to feel attached—that's what sex is for. It's supposed to bond you —when you're doing it right. And for the record, it *didn't* take a long time for me to get over you."

"It didn't?" Generally I appreciated honesty, but I sort of felt like I'd been slapped.

"No. I never got over you, Scarlett," he said. "I don't think I ever will."

TWENTY-THREE

Better Than Anything

Scarlett

Why did this man have to be the absolute most compelling person in the world?

Being alone with him made it feel like nothing else existed, like the three years apart had simply been a blip and that *this* was what real life was about.

In a matter of days, it seemed like Gray had become the center of my universe. I couldn't have stopped myself from touching him if I tried.

Reaching for him, I slid my hand behind his neck and pulled him over me. He came easily, rolling on top of me and fitting his mouth to mine.

And we *were* a perfect fit—so much better than Bryce and I had ever been. Even the way Gray's body weight was distributed over me was perfect, everything aligned just as it was meant to be, hardness against softness, two opposites and yet somehow two halves of a whole.

The scent of his skin was galvanizing, and the feel of his silky hair and tough muscled neck made my fingers ache to touch more of him. I snatched at the buttons of his shirt, slipping my hands inside to the hot skin of his chest and shoulders and back.

Gray's groan was muffled by my mouth as I instinctively spread my legs to make a cradle for him.

Gliding my hands down to his ribcage and flanks, I pulled him harder against me and lifted my pelvis to rub against the enticing ridge of his erection.

A shudder went through his body, and he broke contact with my mouth to move his lips to my neck. "You feel fucking amazing, Scarlett," he whispered.

The velvety softness of his tongue contrasted with the scrape of his bristle against my sensitive skin, and I moaned with arousal and excitement.

"So do you. Better than ever. Better than anything."

After three long years of subsisting on nothing but memories of the passion we'd shared, I would get to have him again in real life.

The anticipation made me nearly frantic with need. I jerked at the waistband of his pants, suddenly frustrated at their existence.

Unable to manage the button with only one hand, I made an impatient noise, and Gray laughed.

But when I gripped the shape of his erection over his pants instead, the amusement converted to raw desire. His pleasured groan filled my ear.

"I'll get it," he panted. "Hold on."

Rising to his knees, he quickly unfastened and removed his pants then stripped off his shirt and underwear.

Suddenly I wished for full daylight. The outline of Gray's body in the moon's glow was a tease. I reached for his taut length, wrapping my hand around him and drawing him back to me.

He felt big and hot and so hard. I loved that he was this hard for me.

"Slow down," he urged with a smile that gleamed in the dark above me. "We've got time. No one's going to interrupt like last time."

Last time.

His reference to our brief interlude beneath the staircase last night lit flames all over my body, particularly between my legs, where I still felt the heavenly sensation of his tongue touching and teasing my most sensitive parts.

I did *not* want to slow down. I wanted more of that feeling. More of *him*.

"I want you," I whispered. "I want to feel you inside me again."

There was a rumble in Gray's chest, a low, masculine groan that sent sparks to my lower abdomen.

"I want you, too." His voice was husky and deadly serious. "I never stopped thinking about you. I dreamed about you, too... all the time. Dreamed about this."

After giving me a slow, soft kiss, he began undressing me.

Leaving my sweater on, he opened the sides of it and worked at the row of buttons running down the front of my shirt. When he had that open, he released the center clasp of my bra and carefully peeled the two halves of it to the sides as well.

Then he sat back and admired his work.

"You're incredibly beautiful, Scarlett. No drawing or painting could ever do you justice."

He couldn't see my blush in the darkness, but he could probably feel it. My skin was feverish and thirsting for his touch. When he cupped his hands beneath my breasts, I shivered with need.

Bracing one strong arm on either side of me, he bent his head and drew one of the tight peaks into his mouth, sucking and bathing it with silky strokes of his tongue. I couldn't stay still.

Twisting and trembling I arched my back to push my breast further into his mouth and ran my greedy hands over the tantalizing lines of his body suspended above me. His chest and abs were sculpted and hard, and the smooth skin stretched over them became covered in chill bumps everywhere I touched.

He was breathing hard now, his breaths like puffs of steam against my sensitive nipples. Sliding my hands down to his lower back, I urged him lower, canting my hips upward in eager invitation.

"Now," I ordered. "I can't wait any more. I've waited so long already."

Gray lifted his head, nodding in agreement as he straddled me then positioned the head of his cock against my opening.

"Oh fuck, you are so wet," he gasped.

"I'm ready for you," I said, as if it wasn't obvious enough.

He didn't plunge inside all at once, rather eased into my welcoming body, stretching and nudging in a gentle invasion that felt better and better with every slow inch.

When he was fully seated, he began a slow and steady back and forth, pressing the front of his body against the front of mine with every delicious downward stroke.

Dipping his head, he kissed me again, his tongue mimicking the actions of his body, thrusting, claiming, consuming me while I met his rhythm and writhed with the excruciating pleasure of his thickness inside me.

It felt so good, so unbearably mind-alteringly unreal, I couldn't stay quiet. Whimpers and cries rose from my throat and blended with the noises of the night wind and the ocean waves crashing on the cliffs nearby.

The sounds seemed to excite Gray. He drove harder, faster, lifting his head and biting his lower lip as his eyes closed and his forehead creased.

His face was severe and beautiful in its expression of ecstasy. Watching him turned me on almost as much as what he was doing to me with his body.

It was like a wildness overtook me. I gripped his shoulders, driving my heels into the cushion of the chaise lounge and lifting myself against him so there was no space between our bodies.

His driving rhythm never changed, just kept pushing me closer and closer with every thrust until suddenly I couldn't move anymore.

Suspended in time and space, burning from the inside out, I went rigid as the luscious spasms rippled through me. And then I shuddered violently, moving faster and faster and clenching my intimate muscles around him, a scream of pleasure ripping from my throat.

Gray drove into me once more, all his muscles tensing as he buried his full length in me and let out a roar, finding his own release and satisfaction.

TWENTY-FOUR

Almost as Good

Gray

Scarlett and I walked back to Victoria's house in what had to be the most scenic "walk of shame" of all time.

The night sky was phenomenal, and the air was filled with the scents of the ocean and of *her*. I couldn't stop touching her, even after we were both dressed again.

As we walked, I kept my arm slung around her shoulders and pulled her in for a kiss every few steps.

Oh yeah, I am gone *for this woman.*

All the day-dreaming I'd done about her after that week in Greece had fallen so short of reality it wasn't even funny. She was even sexier and more addictive than she'd been three years ago.

And the knowledge that she hadn't been with anyone since... well, maybe it was a little cave man of me, but it thrilled the hell out of me. I sort of felt like posting on all my social media that I'd been so good that nobody else's dick would do afterward.

Just thinking about it was making me hard again. Thankfully, when we got back to the mansion, Scarlett invited me to her room.

"Want to come up for a little while?" she asked in a soft, sexy drawl that tickled my ear and sent a shot of energizing heat straight to my groin.

It was all I could do to keep from sprinting up the stairs two at a time.

"Be really quiet when we pass Vivi's room," she whispered. "I don't want her to know."

"Don't want your grandma to know what? That you've invited the big, bad wolf home?" I teased.

When we reached her room and were both inside, I turned and locked the door. Sweeping Scarlett up, I carried her to the bed.

"Now you're in trouble, Red," I warned.

I deposited her on the bed and crawled across it after her, growling. She giggled and kicked at me then let out a little squeal as I grabbed her ankle to pull her toward me.

"Where's that red robe, by the way? I was so fucking turned on seeing you in that last night."

"You mean seeing me *out* of it," she corrected. "I think you have a fetish for fairy tales."

Then she put on this soft little damsel-in-distress voice.

"Oh my, what big claws you have Mr. Wolf. What big *teeth* you have." She breathed in and out in dramatic little gasps. "And what big O's you give."

Fuck. I'd never been into role play before, but this was giving me a boner for the record books. I basically dove for her, getting her clothes off as quickly as possible without ripping them to shreds.

"I'll show you big and bad," I threatened and stripped off her jeans while she wriggled out of her shirt and sweater and bra.

Urging her to lie flat on her back, I eased her panties down her legs and dropped them to the floor.

Now *this* was a sight I could get used to—Scarlett naked and beautiful, spread out before me like a perfect, primed canvas just waiting for my hand.

That gave me an idea.

She reached for me, but I grabbed both her wrists and pushed her arms over her head, pressing them to the mattress beneath us.

I gave her a quick kiss. "Leave them there, okay? There's something I need to do."

She smiled up at me in dreamy anticipation. "What do you *need* to do?"

Stretching out beside her and propping myself on one elbow, I smiled down into her beautiful eyes.

"You know about my tattoo designs, but I forgot to mention my other artistic talent."

"Oh?"

I nodded gravely. "I'm also a master finger painter."

With my right pointer finger, I stroked her mouth until her lips parted. Then I rubbed the inside of her lower lip, extracted my finger, and painted an invisible heart on her chest in the space between her breasts.

A little shiver passed through her. "How does it look?"

"Beautiful," I murmured. "But it needs more."

I tapped her lips, and she opened them for me again, nibbling on my finger then pulling it inside. Feeling her suck on it and swirl her tongue around, I almost abandoned the whole finger-painting idea and begged her to do that to my cock instead. I groaned and pulled my finger out with a little pop.

Then I "painted" some more, this time tracing a figure eight around her breasts, skating close to the erect nipples but not quite touching them. I painted a line down the center of her torso and around her belly button.

Scarlett sighed and squirmed in trembling frustration. I could see she was highly aroused. Her pupils were dilated, her breaths shallow and quick, and her skin was flushed all over.

"Is the painting done yet?" she asked, sounding breathless.

"Almost." I bent to kiss her mouth then her breasts, dragging my "paintbrush" down below her navel and through the whorls of soft hair to her wet center.

Playing with her, I let my fingertip circle the sensitive peak of her sex then slide past it to caress the wet folds.

I lifted my head from her breast. "Know what I'm painting now, Scarlett?"

She shook her head, her breath shuddering. "What?"

"My masterpiece. I'm going to call it *Rhapsody in Scarlett*. People will come from all over the world to see it, collectors will clamor to get it for themselves. They'll offer their fortunes to have it. But I'll tell them it's part of a private collection. Mine."

I slipped a finger inside her, and her inner muscles clenched around it, causing me to inhale a sharp breath. "All mine."

Withdrawing the finger, I finger-painted her slick outer folds then her clit, using soft flicks and nudges circling steadily, while my tongue painted circles on her sensitive nipples.

I could tell my work of art was almost complete when her knees drew up and her back arched. She pushed her bare feet against the mattress, pressing herself into my hand, wanting more stimulation, seeking more complete contact.

Her hips rocked up and she started a chant of *yes, please, oh yes.*

My dick strained against my pants, furious to be trapped in a cage of confining fabric when there was a hot, wet woman nearby begging to be satisfied.

I ignored it, continuing to paint dirty pictures between Scarlett's legs.

When she came it was wild and loud and utterly fantastic. Her hips bucked and her mouth opened in a silent scream followed by an audible one. I was grateful Vivi's room was at the other end of the very long hallway and that the mansion was built of solid marble and limestone.

Just in case, I muffled her screams with my mouth, kissing her and kissing her as the ecstasy moved through her body and left her limp and glowing beneath me.

When she opened her eyes, they were shining.

"Wow," she said.

"Wow is right. I love making you come."

She smiled so big it was almost a laugh. "You are a *very* good artist."

"Thank you. You're an excellent muse."

Rolling onto her side, Scarlett reached for my pants, opened my button and zipper, and delved a hand inside, palming my cock and then stroking me.

"My turn."

I hissed a breath between my teeth, loving the way she touched me. She was confident about it, *knowing* I loved it. In fact, I was loving it a little too much.

I folded my fingers around hers, removing her hand and standing at the side of the bed to step out of my pants and underwear.

She watched me do it, her blue eyes widening and filling with anticipation at the sight of my unrestrained hard-on.

I loved the way she looked at me, the way she touched me, the way she so clearly wanted me. I didn't think it was possible, but my dick got even harder.

She slid back on the bed and let her legs fall open.

Fuck.

There was literally no where else in the world I wanted to be. I climbed over her, almost in disbelief that this was my life, that I was this lucky.

Scarlett stared up into my eyes and reached up to stroke my abdomen and sides in a clear invitation I was so ready to accept.

I wasn't in the mood to go slow this time.

Positioning myself against her, I pushed inside her tightness and heat, and she moaned, her face blissed out. She looked so sexy with that half-lidded smile it was almost enough to make me come then and there.

Of course I wasn't going to let that happen. My new mission in life was to give this woman as many orgasms per day as possible.

Maybe I couldn't have her forever, but as long as I did, I intended to make the time count.

I started to move, keeping my body low and pressed against hers, the way I knew she liked it.

She wanted to feel as much of me as possible, and that's what I wanted too. Skin against skin, our faces aligned, our bodies joined in the most intimate way possible.

Slowly and steadily, pushing deeper with each stroke, I let the friction build then gradually increased the speed and pressure, guiding her toward another crest of pleasure.

When she reached it, gasping and saying my name, it took me about oh-point-two-five seconds to join her.

Afterward we lay together, both breathing hard. I pulled Scarlett against me, loving the feel of her softness and the spill of her silky hair over my shoulder and arm and the warmth of her bare skin against mine.

Inksy was about to strike again somewhere soon, and mamas better cover their little ones' eyes, because I was feeling *inspired.*

Scarlett traced the tattoos on my chest and right shoulder, moving down my arm to the newer ink on my forearm.

"What's this one about?" she asked, scratching lightly over an image of a woman's eyes.

They were her exact shape and shade of blue, which if I'd known I was ever going to see her again in person, I might not have been brave enough to choose.

"I think you know," I murmured into her hair then kissed the top of her head.

"Really? This is me?" she asked, sounding amazed.

"You have pretty eyes," I said, telling the truth but minimizing it.

"These are prettier than mine," she said. "You really are talented, Gray. You sort of blew me off when I said before that you should pursue art professionally, but I mean it—you're almost as good as Inksy."

I had to suppress a snort of laughter. *Almost?*

"That's high praise," I said.

"You're laughing at me, but I'm being serious, Gray."

I stroked her hair and ran my hand down her back, planting a kiss on her forehead then her lips when she tilted her face up to give me access.

"I'm not laughing at you. Thank you for saying that. But as I told you before, art reveals things about the artist's deepest thoughts. I'm sure you saw it in the drawing I did of you last night."

She nodded, her silky cheek moving against my chest. "I *liked* what I saw."

"So did I," I said in the most lecherous tone I could manage.

She tugged at my chest hair.

"Ow." I laughed, and she kissed the stinging place. "I'm not sure I'm ready to share what's in my brain with the world at large."

"Use a pseudonym," she suggested innocently. "Like Inksy does."

That caused a different kind of sting—one to my conscience. I'd always felt completely justified in keeping my alter ego a secret.

But now, with Scarlett, not telling her was starting to feel like lying.

The thing was, she was only interested in a fling. I wanted more. I wanted her to stay, but as far as I knew she would be leaving in a week or two, and we'd never see each other again.

And unless I was certain she was in it for the long haul, how could I trust her with my secret? If it got out, my life would never be the same. I'd be at the center of a publicity nightmare, just like I'd been during my commanding officer's trial.

The last thing I wanted was to be "famous" again.

So I passed up yet another opportunity to come clean with her. Instead, I pointed at a painting on the wall directly opposite Scarlett's bed. It was *Confluence*, the painting I'd given Victoria— the one that had hung in her gallery.

"What's that doing in here?"

Scarlett lifted her head and looked at it. "I asked Vivi if I could move it to my room."

Her tone was nonchalant, but I was burning up with curiosity.

"Why? I thought you said it was only mediocre."

"I didn't say 'mediocre,'" she said. "I said 'decent.' But I've changed my mind."

I raised a sardonic brow. "It's *not* decent?"

"No. It's much better than that." She sat up, gazing at it now. "The more I look at it, the more I see in it. I study it every morning when I wake up before I get out of bed. It's amazing. When the sun hits it, there are all these little details that you didn't notice before. And the colors look different, depending on the time of day."

Scarlett sighed. "To tell you the truth, I've kind of fallen in love with it. I'm going to be really sad when it's sold at auction."

Though it had been only a few minutes since we'd finished making love, I was getting hard again. Listening to Scarlett describing her admiration for my work was one of the most gratifying experiences I'd ever had.

I realized that in spite of all the people out there who weren't my audience—she *was*.

She *got* me.

I also realized I was falling in love with her.

"Maybe you should write Inksy a fan letter," I teased.

"Oh no," she crooned, turning back around and draping herself across my chest. "Are you jealous?"

Scarlett gave me a sultry smile as she ran her hand down the front of my body and became *aware* of my condition.

"Hell no," I said. "After all, I'm the one who's here with *you*."

TWENTY-FIVE

Guardian of the World

Scarlett

I woke up early the next morning, filled with energy.

Last night with Gray had been incredible. He'd slipped out before dawn, promising to come back this afternoon.

He had the day off and said there was somewhere he wanted to take me this evening. Knowing his penchant for surprises, I had no idea what to expect.

I had a little surprise for him as well. When he arrived, there would be a fresh batch of Sweet Scarlett's chocolate chip cookies waiting.

Vivi sat in the kitchen with me, doing a puzzle at the island counter while I measured and mixed and poured. I had the recipe memorized, of course. I'd created it, and every August for the past seven years I'd replicated it several times a day during the Minnesota State Fair, baking literally thousands of cookies a day with my team.

"Something's smelling mighty good over there," Vivi said. "Your taste tester is ready and waiting."

I laughed, pulling the first batch out of the oven. "They need to cool a few minutes, and then you can taste all you want."

"Now there's an offer that catches my interest," a deep male voice said from behind me.

I turned to see Gray walking into the kitchen.

"You don't even know what's on the menu."

He smiled and walked right up to me, kissing my cheek. "Whatever it is, I *know* it'll be delicious."

Conscious of Vivi watching and listening, I widened my eyes and glared a silent *shush* at him.

He just laughed and went to join her at the table.

"What are we working on today? The Sistine Chapel?"

"No. This is Glennray Tutor's work. Scarlett ordered it for me."

"He's a photorealist painter," I said. "I found him on Instagram."

Gray smiled over at me. "Someone's becoming quite the art aficionado."

I shrugged and lifted the platter of hot cookies, carrying it to the table. "I'm picking up a few things here and there. It's the environment. Hanging out with all these art snobs is rubbing off on me."

Gray and Vivi both reached for the same cookie—the biggest one.

"You sure you want that one?" he teased her. "Don't you need to watch out for your girlish figure?"

She snatched the cookie and took a big bite. "No one's watched *this* girlish figure for a long time now. That's one of the joys of living to be eighty-nine—you can eat anything you want without guilt."

Gray selected a (slightly smaller) cookie for himself and bit into it.

"Fuck." He shot a hand out toward Vivi. "Sorry. Excuse my language."

"Was it too hot?" I asked.

"No," he said. "It was too *good*. These are unbelievable. What brand is this dough?"

"That isn't store-bought dough. It's Scarlett's own recipe," Vivi told him proudly.

"You're kidding," he said. "This is literally the best cookie I've ever tasted."

Vivi went on bragging. "Scarlett is *Sweet Scarlett*, the chocolate chip cookie queen of Minnesota."

I shook my head. "That's not exactly true—though I do appreciate the hype job, Vivi."

Directing my attention at Gray, I explained. "I have a booth at the Minnesota State Fair every summer. My cookies are pretty popular there."

"I can see why. I can't get enough of these."

He took another cookie from the platter then a third. I stopped what I was doing and watched him chew. His face looked a little like it had last night in bed, blissed out and somewhat disbelieving.

Picking up his phone, he tapped the screen a few times.

"This article says they're more than just 'pretty popular.' It says you sell out every day of the fair and calls your cookies a 'Minnesota tradition.'"

Reading on, he said, "It says people are clamoring for grocery stores to carry your cookies and there's enough demand for you to open franchises. Scarlett—this is a big deal. Why didn't you tell me about this?"

"Have you told me every last detail about your life?" I challenged with a raised brow.

Gray got quiet.

"Scarlett's sister and her roommate have told her the same thing," Vivi said. "I think she should quit that boring office job she hates, move to Eastport Bay, and make cookies full-time."

"I can't move, Vivi. And I can't quit. My stepdad counts on me. Besides, starting a business from scratch takes money."

It was my grandmother's turn to get quiet. She went back to her puzzle, taking another cookie from the plate and munching it as she searched for the right fit.

Gray apparently wasn't ready to let the subject rest.

"Would you?" he asked. "If money *wasn't* an issue. Would you like to have your own business?"

"Well of course I'd *like* to. This is what I enjoy doing more than anything else. But there's still the issue of my job at Mixitall."

"And there's no one else who could do that job better?" he asked.

"Well…"

I'd never really considered that before. In truth, I *wasn't* the best person for the job at Mixitall. I kind of sucked at accounting.

I mean, I worked hard and got the job done, but it had never come naturally to me. A real accountant could probably do what I did each day in a third of the time.

There was a bubbling sensation in my chest, and it didn't feel terrible. It was a sort of light, airy feeling.

But then the bubbles popped. David liked the idea of working with family. He *trusted* me. He'd been disappointed when Maddie left the company to stay home with her kids.

He would hate the idea of hiring a stranger to do the books. I was afraid it would break his heart-and my mom's—if I quit.

In fact, they were hoping I'd take over the company one day.

"I don't know. Maybe," I admitted. "But David relies on me. As good as he's been to me, I don't want to let him down. It's a family business. My mom works there, too, part-time. My sister did, but she left, so I feel like it's all on me."

"I respect that," Gray said. "You're loyal to your family. That's a great thing. You should also be loyal to yourself, though—to what *you* really want in life. Because ultimately, you're the one who's got to live it. Eventually David's gonna retire. Your mom's gonna retire. When they aren't there anymore… would you still want that job? Do you *want* to run that company someday? Or will you wish you'd pursued your own dream?"

Vivi spoke up. "After what happened with Stuart and your father—I can tell you this—I would never encourage a parent to pressure their child to give up their passion in favor of the family business. I'm sure your mother and stepfather, if they're as loving and supportive as you say they are, wouldn't want that either. Do they know you're unhappy in your work?"

"I'm not unhappy," I said. My voice lost some of its vigor as I added, "I'm just not *happy* happy."

I pulled the next batch of cookies from the oven and tried not to think about the significance of that admission.

While they cooled, I went upstairs to change and get ready for whatever Gray had planned for us. My phone beeped with a text notification. It was from Maddie.

-Now a good time to talk?

I hit the little phone symbol beside her name. My sister answered immediately, a laugh in her voice.

"I guess that's a yes," she said.

"Hi. I miss you. How are you?"

"Great. Busy. Trina's having fun at the pool every day and looking forward to starting second grade. James is talking non-stop and climbing literally *everything*. How are you? How are things with the grandmother?"

"Vivi. She's awesome, actually. We're having fun together, and I'm trying to help her as much as I can while I'm here."

"Of course you are."

"What does that mean?"

"Just that you're a caretaker. You're always trying to make sure everyone else is okay," she said. "I was watching Trina with James the other day, and it made me think of us when we were younger. She's only four years older than him, but she's like a second little mommy to him, always trying to teach him things and take care of him."

"So sweet," I said.

"It is. And it's normal. But Mom told me you were like that even before I was born—with your father. She said your roles were kind of reversed, that he was so hurt, and you were always trying to take care of him instead of the other way around."

"I don't even remember that," I told her.

"It's a lot to ask of a kid," she said. "You weren't much older than Trina. Situations like that when a child has to 'parent' their parent can have a lasting effect. They can turn you into a pleaser."

"You think I'm a pleaser?" I asked in a state of semi-shock.

"Well, you're doing a job you hate just to make Mom and David happy. You go out with guys you don't even really like just to make *them* happy. It's okay to want things for yourself, you know. When I decided I wanted to be a stay-at-home mom, I knew Mom and Dad would be disappointed I was quitting work at Mixitall, but I had to do what was right for *me* and my family. I'm not sure you're doing that. Hold on—James is halfway up the bookcase, the little shi—pbuilder."

There was background noise of footsteps and then a very angry toddler who was less than grateful for having his life saved.

Maddie picked up the phone again. "Sorry about that. He's in time out. So, as I was saying, *your* needs are just as important as everyone else's. But it's like you're the self-appointed guardian of the world, and the thing I realized is... you can't save the world unless you take care of yourself first. You know that oxygen mask announcement the airlines make at the start of every flight? If you're not okay, how are you supposed to save anyone else?"

"I *am* okay," I promised her.

"Okay, if you say so. All right... now tell me about this Gray guy..."

TWENTY-SIX

What Makes You Tick

Scarlett

That evening, I got into Gray's car with several dozen cookies boxed up in my lap.

He hadn't told me where we were going, but he assured me they'd be appreciated. On the ride to our mysterious destination, he brought up the cookie business idea again.

"You know... if taking Sweet Scarlett's nationwide is something you'd really like to do, I could help with the startup costs. I've got some money saved, and I could be sort of a silent partner. Or, if you'd rather, it could be a loan—"

"No."

It was really sweet of him, but how could he make an offer like that? He hadn't really known me that long. It was far too much of a risk, and what would be in it for him?

"Thank you, but I couldn't ask you to do that."

"You didn't ask," he said. "I offered."

"I know, but you shouldn't have."

His right brow lifted. "You're telling me what I can and can't do with my money?"

"No, of course not, but I don't think you realize how much it would take to get a company like that off the ground. I researched it once. It's a lot, and no offense, but how much could you possibly make as a security systems installer?"

He barked a sharp laugh. "You make it sound like I work with the Geek Squad at Best Buy. There's a little more to it than installation. And you'd probably die of shock if I told you some of the names that have hired me to set up security in their homes—not that I *would* tell you. Our non-disclosure agreements are ironclad. Let's just say these clients can afford to pay for top quality work and expertise."

"I'm not doubting your skills and expertise, and I'm sure Wilder pays you well. I'm just saying I don't want you to risk *any* of your money on me when it might not pan out."

He glanced away from the road to pin me with an intense look. "Maybe I think you're worth the risk."

My pulse quickened as it always did whenever I was the subject of Gray's acute focus.

"I just hate to see you let your dream die," he said. "It bothers me to think of you stagnating in a place you don't feel fulfilled when you could be following your passion."

"I could say the same to you," I countered. "I know you like working with Wilder and the other guys from your team, but it's not your passion. You're not following *your* passion either."

He frowned.

"That's different."

"How?" When he didn't answer, I said, "I'll make you a deal, when you put your money where your mouth is and start living your dream, I'll think about leaving my job and making Sweet Scarlett's into a fulltime business."

The rest of the drive was *very* quiet.

I was shocked when we reached our destination. It wasn't an art exhibit or a fun show or some charming restaurant with a great water view.

Gray pulled up and parked outside the Ocean State Training School.

A collection of flat-roofed brick buildings surrounded by high chain link fencing, the facility housed the state's juvenile correctional services—otherwise known as juvie.

"We're at the juvenile detention center? Do you know someone in here?" I asked.

"I know lots of someones in here—my students."

My jaw literally dropped. "You're a teacher?"

He smiled. "Not like you're thinking. The actual teaching is a once-a-week thing for me. I started an arts non-profit that holds programs here at the detention center. I found different people to come and teach photography, pottery, drama, creative writing, all kinds of stuff. I'm helping the guys who want to learn to draw."

"Learn to draw what?"

"Most of them are creating graphic novels. Some are doing self-portraits."

We got out of the car and walked toward the facility's entrance.

"As I discovered, art has tremendous potential to help unlock your emotions," Gray said. "That's an important thing for the kids in here because unless you address the underlying emotional issues behind their crimes, you can put all kinds of services in place, but they won't necessarily be able to benefit from them. Self-expression and creativity aren't just fun—they're vital. And when the kids are recognized for doing something creative and *good*, they're more motivated to move forward with education and counseling. Some of them are even pursuing careers in art."

"That's phenomenal."

His smile was wide. "I think so. I'm proud of them. Since I've been working with the kids here, five of my students have been accepted at Rhode Island School of Design, one to Mass Art, one to Savannah College of Art and Design, and a few to other art schools. All of them are from poor backgrounds and going on scholarship."

I was blown away. "Gray... you literally changed their lives."

"They changed their own lives," he said. "But I hope by

enabling them to express and discover themselves through art, maybe I helped them *want* to change."

Gray and I went through the required entry procedures—I was admitted as his "assistant"—and we went to a classroom that had been prepared for the drawing class.

I sat at the back and observed for the next hour as Gray worked with a group of eight guys, demonstrating drawing techniques and working with each student individually. He checked the progress of projects they'd started previously and praised the work they'd done.

Several times I had to fight back tears. The incarcerated boys were so excited about what they'd created, so proud of themselves, so clearly *into* it.

And that had to be because Gray was so invested in *them*. It was obvious he really cared about them.

And I accused him of not following his passion.

I felt like an idiot. Maybe Gray wasn't creating art for a living, but he was helping these young guys create better lives for themselves.

That was passion.

While they worked, the boys wolfed down the cookies I'd brought. They'd had to go through metal detection and visual inspection before being allowed in, of course, but watching how the teens enjoyed what *I'd* created made me want to bring them a fresh batch every day.

When we left, I thanked Gray for letting me come along.

"That was really special. Thank you for sharing that part of your life with me."

He looked at the ground, but I could see a pleased expression sneak across his face. "It's nothing."

"No, it's something, Gray. Remember I told you how important transparency is to me? It means a lot that you'd show me something that's meaningful to *you*. I know we're only having a fling, but I like seeing what makes you tick."

"You know what really makes me tick?" he asked with a rascally grin. "Pie. I'm starved. How 'bout you?"

"I could definitely eat. And pie sounds amazing. Want to go to Nooky's so I can try that famous chocolate cream pie you were telling me about?"

"Absolutely. But I have an even better idea."

"What could be better than chocolate cream pie?"

"You'll see. Or actually… you won't."

"What does that mean?"

"Just wait."

We pulled up to Nooky's, and Gray asked me to stay in the car while he ran inside. I assumed he was getting a pie to go. Honestly, I was a little disappointed—it would have been nice to eat inside the cute railcar-styled diner.

But he came out minutes later with no less than ten pie boxes.

"I'm not *that* hungry," I joked when he'd stashed them in the back and gotten into the car.

"You don't have to eat them all tonight," he said. "But you do have to *taste* them all tonight. We're going to play a little game."

"Oh really? And what is this game? We're not going to throw pies at each other, are we?"

"Why would we throw them at each other? That's a waste of good pie. Don't worry, it's not going to be messy or painful. It'll be fun," he promised.

When we got back to the house, the first floor was deserted, and the kitchen had been cleaned up from dinner.

Gray put the stacks of pies on the counter. I ran upstairs and saw Vivi's door was closed. When I came back down, he was rifling through the coat closet.

"What are you looking for?"

He pulled a lightweight scarf from the closet. "This."

What was going on? What kind of game involved pie and a scarf?

I found out when we went back into the kitchen. I slid onto a stool at the island, and Gray stepped behind me.

"Close your eyes please."

"What? Why?"

"So I can blindfold you." He said it in a *no big deal* tone of voice.

"Um..."

"Don't worry. I promise... this will be fun. It's just a little taste test. We're going to find out how much of a pie connoisseur you are."

My belly simmered with excitement as Gray tied the scarf around my eyes.

"We've got ten different kinds of pie here," he said. "Let's see how many you can identify."

"Oh, come on now. This is going to be too easy."

"As easy as pie?"

"Hahaha," I said in a flat tone.

I heard the sound of the boxes being opened, a drawer opening, and the soft clink of silverware.

It was strange to be in the same room with Gray and not be able to see what he was doing, whether he was looking at me or not, how close he was.

"Ready?"

I jumped a little. Judging from the sound of his voice, he was *very* close. "I guess so,"

Wow was I nervous. I giggled, though nothing was particularly funny.

"Okay, open up. Here comes the first bite."

I opened my mouth, and Gray placed a bite on my tongue. A blend of flavors stimulated my tastebuds. Flaky, buttery crust, sugar, some kind of sweet-tart fruit. After chewing and swallowing, I ventured a guess.

"Cherry pie?"

He laughed and made a sound of frustration. "That one *was* too easy. Okay, get ready for the next. I'm keeping score by the way."

"What happens if I get all ten of them right?" I asked.

"You won't."

"What if I do? What do I get when I win?"

He didn't answer right away. I assumed he was thinking of a suitable prize.

"If you get them all right," he said, "then I'll take you swimming at the best swimming pool in town."

"Oooh, sounds nice. And what if I lose?"

"If you get the majority of them wrong, you have to swim with no suit on."

TWENTY-SEVEN

Strip Pie-Tasting

Scarlett

"What? You want me to skinny dip?" I reached for my blindfold, intending to take it off.

Gray's warm fingers wrapped around my wrist, stopping me. "Relax. I don't mean in the ocean. Nowhere public. Here—in Vivi's indoor pool."

"This house has an indoor pool?"

"Mmmmhmmm," he hummed. "She's invited me to use it anytime I want to. It's on the lowest level, heated of course, salt water. It's great for your skin, and I seem to remember you're a fan of swimming au naturel."

"I'm glad *you* remember that night. Or maybe I'm not," I joked, still somewhat mortified at the memory of my drunken midnight dip.

"I do. And I'm *definitely* glad I do. I'm looking forward to a swim where I'm *allowed* to touch you. It was torture for me that night at the resort—you looked so fucking good. And I had to be a gentleman. You didn't make it easy."

Chill bumps spread across my skin, and my breath caught before resuming in a lighter, faster pattern.

"Okay, I agree to your terms." I let my hands drop to my lap, opening my mouth.

Gray placed the next pie sample inside. This one had a graham cracker crust. Crumbly and sweet, that was my favorite kind of pie crust. The rest of it was harder to identify.

It wasn't chocolate, that was for sure. I tasted cream cheese, vanilla, some kind of nuts... "Praline pecan cheesecake?"

Gray's gasp was audible. "What are you, some kind of ringer? I've been duped. I thought I was dealing with a rookie. I think you're a professional pie-taster in addition to being a bookkeeper."

"No, but I *am* a baker. I know my baking ingredients."

"Okay, well you're two for two, but there are still eight more to go. Here comes the next bite."

This one was tough. There was a traditional graham cracker crust, but the filling was decidedly non-traditional. It was creamy and tasted good, but I couldn't place the flavor.

"Is it some kind of pudding?"

Gray made a funny buzzer noise. "I'm sorry. That. Is. *In*correct. It's an avocado pie."

His kiss soothed the sting of defeat.

It felt particularly decadent to kiss him with a blindfold on. I'd never participated in any sort of kinky sex, but suddenly I could see the allure of it. With my vision taken out of play, my other senses felt heightened.

My nose was filled with the scent of sugar and fruit, and Gray. My ears picked up on the smallest change in his breathing pattern, the way his breaths grew shallower and more rapid as the kiss went on.

The taste of him—always a pleasure—was heightened by the combined flavors of the different pies lingering on my tongue. I squirmed on my bar stool, restless and eager to feel and taste more of him.

"Since you appear to be *losing* this game, maybe you should go ahead and take off an item of clothing," he murmured against my lips. "In fact, I think that's a great idea. Instead of strip poker we'll play strip pie-tasting."

"You wish," I said, but then on impulse, I kicked off one of my shoes.

Though I couldn't see his face, I could almost *feel* Gray's approval. "Now we're talking," he purred.

"Since we're changing the rules mid-game here, I have a new one to propose," I said.

"Oh?"

"If I win—which means you lose—then *you* have to strip for *me* and skinny dip while I get to keep my clothes on."

After a moments' hesitation, Gray agreed. "You're on."

There were several more exotic pie flavors, which I failed to guess, and then a couple of easy ones I got right.

It was down to the last bite, and I was down to only my sundress, having already removed both shoes, my bra and panties, and my necklace.

"It's strawberry," I said with confidence.

"Ehhh." He made the buzzing noise again and spoke like a game show host consoling the last-place finisher.

"I am so sorry, but that is not correct. The right answer is strawberry-*rhubarb*. We have a lovely consolation prize for you."

He kissed me again, a quick one this time but still delicious. "And now if you'll please remove your dress, we shall proceed to the pool."

I yanked off the blindfold. "Hold on a minute. That was very close. I was partially right. I think we should call it a tie."

He narrowed his gaze. "What about the prize distribution? I mean, I've almost got you naked already."

I laughed. "It's only right that you get naked, too. I'll give you a head start down to the pool. I'm going to go upstairs and grab some towels and something to put on afterward."

"Okay that's fair," he conceded. "I'll see you down there in a few minutes."

With a silly eyebrow waggle, he added, "Wear the red robe."

* * *

By the time I made it to the lower level, which contained not only a gorgeous pool but a sauna and a luxurious changing room with shower, my courage had waned a bit. I felt self-conscious in only my robe.

This wasn't a bedroom behind a locked door. It was an open pool area. There was the chance—slight but real—that someone could walk in on us.

Gray waited for me, barefoot but still fully dressed.

"Cheater," I accused. "You were supposed to strip, too." I relaxed a little, assuming I was off the hook.

His grin was slow and deadly sexy. "Oh, I plan to honor my side of the bargain. I just thought you'd like to watch."

Oh my God.

I felt light-headed, like I might pass out. Either it was the mother of all sugar-crashes, or this guy produced the most potent pheromones on Earth.

"What if Vivi or Stephanie were to walk in?"

"Stephanie doesn't swim, and the elevator doesn't come down to this level, so Vivi's not going to walk in," he promised.

He ran his gaze over the robe. "You know how much I like that, Red, but it's gonna have to come off."

I bit my lower lip as goosebumps chased each other across my skin, and my heart played my breastbone like a hi-hat drum.

"You first."

"You sure drive a hard bargain for someone who lost," he said.

"It was a *tie.*"

He grinned. "Fine."

Keeping his eyes locked with mine, Gray unbuttoned and unzipped his jeans, shoved them down, and let them hit the tile pool deck. Then he grabbed the bottom of his shirt and dragged it up and over his head, exposing his chest and sculptured shoulders and those delineated, highly lick-able abs of his.

That left only his underwear, which were dark gray and form-fitting.

And the form they revealed was *impressive*—long, and thick, and straining against the stretchy fabric.

My heart fluttered, stealing my breath.

"Okay, your turn now, Red."

Feeling self-conscious about walking through someone else's house in nothing but a robe, I'd put on a pair of panties and a matching bra.

When I opened the robe, and Gray saw the lingerie set, he took a deep breath and shook his head like someone observing a wonder of nature such as a waterfall or a sunset.

"Cheater yourself," he accused with a raised brow. "You put some clothes back on."

Though I was struggling for breath, I managed to say, "I thought *you'd* like to watch."

Where had *that* come from? And who was I?

It was like Gray had reached back in time and dragged the un-honeymoon me here from the Greek islands. My sense of confidence and my sexuality were reawakening—thanks to him.

I could have sworn I heard a growl. "You know I would."

Shedding the red robe, I tossed it onto a nearby chair. Gray sat in another chair, watching. Waiting.

Feeling wobbly but excited, I slid the bra straps down my shoulders, then unfastened the band. The bra dropped to the floor.

Gray smiled and leaned back in his chair, rolling his lips in then out as he crossed his arms under his chest.

Encouraged by his appreciative expression, I hooked my thumbs under the top band of my panties at each of my hips. I paused, letting him wonder—letting myself wonder—If I'd actually do it.

My heart was pounding so hard he could probably see it vibrating my chest wall.

I slid the panties down and stepped out of them.

Gray blew out a long breath, like a silent whistle. "Scarlett... you are stunning."

He stood and slid his own underwear off his hips, freeing his erection.

Talk about stunning.

I dove into the water, enjoying the bracing sensation of its coolness on my overheated skin. A splash sounded behind me a second later, and then his strong hands were on my bare skin, hot even compared to the heated water.

He slid them over my legs, over my bottom and stomach. I stopped swimming away from him and fanned the water with my hands to swirl toward him.

Looping an arm around my waist, Gray clamped our bodies together, then kicked hard toward the surface.

We broke it and locked mouths, barely taking a breath before giving into the desire to devour each other. He kept a loose hold on me with one arm and stroked the water with the other, moving us toward the shallow end of the pool.

"Do you want to get out already?" I asked.

"Nuh uh." He shook his head, a wicked smile on his face. "I wanted to do... *this.*"

With his hands on my waist, he set me on the highest step of the pool stairs. In this position, the water came to just below my belly button. Gray flattened his body, floating as his hands gripped my knees and his legs stretched out behind him.

"I didn't get to finish what I was doing the night I drew you at the fountain." He licked his lips.

I looked around, suddenly nervous.

"Here?"

He nodded, his eyes narrowing in sexy menace. "Here. Now. All you have to do is let me."

Rapid breaths lifted my chest, and my nipples hardened. The area between my legs grew hot and achy, desperate to accept what he offered.

Apparently, it was possible to get wet even underwater.

I nodded slowly, and Gray dragged himself forward until his head was positioned directly over my lap. Then he stroked my legs apart and lowered his face into the shallow water.

The contrast of his hot mouth to the relative coolness of the pool water was stimulating. What he did with his tongue was even more electrifying.

My clit had its own heartbeat now, throbbing in steady, ecstatic pulses as Gray licked and sucked, opening me gently with this thumbs and thrusting a big finger inside me while his tongue stroked me on the outside.

Within seconds I was writhing and panting, pleasure streaking through me in little comets as I came hard on his lips before he even needed to surface for a breath.

TWENTY-EIGHT

Private Donor

Gray

Floating on her back, Scarlett looked like a water fairy, her skin luminous and her hair rippling around her in a golden cloud.

The problem with fairies was they were wicked hard to catch. Even if you could manage to capture one, they were nearly impossible to hold onto.

More and more often, I thought about the fast-approaching expiration date of our "fling." I wasn't sure about Scarlett, but I was falling hard.

I'd had more fun with her than I'd ever had with any woman. I was more attracted to her than I'd been to anyone in my life. I loved her voice, her body, her laugh. I loved her cookies.

The idea of her leaving made me feel like I was going to shrivel up and fade away no matter *how* much I worked out.

"I could get used to this," she said and sighed, a long, soft, happy sound that curled around my spinal column and sent zings of sensation to every extremity—including my dick, which should have been pretty fucking satisfied at this point but somehow wanted more.

"Why don't you?" I suggested, working hard to sound

nonchalant. "If you moved to Eastport Bay, you could visit Victoria's pool every day."

My heart thumped as I added, "Plus, you could see her every day. And *me*."

"If *you* moved to Minnesota, you could start an arts program in the juvenile detention system there," Scarlett countered in a blithe tone. She did a couple of lazy backstrokes, propelling herself away from me.

Swimming to the side of the pool, I hoisted myself out, toweling off.

Scarlett stopped her lazy float, letting her feet drift to the bottom of the pool.

"Speaking of that... you know Vivi's assigned me to find worthwhile charities to donate her money to. I was thinking, your arts non-profit would be a great cause. You could expand it to a *bunch* of other states, maybe even take it nationwide."

"No thank you," I said politely.

She blinked and cocked her head to the side as if wondering whether there was water in her ears.

"No?"

"No. Thank you. I appreciate it, but it's not necessary."

She swam to the steps in the shallow end. "But... how can you tell me I should expand my business—which is just baked treats— and then flat-out refuse to even consider expanding your amazing program? Especially when I'm offering you the money that could make it possible?"

"I'm not opposed to expanding the program," I said. "In fact, I've *been* considering it."

I'd spent a *lot* of time thinking about it actually.

Though I felt a strong sense of loyalty toward Wilder and the other guys at Viridian, I honestly spent way more time thinking about my "side gigs"—the detention center program and my work as Inksy, which paid for it—than I did my full-time job.

Scarlett wasn't aware of any of this of course.

"So, it's money you're opposed to," she said.

I smiled. "I'm not opposed to money—you just don't need to give me any of Victoria's. Give it to another program or charity. There are so many that are worthwhile."

She got out of the pool and grabbed a towel, covering up that body I could never get enough of.

"You know Vivi would want you to have it," she said as she dried off. "If that's what the problem is."

My smile widened. She was a persistent one when she got an idea in her head. "There isn't a problem. Can we just drop it?"

She didn't drop it.

"Is this about pride or something? You don't want to take charity?" she guessed. "Because if that's the case, you should think of all the incarcerated kids who don't have access to something like this."

"I am thinking of the kids. It's *not* about pride. The program is fully funded."

"Oh." She pulled the red robe back on and cinched it at the waist. It made her look like a slice of delicious red velvet cake, soft and sweet and oh so tempting.

Unfortunately, I couldn't take a bite. I was already fully dressed again—in the clothes I'd been wearing all day. I needed to go home and shower and change before work in the morning.

"If you do expand the program, you're going to *need* more money," Scarlett reasoned. "What are you planning to do? Hold fundraisers?"

She smirked. "Or what? You've got a rich grandma, too?"

I walked over to her, kissing her wet forehead and then her nosy little nose. "No and no. Don't worry about it. I told you there are no money problems. Can't you just accept that?"

"Sure I can. If you want us to stay strangers. I thought you wanted to be closer."

"Yes." I bent to kiss her mouth. "I do. I'm sorry."

The kiss only lasted a few seconds before she broke it and made eye contact again. She stretched up on her toes and locked her fingers around my neck

"I don't understand why you're being so weird about this. Changing kids' lives through art is important to you, and I'm only trying to help."

"Look, we've got a private donor, okay? He wants to remain anonymous."

I was fighting not to sound irritated. Scarlett's questions were innocent. She was being kind and generous, but she was also getting very close to my secret.

As she'd pointed out earlier, my job at Viridian paid well, but it didn't pay *that* well. Navy SEALs didn't exactly make big bucks either. So how could I explain the funding of my arts program?

"I see," she said. "And this 'private donor' is willing to supply any and all funds the program might need as it expands?"

"Yes. Exactly. Satisfied?"

"So, when were you thinking of starting the expansion?" she asked.

"When I have time," I snapped. "I've got a full-time job with Viridian, remember?"

She recoiled, clearly stung by my confusing reaction and unwillingness to discuss the subject. I couldn't though. Not when she was still talking about going back to Minnesota.

"I get it," she said, but her expression had clouded over, and she'd pulled away from me.

I wanted to grab the belt of that robe and drag her back to me, but she wanted answers I couldn't give. I didn't know what to do.

"Sorry. I'm just... tired I guess."

What a weak-ass excuse.

"Listen, I've been meaning to mention I'm going to be going out of state on a consult and install. I have to leave tomorrow. So I'm afraid you'll have to handle the final arrangements for the art auction. I've got all the pieces appraised and logged for the program. I've already hired an auctioneer, and Viridian will provide security. If you and Victoria could handle sending invitations and hiring a caterer, that would be great."

"Okay. Sure. We'll take care of it," she said. "How long will you be gone?"

Too long.

I didn't want to leave at all. I wanted to stay here—with her—and enjoy every minute I could squeeze out of our fling. I wanted to spend more time working on the arts program and be around to help Victoria, too.

But I *did* have a job. It was demanding. I didn't need the money, but I'd made a commitment to Wilder.

And as Scarlett had said, sometimes you couldn't just walk away from your obligations.

"A week. Maybe two," I answered.

Her face fell. "The auction is in two weeks. After that, I'm going back home."

"I know. I'll try to finish it as quickly as I can. I wish I had a choice about it."

Scarlett shrugged and stepped back. "I guess some things just can't be helped."

TWENTY-NINE

Heart Trouble

Scarlett

It was time to end it.

How could I have entertained the idea of quitting my job, moving here to Eastport Bay, and starting a cookie company—and starting a life with Gray? (Because, come on, who was I kidding? That's what I would have been hoping for by moving here, that we would be pursuing our dreams *together*.)

But some things *couldn't* be helped. I hadn't been able to help falling in love with him. And he was *still* keeping secrets.

It was more than just an anonymous donor or his failure to mention that he'd be leaving tomorrow. Possibly for *weeks*.

He was closing himself off and hiding from me, and I refused to live that way.

I stomped up the stairs from the pool with Gray close behind me. When we reached the first-floor entry hall, he tugged the back of my robe.

"Hey—Scarlett. Slow down."

I stopped and turned around.

"Are we good?" he asked.

"Yes. I think it *is* good, actually. It's for the best that you're leaving tomorrow," I said.

At his hurt expression, I explained. "I'm afraid I did it again. It's not your fault. We tried the casual sex fling-thing, but as it turns out, I'm just not built for it. If we keep at this, I'm not sure I can survive it. So, let's just call it now, okay? You're leaving tomorrow. The timing is perfect."

Gray stepped closer, trying to enfold me in his arms again. "Don't do this. Please. I have work. You understand that."

I wiggled away. "Yes—I do. I have work, too. Which is why in two weeks, after the auction, I'm leaving. We'll never see each other again. So it makes no sense to continue this... whatever it is we're doing. We might as well stop it now. The fling is officially over."

His brows pulled together. "I don't want it to be over."

"Well, if there's one lesson I've learned in life, it's that we don't always get what we want," I said.

Vivi appeared across the cavernous, echoey space, stopping me in my tracks. She must have just gotten off the elevator—which we didn't hear because we were on the lower level—skinny dipping.

"What's that dear? Leaving? Where are you going?" My elderly grandmother suddenly seemed to have the hearing of a bat.

Tugging the robe tighter around me, I smiled and went to her.

"I was telling Gray I have to leave soon, go home, go back to work. And he's leaving tomorrow for a job out of state. He'll be gone for a while. We were saying our 'goodbyes.'"

"No," Gray said sternly. "That's *not* what we were doing. We were just discussing our scheduling challenges, but we'll work it out."

"There's nothing to work out," I insisted. "It's late, Gray. You should go home and pack."

"Scarlett... please."

Vivi made a small sound, almost like a baby's cry, then she staggered back a couple of steps, clutching her chest.

Gray and I both rushed toward her.

"What's the matter Vivi?" I yelped.

Gray put his arm around her for support. "Are you okay?"

She shook her head, appearing confused. "I'm not sure. I feel funny. I think it's my heart."

"Is that why you came downstairs?" I asked with concern. "You weren't feeling well?"

Now I felt horribly guilty for engaging in aquatic woo-woo instead of going to check on her when we'd gotten back from the detention center.

She didn't answer me, just shook her head and went limp in Gray's arms. He lowered her gently to the floor and put his ear to her mouth while feeling for a pulse in her neck.

My hands covered my lips, which were trembling. "Oh my God. What's happening, Gray? Did she have a heart attack?"

"I'm not sure. She's breathing. Call 9-1-1."

I looked around me in a panic. "My phone's in my purse. It's up in my room."

He pointed to the office door across the hall. "Use the house phone."

I ran to the office and called for an ambulance. It arrived within minutes, and Gray and I climbed into the back of it with Vivi for the ride to the hospital.

She looked okay to me, like she was simply sleeping, but what the hell did I know?

An EMT was also in the back with us. He put an oxygen mask over her face and started an IV line.

He asked a steady stream of questions about her age and general health, her diet and hydration level—things I wouldn't have had a clue about before coming to stay here.

I answered them all, clutching one of Vivi's hands while Gray cradled the other. Once our gazes caught and held for a moment, but I looked away, back to Vivi.

What was I going to do if something happened to her? I had *just* found her. There was so much more I wanted to know about her and tell her about me.

So much lost time to make up for.

When we arrived at the ER, Gray and I followed the gurney inside. An admitting nurse asked some more questions while Vivi was taken into a curtained-off room.

"Can I go with her?" I asked.

"Family only," the nurse said.

"We're family," Gray said and started to follow her.

I turned to look at him. "You can go home. I've got it from here. I know you need to get ready for your work trip."

"Fuck work," he growled.

"Really. It's okay," I said in a gentler, less businesslike tone. "You said the trip was important. Besides, I'm her blood relative. You're not."

Gray's eyes were glittering. I couldn't tell if he wanted to hug me or strangle me.

"Don't cut me out, Scarlett," he pleaded. "I love her, too."

"So? You act like 'love' stops people from leaving. Men say they love you and leave *all the time*."

"Not me."

"No, not you," I agreed. "You've never even said it."

Spinning away from him, I followed the nurse to the unit where Vivi was being treated. She pulled back the curtain, and I entered.

Gray followed. I shot him a hostile look but didn't say anything.

Vivi was hooked up to an IV bag and several monitors. The slow, intermittent beeps of a heart monitor caught my attention.

"How is she doing?" I asked the person attending her. I wasn't sure if the woman was a doctor or a nurse.

She looked up from the clipboard she was holding. "Hi. I'm Dr. Arena. I'm an emergency medicine specialist here at Eastport Bay Hospital."

She offered a handshake to me and to Gray, and we introduced ourselves.

"Your grandmother is stable right now," the doctor said.

"She might have had a mild heart attack. We're not sure yet. We'll have to run some tests to determine how much damage might have been done. Don't worry. We're monitoring her closely, and we're going to admit her. Just waiting for a room right now."

She looked down at the paper on her clipboard again.

"Her records don't show any history of cardiovascular disease, but of course, at age eighty-nine, a lot of things can happen out of the blue. Do you know if she did anything outside of her usual routine today? Was there a lot of excitement? Anything disruptive or upsetting?"

Gray and I exchanged guilty glances.

"It's my fault," he said. "I upset her."

"No, it was me. We were bickering, and I mentioned the fact that we'd both be leaving town soon," I said.

"You're married?" the doctor asked.

"No. *No*, we're... just friends," I told her.

The doctor smiled. "I highly doubt overhearing some bickering between friends could lead to myocardial infarction. It's more likely she's got some blockage in her arteries. Like I said, we'll be running some tests and keeping an eye on her. I am a little concerned to hear you say you're both leaving town. Is there anyone to take care of her when she's released? A hospitalization at this age is stressful to the system. Elderly people can lose some of their mobility simply from being off their feet for several days and in an unfamiliar environment."

"I can stay with her," I said without even hesitating to think about it.

"I'll be here," Gray said. "I'm cancelling my trip."

I gave him a sharp glance. "But... how can you..."

"I can, and I will."

Well, okay then.

The two of us stayed in the emergency department with Vivi until a room opened up on one of the floors. Gray and I followed the gurney through the corridors and into a large elevator then

through more twisting and turning hallways as she was transferred to an inpatient room.

Once she was settled, he went to the padded chair near the
window and pulled it out flat into a single sleeper then turned and
faced me.

"Why don't you stretch out and get some rest?"

"Are you going back to your place?"

He looked at me like I'd just asked if he planned to drive his
new Mercedes through a hailstorm.

"I'm not leaving. I'm going to call Wilder. Then I'll find us
some water and vending machine provisions. I'll bring them back
here before I find a spot in the lobby to grab a few hours of sleep.
Doctors usually do rounds super-early in the morning, like six
o'clock, so I'll be here for that."

I nodded, my throat feeling thick. "Okay."

My belated "thanks" was so quiet, I wasn't sure Gray had
heard it, but he turned back around before disappearing through
the doorway and gave me a nod and a sad smile.

THIRTY

Love, Harold

Scarlett

The next morning started early, as Gray had predicted.

Vivi was awake and alert though still connected to the IV and monitors. A team of doctors came into the room, introduced themselves, and told us that the tests they'd run on her so far were inconclusive.

"It doesn't appear at this point that you sustained any damage to the heart muscle, Mrs. Hood," one of the men said. "But heart attacks often present differently in women than they do in men. Because of that and because of your age, we're going to keep you here a few more days, run a few more tests. We want to be sure before we release you."

"Of course. Thank you. That's great," I said.

"I think that's a fine idea," Vivi agreed. "Besides, I haven't gotten my hospital Jello yet."

When the doctors had all left, Gray went in search of coffee, and I moved to the bedside, taking Vivi's hand.

"You scared me, you know."

Her grip on my fingers felt weak, and her voice was barely above a whisper.

"No reason to be scared. If it's my time, it's my time. I'm

worried about you, though. What were you and Gray fussing about last night?"

"Nothing," I assured her, not wanting her to worry. "Everything's fine."

"A little lovers' quarrel perhaps?" she asked with a wink.

My jaw fell open.

Vivi laughed, a papery sound. "You didn't think I knew? I'm old, not blind, deaf, and senile. Even if I was, I'd still be able to tell you two are in love. I wouldn't worry about the spat. These things have a way of working themselves out."

I stroked her soft, white hair, shaking my head at her misunderstanding. "Vivi... I really don't think—"

"Miss Hood?" A nursing assistant peeked into the room. "There's someone who's asking to speak with you in the hallway."

"Oh. Okay, sure." I leaned over and kissed Vivi's cheek. "Be right back."

I stepped into the hallway, expecting to find a nurse or doctor who had information about Vivi's case they wanted to share with me privately.

The person waiting there was actually the last one I'd ever have expected to see.

"Bryce?"

My former fiancé gave me a sympathetic look and stepped forward to hug me. I was so shocked, I let him.

You know what? Maddie was right—he *did* smell like hot dog water.

"How are you, sweetheart? I came as soon as I heard."

When he released me, I stared at him. "What are you doing here?"

"I went to the mansion first—wow, what a place. That must have cost some big bucks. The housekeeper there said your grandmother had been brought here, and you went with her. Is she okay?"

I nodded, feeling numb. "She's doing alright. They're running tests."

Staring some more, I tried to get it through my head that my ex had flown halfway across the country and was standing in front of me.

"Is something wrong?" I asked him. "Did something happen at home?"

"No, your family's all fine. I'm fine," he said, "Actually, no, that's a lie. I'm not fine. I haven't been fine since I lost you."

"Lost me? You didn't *lose* me, Bryce. You returned me for a full refund."

"The biggest mistake I ever made," he insisted.

"I've been doing a lot of thinking," he said. "And here's the thing—you're the love of my life, I can't live without you. I want you to give me another chance. I want to *be* there for you... till death do us part this time."

From behind his back, he produced a bouquet of mums and daisies that had obviously been purchased at the hospital gift shop. In fact, there was a card nestled in the vase with the hospital's logo—and the inscription, "For Patty. Get well soon. Love, Harold."

Noticing it, Bryce snatched the card out and dropped it on the floor. "Not sure how the florist got that confused."

He shoved the vase of stolen flowers at me. "I know it's been hard on you since we broke up. And I know you're not with anyone. You've been single since what *should* have been our wedding night. But you don't have to be lonely anymore."

Just then, Gray rounded the nurses' station holding a cardboard tray containing two cups of coffee in one hand and his phone in the other.

"Actually, she's been with *me* since your non-wedding night," he announced, setting the items on a counter and coming to stand beside me.

"Thanks for that, by the way," Gray said to Bryce. "I never would have gotten the chance to propose to this amazing woman if you hadn't fucked up so thoroughly."

"Propose?" Bryce yelped.

I shouted the question just as loudly inside my head.

"I'm her fiancé," Gray calmly lied. "We're getting married."

My *ex*-fiancé's gaze fell to my bare left ring finger, and Gray noticed.

"We're still picking out the ring," he explained. "I want her to have the perfect one. We were planning to fly to LA and New York this weekend to look at two different choices. Vivi's little scare here might put that off for a bit."

"What are you, some kind of billionaire?" Bryce emitted a snort-laugh.

Gray's expression stayed cool. "My financial status is none of your business. The only thing you need to know is I've got everything it takes to make Scarlett happy and take care of her. She doesn't need you—or want you."

He looked down at me, sliding his arm around my shoulders and silently willing me to go along with the ruse.

"Right babe?"

THIRTY-ONE

New Lease on Life

Gray

For a minute, I thought Scarlett was going to leave me hanging and demand to know what the hell I thought I was doing.

Not that I had an answer to that question.

I'd seen that ass of an ex of hers, overheard enough of the conversation to identify him, and autopilot had taken over.

Even now, I was acting more on impulse than intellect. I glared down at the guy, pulling Scarlett against my side.

Feeling her heartbeat thump against my ribcage like a frightened rabbit's, I was torn between the urge to pick her up and carry her out of here and the powerful desire to pound this motherfucker's head into the linoleum hospital floor.

The thing was, most of what I'd said was true. I *did* want to make Scarlett happy. I *did* want to take care of her.

I sure as hell didn't want this fucking guy anywhere near her—especially not when she was upset about Vivi's health scare last night. If he thought he was going to move in for the kill when she was emotionally exposed, he had another thing coming.

"Scarlett? Is this true?" Bryce asked.

She nodded up and down woodenly, probably in shock.

Finally, she spoke. "We met in Greece—at the resort, the day you left."

"You met him on our wedding day?" The guy's face turned purple with outrage.

"I spent the night, in fact," I added in a helpful tone. "Nice bungalow you picked out."

Bryce glared at me then lasered in on Scarlett. "You slut. My bed wasn't even cold."

I gritted my teeth and clenched the hand that wasn't holding Scarlett.

Not worth it. You can't do her any good from jail.

Scarlett, who seemed to have snapped out of her shock-stupor, smirked. "Well, it wasn't exactly burning up when you were *in* it."

Now Bryce was literally shaking with righteous indignation. "How dare you. And to think I flew all the way out here to support you. I was prepared to help you care for your grand-mother in her dying days and even willing to move out here if you wanted to live on the family estate."

Ah. It was all becoming clear. Old Bryce had obviously gotten wind of Scarlett's reconciliation with her paternal grandmother and done a little research, discovering that the Hood family tree was blooming with money.

"How generous of you," Scarlett snapped. "You might be interested to know that after my grandmother has enjoyed a *much* longer life, she'll be leaving her money to charity—all of it. Marrying me wouldn't get you a promotion you didn't deserve, and it's not going to get you a fat inheritance either. So, you can just hop back on a plane. Unfortunately, you'll be flying coach— there's no gold to dig here."

Bryce's eyes slit, making him look like the snake he was, and he hooked a thumb in my direction.

"Like *this* guy's interested than anything other than your money. You stupid bitch."

Fuck it. It'll be worth some jail time.

I stepped up close to the guy, looking down at him with my chest to his nose. "I think it's time you left—this hospital *and* your job at Mixitall."

"What?" he said, but his tone was much less confident. "You can't force me to quit my job."

"You're right. I can't force you to. But I can strongly *advise* you to."

Bryce looked a little less irate and a lot more unsure of himself. His eyes kept flickering away, unable to maintain direct contact with mine.

"And if I don't?"

"Let's just say it wouldn't be the first time I made a trouble-maker disappear."

My menacing tone left no doubt I meant every word of what I was saying. "Oh—and you'll never see or hear me coming. I can lie in wait for days without sleeping, eating, or taking a bathroom break."

The man's eyes widened in horror as he backed away. "You're crazy."

"You bet I am," I assured him.

And that was the last we saw of Bryce. He turned and sped away without a glance back at me, or more importantly, at Scarlett.

She wore an expression I'd never seen on her before. "Wow. That was... that was amazing. I guess I'd better call David and tell him to start looking for a new robotics technician."

"Sorry about that," I said. "Maybe I got a little carried away there with the threats."

She turned and walked back into the open door of Vivi's room, motioning for me to join her. "No. Not at all. He doesn't take a hint very easily, so apparently a bit of terror is what it takes. Thank you so much, by the way."

"Anything for my lovely bride-to-be," I said.

She rolled her eyes at me before turning to face Vivi.

The older woman was sitting up, the back of her hospital bed raised to its full upright position. Her eyes were alert and bright, and she was smiling ear-to-ear.

"Vivi," Scarlett said with obvious shock. "Should you be up like that? Do you need something? What's going on?"

Clasping her hands beneath her chin, Victoria looked from Scarlett to me then back to Scarlett.

"I can't even tell you two how happy you've made me. I've been hoping and praying for this."

Scarlett and I looked at each other, baffled.

Vivi went on, "I have to be honest, last night I thought I was a goner. But today... hearing your big news has given me a new lease on life. It's a miracle, I think."

"Big news?" Scarlett asked. "What big news, Vivi?"

Her grandmother gave her a knowing smile. "Your engagement dear. Your secret is out. These old ears are still good for something. I heard everything you said to that scoundrel out in the hall, and I approve a hundred percent."

She picked up her phone from the bedside tray table and scrolled through her contacts.

"I know the *perfect* person to help plan the wedding—unless you want to do it all yourself—but a big wedding is a lot of work. You'll need help. You can hold it at the mansion. You know, I was starting to think that ballroom would never be used again—at least while I was alive. I once told Gray I wanted to dance at his wedding, and now I *can*—as the grandmother of the bride!"

She looked like she was ready to get up and dance right now, in fact. How was that possible when just this morning she seemed so weak and fragile?

"But Vivi..." Scarlett began. She darted her eyes at me and bit her lip. "I think you misunderstood."

The light in Victoria's eyes dimmed a bit, and she sank back into the pillows. "What do you mean?"

Her heart monitor slowed, and maybe it was my imagination, but did it skip a beat or two?

I stepped forward, putting a big smile on my face. "What Scarlett is trying to say is that we *were* planning to elope. But if you're up for helping to plan it, of course we'll get married at your house. In fact, we'd love it."

Victoria threw up her hands and let out a cheer.

"Yay! Oh, thank you, Gray. Thank you, Scarlett. This really is a dream come true—a fairytale wedding at Indigo Point with the world's most beautiful bride and most handsome groom. The first time I saw you two together, I *knew* it was a match made in Heaven. And now that I have a reason to hang on... I think I can put off going to that Great Beyond a little longer."

While Vivi's cheeks were suddenly pink and full of life, Scarlett was pale.

She was clearly conflicted about what to do—tell Vivi the truth and take the chance the disappointment would crush her and sap her will to live—or go along with the ruse... and pretend to agree to marry me.

I honestly had no idea which way she would go.

THIRTY-TWO

Still a Good Liar

Scarlett

What was happening?

My head was spinning, and my belly was nauseous—*before* I'd had any hospital coffee. I'd been catapulted from the unreal experience of having Bryce try to win me back to the even more unreal experience of being "engaged" to Gray.

All within the past ten minutes.

"Gray? Want to go downstairs and get a cup of coffee with me?" I wheezed.

He looked down at his hands, apparently just now realizing he'd left our cups in the hallway, then back up at my urgent expression.

"Sure. Yeah." Turning to Vivi, he said, "Victoria, we'll be back in a little while."

She smiled and waved, picking up her phone. "Good. That'll give me a chance to call Meghan. She's the best wedding planner in Eastport Bay. She'll help us set everything up."

Nodding noncommittally, I rushed out of Vivi's hospital room with Gray close behind me.

Once in the hallway, he went to the tall counter at the nurses' station. "Hey—someone took our coffee cups. I guess we actually *will* have to buy some more."

"I don't care about coffee," I practically yelled, then realizing I was in a hospital ward, lowered my voice. "How can you think about coffee at a time like this?"

"A time like what? Are you okay?" he asked.

"Well, let's see, I'm not sure. Was it just my imagination, or did we just agree to participate in a large society wedding at Vivi's house—*as the bride and groom?*"

"No, that did happen," he confirmed.

"And *why* exactly did we do that?" I asked, feeling a bud of panic preparing to bloom in my chest.

"You saw her," Gray said. "She basically had an instantaneous recovery when she thought we were engaged. The anticipation of a wedding will be amazing motivation for her to get well and do her physical therapy. On the other hand, if we tell her the truth... who knows what'll happen?"

I turned to look at him with bugged out eyes. "If we *don't* tell her, then what happens? We let her spend time and potentially a lot of money planning a wedding that's never going to take place?"

We certainly weren't going to carry it as far as getting married to make Vivi happy. For one thing, that was just crazy pants. For another, I was *not* interested in being a bride again.

Seeing Bryce had reminded me of what happens when you trust someone to be there for you for a lifetime.

I had no intention of putting myself in that precarious position ever again.

"We have to explain it to her, Gray. The longer we let it go, the worse it'll get."

He nodded, looking like he was mulling it over. "You're right. But I think we should wait at least until she's out of the danger zone and home from the hospital. You agree?"

I blew out a short breath. "I don't know. I guess so. She's already calling a wedding planner, though."

"Relax. It's a few days. How much damage can she possibly do in such a short time?"

* * *

Three days later

"This is like a runaway train," I said to Gray, following him as he carried yet another bunch of delivery boxes from the front door to the ballroom. "What *is* all this stuff?'

Gray had delayed his work trip and taken a few days off so he'd be able to visit Vivi frequently and to help me "house-sit" while she was in the hospital.

It felt more like an Amazon warehouse than a house. Several times a day, deliveries arrived.

"Victoria's been doing a little online shopping, I guess," he said.

"A little? It looks like she's buying out the entire inventory of every bridal shop on the East Coast. She's spending a fortune."

"She *has* a fortune to spend," Gray pointed out. "It's her money. She's having fun."

"Well, make sure to save the receipts for when all this stuff has to go back. And take pictures of everything will you, so we don't lose track?"

"I can't find my phone," he said.

"What?"

"My phone. I'm not sure where it is—I haven't seen it since the morning Vivi was admitted."

"Did you check your car?"

He turned to me with a *duh* expression.

"Well, it must be around here somewhere—or maybe it's in her hospital room," I said. "One thing's for sure—Vivi has *her* phone, and she's getting excellent reception."

I spun in a circle, looking at the sea of boxes.

"I don't even know why she's ordering things already. I told her the 'wedding' would have to be at least a year from now."

"I guess she's just excited. And maybe she's not sure what things will look like a year from now—none of us do," Gray said.

"I do. I'll be back in Minnesota, working at Mixitall, sharing an apartment with Julianna."

For some reason that mental picture produced an almost violent sense of aversion.

Stepping up close to me, Gray put his hands on my hips and lowered his head. "If that's the case, I know what *I'll* be doing—missing you terribly. Try not to worry so much, Red. Try to relax. Want to take a break and go for a swim with me?"

"No," I yelped, leaping back from him.

Swimming plus Gray equaled guaranteed sexy times, and I could *not* allow myself to indulge in any more of those with him. Not now that we were "engaged."

It would only add another layer of confusion on top of what was already a tangled mess of crossed wires and emotions.

"I told you it's over," I said. "Just because we're engaged, that doesn't mean we're going to have a fling."

He pressed his lips together and blew out a short breath through his nose, clearly trying not to laugh at the absurdity of my statement.

Apparently he lost the battle. Throwing his head back, he laughed out loud then leaned forward and rested his hands on his knees with his head hanging down, overcome with hilarity.

I started laughing, too, suddenly unable to contain a flood of giggles.

It was just all so ridiculous—the two of us standing in a massive ballroom, surrounded by boxes, arguing over the rulebook of our fake engagement.

When I thought of it, I couldn't deny that it was funny.

And then the RSVP's started coming.

I walked into the mansion's kitchen that evening, holding a large stack I'd just retrieved from the mailbox.

Gray stood at the kitchen island where he'd just set down a white handled paper bag. He pulled out the takeout containers one by one as I used Vivi's silver letter opener to slit the top of one of the identical envelopes.

"You are not going to believe this," I said, reading the card.

"What?"

"Vivi has apparently planned an *engagement* party—for *this* weekend. That must be what she's been ordering all this stuff for."

He shrugged. "She mentioned she might do something like that."

"What? You *knew*? Gray... this is getting out of hand. We have to tell her."

"No, we don't," he argued. "Not until she gets home. What's the harm in a little party?"

"What's the harm? It's a lie, Gray. All these people..."

I sifted through the pile of envelopes and started reading off the names. "... the Bestias, and the Reeces, Reid Mancini, the founder of StillYours-dot-com, some prince and princess who apparently live on this street, that hot Nauticals player Presley Lowe, and Jade—oh my God, do you think that's the real Jade?"

"It is," he confirmed, smiling. "She's married to my best friend, who happens to be the brother of that hot Nauticals player."

"Well, that's great, that's just great. We'll be lying to my sports hero and my favorite singer of all time—to *all* of those people—if we stand there smiling side by side at an engagement party when we're not even engaged."

Again, he shrugged. "Who cares? You don't even know those people. If you go back to Minnesota, you'll never even see them again. I'm the one who'll have to deal with the fallout later, and I don't give a shit."

He opened a clamshell container filled with seafood scampi and slid it toward me on the countertop. The fragrant steam rose to my nostrils, making me ravenous.

"Look, Victoria's told me how much she used to love hosting

big events," Gray said, digging into his own takeout container. "This may be the last one she gets to do, and she's having a great time planning it. Do you really want to take all that away from her —along with her will to live?"

"That's not fair," I said, speaking around a scallop in my mouth.

"Just go with it. Parties are fun," Gray said. "Vivi's apparently hired staff to run the whole thing. All you have to do is show up."

* * *

On Friday, Vivi came home from the hospital. She was using a wheelchair, which was a little shocking at first.

"Don't you worry about this old contraption," she told us. "I'll be up and dancing by your wedding day. Not in time for your engagement party, unfortunately, but maybe we can get out the glue gun and bling up this chariot a little. Then I can call it an accessory."

"About that... it was quite a surprise to find out there was a party this weekend," I said in the understatement of all time.

"I thought you liked surprises." She winked. "I know I do. Finding out you and Gray were going to get married was the best surprise of my life."

A big, fat anxiety worm slithered in my gut, but I forced a smile. "I think the whole thing caught us off guard as well."

"You know what they say about love," Gray said. "It can strike when you least expect it."

His eyes glowed with a great approximation of conviction. He was *still* a good liar.

"Like a rattlesnake," I added. "Vivi... it's amazingly kind and generous of you to do all this for us, but are you *sure* it's a good idea to have this party when you've just gotten out of the hospital?"

"Absolutely. It's the best medicine possible. I feel invigorated like I haven't felt in years—decades even. Besides, it's the perfect event to get potential bidders excited for the art auction. They'll get a preview and having many of them here together will stoke the fires of competition. I even sent an invitation to Inksy."

THIRTY-THREE

Full Recovery

Gray

Scarlett and I both did a double-take.

"You did?" she asked.

"How'd you do that?" My pulse tattooed the inside of my neck veins. "When no one knows who or where he is?"

"I messaged him on Instagram."

Victoria's smile was confident. "I'm sure he likes a good party. People are saying he might live around here. And I posted on my Insta feed that his painting *Confluence* would be part of the auction next week. There's been a lot of interest. I'm hoping I'll be able to persuade him to donate a few more pieces for the auction."

"I thought you weren't going to sell that one," I said, trying to hide the hurt in my voice.

Victoria gave me an understanding smile. "I love it. It's my favorite in my whole collection, but as they say, 'you can't take it with you.' Even if I live ten more years, I'll be living in a much smaller place. The painting is quite large, and it really should be displayed in a gallery space with proper lighting and security. I doubt the dining hall at Shady Acres will be the right place for it."

"Vivi, you don't really want to go live in a retirement home, do you?" Scarlett asked.

"Why not? It's like a college dorm, but for old biddies like me. Everyone's around your own age and has similar interests and concerns. I'll have company every day and all the cards and Bingo I can play. Indigo Point is a big house for a big family. You're planning to go back to Minnesota, Scarlett, so you won't be here to share the space with me much longer. Stephanie has been wanting to retire for years, but I know she feels guilty about leaving me alone. I want to go—and I appreciate you helping me downsize with the house sale and the auction."

"Well, I wouldn't get my hopes set on Inksy showing up," I warned Victoria. "He's been protecting his identity for years—there must be a good reason."

"I can tell by his art that he has a good heart. If he thinks it's the right thing to do, he'll come."

Great. One more reason to be nervous about the party. Since my phone had gone missing, I hadn't checked my Instagram messages for several days or seen Victoria's post.

But the art world had.

Which meant there was likely to be a mob scene outside the gates tomorrow night.

* * *

On Saturday night, I arrived for the party a couple hours early to help with last minute preparations. Already, a crowd had formed outside the gates.

Finally giving up on finding my lost phone, I'd gotten a replacement, and when I checked Instagram, the reason for the siege became clear.

Vivi's post had more than six thousand comments and more than forty thousand likes. In it, she'd not only announced *Conflu-ence* would be going up on the auction block, she'd hinted that its creator, Inksy himself, might make an appearance here tonight.

What is that old broad up to?

I hadn't seen her or Scarlett since arriving at the mansion. Both ladies were upstairs behind closed doors, presumably getting ready for the party.

The elevator rattled down, and I went to help Victoria maneuver the wheelchair out of it. She was dressed in a sparkling long dress, a light pink that matched her lipstick and made her skin look radiant. With it she wore a dramatic diamond necklace and drop earrings. Her hair was swept up into a regal rolled chignon.

"You look amazing," I told her honestly. "Prettiest I've ever seen you."

"This is the *happiest* you've ever seen me—and it's all because of you and Scarlett. When are you going to give it to her?" she asked.

I put my finger over my mouth in the time-honored signal for *hush*. "Later. When the moment is right. Don't spoil the surprise."

"Oh goodness, not another surprise. My heart can't take it."

We both looked up to see Scarlett standing at the top of the staircase. I literally went breathless at the sight of her.

She wore a form-fitting hot pink cocktail dress and strappy nude-colored high-heeled sandals that made her legs look spectacular. Reaching the bottom of the stairs, she walked over to us.

"What are you two whispering about?'

Before I could say anything, Vivi provided a cover story.

"Now that you caught us, we might as well tell you. Jade is going to sing a song for us tonight—or rather for you two lovebirds. She's a personal friend of mine," Vivi bragged.

"You are kidding me," Scarlett squealed and ran to her grandmother, hugging her.

It worked like a charm. She was thrown completely off the trail. Victoria might have made a good SEAL herself back in the day—she had nerves of steel.

Now if I could get through the night without losing *my* nerve.

The limos started arriving at seven. Before long, the ballroom was filled with laughter, chattering voices, and music. Victoria had hired a jazz band to play for the event. They were a group I'd actually heard on satellite radio before.

When Mrs. Hood did something, she did it right.

She seemed completely in her element, conversing easily with lawmakers, royals, professional athletes, and billionaires as well as the "little people" like me and my former SEAL buddies.

"Gray, Scarlett, I'd like to introduce the crown prince and princess of Aubernesse, Alexander and Cinda Wessex. And this is Alex's brother Cameron and his sister Jane."

I extended my hand to each of them. "Gray Lupine. Pleased to meet you. I believe my company provides your family security services when you're here Stateside."

"Yes, that's right," Alex said. "Viridian has been excellent."

He shot his brother a look. "Especially when Cam needs to be pulled out of some scrape or another. Which is quite often."

The younger Wessex prince offered a dazzling grin as he executed an elaborate bow. "Always happy to keep the bodyguards employed and busy."

"Almost as busy as you keep the American girls when you visit," his sister teased.

Jane offered congratulations to Scarlett and me. "Will the wedding be here in Eastport Bay? I'm in medical school just up the road in Boston if you need any help in the planning. I just love weddings."

Scarlett looked uncomfortable but maintained the subterfuge. "Thank you so much. That's very kind. I believe my grandmother's heart is set on having it here at Indigo Point."

After a few minutes the Wessex family said their goodbyes, and Presley Lowe walked over.

He looked quite different tonight from when I'd seen him at

the Nauticals training camp. With his six-foot-five height and all cleaned up, wearing a tux, he could have passed for a male model.

"You want to introduce me to your bride to be," he asked, "or are you too afraid she's gonna realize she's been settling for cold cuts when she could have ribeye steak instead?"

"Well, you *are* a meathead," I said. "Scarlett, this is my friend Presley Lowe. He's Wilder's brother."

"It's nice to meet you Presley." They shook hands.

I was gratified to see she didn't have visible drool on her lips like many of the party guests checking out the famous football player.

"Nice to meet you, too," he said. "I was just kidding about that cold cuts thing—Gray is at least tenderloin."

She smiled obligingly, and Pres leaned close to me, whispering as he stared across the room. "And who is *that* petite filet mignon?"

Snorting at his joke, I followed his gaze to Jane Wessex, who was now deeply in conversation with best-selling author Jack Bestia and his wife Bonnie.

"*That*—is on a whole different menu, my friend," I said. "I'm not sure you can even afford the appetizers. She's a literal princess."

"No shit," he said, never taking his eyes from her. "Does she speak English?"

"A whole helluva lot better than you do. Want me to introduce you?'

Suddenly the enormous football player looked nervous. "I don't know. I'm not sure what I'd even say to her. It's easy to talk to the football groupies. They already know who I am and want me before I say a word. This girl, though..."

"Would it help if I told you she's a student?"

"She looks older than college age."

"A med student," I corrected. "At Harvard."

He turned and gave me a droll look. "Yeah, that helps a ton.

She's a royal *and* a genius. I'll see you guys later—think I'll go hit the closest sports bar and find a girl more my speed."

Stephanie rolled Victoria's wheelchair back over to us.

"Do you mind if I steal your fiancé for a dance, Scarlett?" Victoria asked.

"By all means," Scarlett said.

I pushed her chair out into the middle of the floor, and Victoria danced while sitting, wiggling her hips and shaking her arms above her head, laughing loudly.

She'd certainly made a full recovery.

She seemed *so* healthy, in fact, I started getting suspicious. After running every test they could think of, the doctors had proclaimed her completely healthy and discharged her.

Quite the comeback there, granny.

Victoria's heart attack scare might have been faked, but the results of it were genuine. The house was filled with life, guests were raving over the pieces in her art collection, eager for the auction—and Scarlett and I were together.

As far as anyone knew.

Though we stood together, holding hands and accepting congratulations, she was still keeping me at a distance emotionally. I hoped that was only due to the awkward circumstances and not because she didn't love me.

Because I sure as hell loved her.

Yes, I'd pulled the engagement story out of thin air when Bryce had shown up, but I hadn't been exactly sad Victoria had overheard us talking about it and had gotten confused.

In fact, I'd been pretty fucking thrilled.

I just wished I knew how Scarlett really felt about it. About *me.*

And I was terrified of how she'd react when I gave up my most precious asset—my anonymity—and finally confessed my secret to her.

I'd find out soon enough.

THIRTY-FOUR

His Muse

Scarlett

I stood by the ballroom's open French doors, breathing in the ocean air and seeking out the cooling breeze so I didn't have a panic attack.

The whole ballroom scene was... overwhelming. It was beautiful and exciting and *talk* about new experiences—this was one to literally write home about.

But it was so different from my ordinary life. I felt like a fraud for multiple reasons—not the least of which was the lie Gray and I had told.

It had created *monumental* consequences.

For instance, at this very moment, Jade, the world-famous singer/songwriter, was performing a song she'd written for Gray and me as a celebration of our "love."

When the song ended, he leaned over and dipped his head close to my ear. "Take a walk with me."

Wanting desperately to escape the applause and the dewy-eyed looks people were sending in our direction, I nodded rapidly and took his arm. He led me out onto the mansion's wide rear terrace and down the steps to the moonlit lawn.

Every tree on the estate had been decked with glowing lanterns, transforming the yard into a fairyland.

Tugging at my hand, Gray pulled me a few steps toward one of the large European weeping beech trees.

It had to be more than a hundred years old judging from its size. The majestic tree's branches spanned as wide as a normal-sized house and were so thick with leaves, that once underneath them we couldn't even see the party guests talking and laughing and drinking on the mansion's balconies above us.

Hanging from one of the thick branches was a tree swing.

"Get on. I'll push you," he said.

I sat on the wide, smooth wooden seat and grabbed the rope supports on either side of me. Gray walked around behind me and put his hands on my waist.

For a few moments he just kept them there, and I felt them trembling. *What* was going on?

Then I felt pressure from behind, and I was in motion, soaring toward the dark night sky. Behind me, Gray started humming the song Jade had just finished. Then he sang one of its verses.

Before you knew you needed me... you did.
Before you knew I loved you... I did.
Before we knew each other's names
Before we knew each other's pain
I did. You did.
I do.
Will you?

His voice wasn't polished and perfect like hers, but to me it was beautiful. Each note pulled at my heartstrings.

As his singing faded, Gray walked around in front of me. The swing slowed, then stopped.

And he got on one knee.

My heart performed a double somersault. "What are you doing?"

He didn't answer, just gave me a smile and pulled something from his pocket, holding it out to me.

The facets of the platinum-set diamond glittered like mini-bonfires in the light of the lanterns hanging all around us. It was absolutely magnificent.

"It belonged to Vivi," he said. "I was going to buy a ring, but she insisted you have this one. It's her favorite."

My mouth went dry, and my throat ached. "Isn't this going a little far to support the story?"

The sincere way my heart was reacting to the fake proposal was almost cruel. I fought back tears.

"We can't keep doing this, Gray. *I* can't keep doing this. It's gone too far. We have to call it off. We have to tell the truth."

He nodded. "You're right. I do want to tell the truth—all of it. And when I'm finished, I hope you'll let me slide this onto your finger."

Rising to his feet, he offered his hand to pull me up. When I was standing, he took me into his arms, looking down into my eyes as he spoke.

"Scarlett... I might not be able to say it as well as the song did... but I felt every word of what she said. The way I feel about you would fill up albums—racks of albums—old vintage record stores full of albums."

"The way you... feel?"

"Yes. I love you, Scarlett. *Not* in a fling way—the no-sex kind *or* the with-sex kind. In a forever way. I want the engagement to be real. I want you to stay here in Eastport Bay. I want you to marry me."

Overwhelmed and probably in shock, I struggled for words.

"Gray, I..."

"Before you answer... there's something I need to tell you." He swallowed, his Adam's apple traveling the length of his throat. "Something I maybe should have told you a long time ago."

"Ooookaaay…" I dragged the word out, waiting.

Just then, a small group of about five people ran out of the back door of the house onto the terrace. Looking around, one of them pointed at us.

"It's her. I told you it's her," a woman shouted. She held up her phone so the others with her could see the screen. "This is the girl who's getting married, the one the party's for."

"It is her," the guy next to her said.

What was everyone yelling about? Were they looking at a picture of me online? Why? It wasn't like I was famous or anything. I'd been mixing with party guests all evening, and no one had seemed that excited.

"That means she knows him," the woman said. "She *knows* who Inksy is."

"Hell, based on that drawing, she's fucking the guy," one of the men said.

Pounding down the stairs toward us, the group started shouting questions. "Do you know Inksy? Who is he?"

"What's his real name?" a man shouted.

"Are you lovers?" someone else demanded to know. "Are you his muse?"

Instinctively I backed away. Gray stepped in front of me and held out an intimidatingly large hand.

"What's this about? What's going on?"

The woman turned her phone around and held it so the screen was facing us. "This is her, right?"

Craning to see around his large frame, she spotted me. "It looks just like you. It has to be you."

I gasped at the same time I felt Gray's body stiffen in front of me.

He stepped forward and snatched the phone from the woman's hand so he could look at it more closely.

I didn't need to.

I'd recognized the image immediately.

It was a photo of the drawing he'd done of me. Naked.

Somehow the drawing had been posted online, and the woman had come across it.

"Give that back," she demanded.

"Where did you get this?" Gray asked, sounding furious.

"At Verizon. And it cost a fortune—give it back."

He handed her the phone. "I don't mean the phone. I mean the picture. Where did you find it? How did it *get* on your phone?"

"Somebody texted it to me," she explained, seeming annoyed with him. "It's gone viral—everyone's speculating it's an authentic Inksy. When I saw it, I compared it to online photos of his other work. I think it *is* an Inksy."

Leaning to the side to see around Gray again, she said, "Which means *that* woman knows who he is."

Gray turned around to face me. I knew the second I saw his eyes—it was true.

I *did* know who Inksy was.

Gray.

He was the reclusive artist who'd created street art under the cover of night around the world, whose works now sold for millions if not tens of millions of dollars apiece. He was the one who'd painted that piece worth twenty-five million in Vivi's gallery.

He must have been the one who'd gifted it to her, too.

All along, as I'd been falling in love with Inksy's art—and with Gray—they'd been one and the same person.

And he hadn't told me.

He'd lied to me.

Again.

THIRTY-FIVE

Let Me Explain

Gray

Oh shit.

This was *not* how I'd wanted Scarlett to find out about my alter ego. I'd been seconds away from telling her myself, but now, based on the expression she wore, it was too late.

A few minutes ago, the tears welling in her eyes had been inspired by joy. Now, they were byproducts of betrayal.

She pushed at me, forcing me to take a step back. "You *promised* me. You said there would be no copies of the drawing."

Now the tears spilled over, breaking my heart. "And then you put it up online to what—help further your mystique? Drive up the prices of your art even more?"

I stepped forward again, reaching for her. "Scarlett. Let me explain."

She recoiled from my touch. "You could have *explained* anytime during the past few weeks. But you didn't. You just let me play the fool and blather on about 'Inksy's' art, even when you took me to see the mural."

Her hand came to her forehead. "Oh—that's why you kept putting it off that day, isn't it? You put it out there for the world to see and *still* you were trying to hide it from me."

All around us people had lifted their phones to record the disastrous scene. Drawn by the commotion, more people were drifting out of the house and crowding onto the terrace to watch the drama unfold.

There among them was Victoria in her wheelchair.

Guess the jig is up. After all I'd done to protect my anonymity over the years, it ended today.

And I don't even care.

The realization shocked me. Compared to the imminent possibility of losing Scarlett, the loss of my privacy was nothing.

"I put it out there for the world to see because I couldn't contain myself," I explained. "I had all these big feelings for you. They were coming out of my pores—and you didn't want them. Or at least I didn't think you did. I told you art is my therapy. It's the only way I know of to express feelings that are too powerful to keep inside. And Scarlett... the way I feel about *you* is the most powerful thing I've ever felt in my life. I *love* you."

She crossed her arms over her chest. "And I suppose all this 'love' is why you lied to me about who you were—and about the drawing, too. I thought being stood up at the altar was the most embarrassing moment of my life, but you make Bryce look like a sweetie."

Turning, she sprinted toward the house, running up the stairs and pushing through the accumulated crowd to get inside.

"Scarlett! Scarlett, wait..."

I ran after her, but instead of stepping out of my way as they'd done for her, the onlookers moved into my path, trying to talk to me, pulling at my clothes, some asking for autographs or pictures or taking video.

In no time at all, our private lives would be playing on screens across the world, thanks to my new notoriety.

And then—oh God it was going to happen, I knew it just like I knew I could never live down my past.

People would make the connection to my infamy as one of the

SEAL team "traitors" who'd testified against their commander, and my nightmare would be complete.

More importantly, Scarlett would be drawn into it and suffer the second-hand shame.

I didn't blame her for running away from me.

And that's why I decided to stop chasing her... and let her go.

THIRTY-SIX

A Part of Me

Scarlett

There was a knock at the door to my suite.

I stopped folding clothes and turned to glare at it. "Go away, Gray. I don't feel like talking—*or* posing nude."

"It's Vivi, dear."

Fantastic. I was just thinking I could use a little more humiliation tonight.

I rushed to the door and opened it. "Sorry about that. I thought you were... you know."

She rolled her chair into my room. "I know."

Peeking into the hallway and checking one direction then the other, I drew back into the room and shut the door.

"Is... everyone gone?" I asked.

"If you mean is Gray gone, yes, he is. Everyone's left. The party's over... in every sense of the word I suppose. Why did you two pretend to be engaged?"

Going to sit on my bed, I faced her. "I'm sorry. It just sort of happened. Gray pretended we were engaged when my old fiancé showed up. He was trying to help me get rid of him, and it worked, but then you overheard."

I threw my hands out to the side then let them flop to my lap.

"You were so happy, and it seemed to make you feel more energized. We were both worried about you possibly having a relapse of your condition if we told you it wasn't real. And then you planned this amazing night, and we didn't know how to get out of it."

"And is that what you wanted?" she asked. "To get out of it?"

"Of course," I blurted, but then I got quiet. Now that it was over, I didn't feel relieved. I felt sort of the opposite.

"I'm not sure," I admitted. "I've spent so much of my life focusing on what I *needed* to do and should do and what other people wanted me to do, I think I've kind of lost touch with what I want."

She nodded. "Well then, you know what your next step is. You need to *figure out* what you want."

I reached for her hand, and she gave it to me. For a few minutes we just sat with clasped hands in the quiet room.

"I have to go home," I said. "I can't think clearly when I'm this close to Gray."

Her hand squeezed mine. "You know, that *could* be an indicator of what you really want."

"It could also mean that my girl parts have been doing all my thinking for me, and I need to let my brain have a turn. Sorry— that may have been TMI. Sometimes I forget I'm talking to my grandmother."

She let out a loud guffaw. "You don't get to *be* a grandmother unless your 'girl parts' have seen a little action. It may have been a while, but I do know what you're talking about. I'll just say one more thing about it—while you're letting your brain mull it over, don't forget to let your heart have a say."

"I really love you, you know that?"

She nodded, her misty eyes matching mine. "I know. I love you, too. I always have."

I swiped at an escaped tear on my cheek. "I'm sorry to be

leaving before the auction, but I just can't be around him right now, you know?"

She patted my other hand. "I know. And you've already done more to help me than I ever could have expected. You've been the answer to my prayers, and this time with you has been more precious than I could ever express. I'm sure Gray will handle the auction just fine on his own. Will you promise to come back and visit me soon? No matter what you decide about him?"

"I will. I promise. I'm going to miss you so much." I leaned forward and hugged her, breathing in her soft, powdery scent.

She patted my back. "I'll miss you, too, honey."

When the embrace ended, Vivi reached into the leather pocket hanging from the side of her wheelchair and pulled out an envelope.

"This is for you."

Holding up my palms, I shook my head. "No. You don't have to give me any money. That's not what I came here for. Helping you with the estate stuff was my pleasure."

She smiled and extended the envelope to me again. "It's not a check. Just a little light reading for the airplane ride home. Don't open it till you board, okay?"

* * *

For the sixth time in the past hour, I checked the clock on the wall in front of my desk.

The minutes dragged like a banana slug crawling through tar. I'd been home for almost a week, but it seemed more like six weeks, and my workdays at Mixitall felt about twice as long as they used to.

Admittedly, without Bryce here, work was a *little* more tolerable, but I kept thinking about my cookie business and what Vivi and Gray had said about following my heart.

My heart was definitely not in this job or even here in Anoka. It was back in Rhode Island. With Gray.

And when I'd opened Vivi's envelope on the plane, suddenly anything—and everything—had become possible.

It was mind-boggling. And scary. And exciting.

And *scary*.

"You okay kiddo?" my stepdad David asked as he walked into my office. "You look about a million miles away."

No, only 1400 miles, actually.

"I'm fine," I said. "What's up?"

"Listen, I ah... wanted to talk to you about the income and expenditures report for this month."

He sat down in the chair in front of my desk and handed me a printout of the report I'd turned in to him earlier today.

Leafing through the pages, I immediately spotted what had concerned him. I'd made a major error.

"I am so sorry. I'll fix it and get it back to you before I leave here tonight. I wish I could plead jetlag, but I'm not sure that works for a domestic flight that was six days ago. The truth is... I've been a little distracted since I got home."

He chuckled, wearing a sympathetic smile. "You don't say. That isn't the only reason I stopped by. Your mom and I want to take you out to lunch."

"Oh. Okay sure. Let me finish up this one thing, and I'll be ready to go."

As we walked past the receptionist's desk on our way out, Regina stood and called out to me. "Scarlett—there's a delivery for you."

She waggled her eyebrows and lifted an arrangement of poppies to the raised counter in front of her desk. They were stunning—bright citrus-colored blooms interspersed with some bougainvillea and eucalyptus. I walked over to her, feeling like my legs were made of noodles.

"Somebody sure likes *you*," Regina said.

"Who are they from, sweetheart?" Mom asked.

I didn't even have to check the card. I already knew. Only Gray would send these to me.

Only he would remember a single conversation during which we discussed my favorite flower.

With trembling fingers, I picked up the envelope that came with the flowers. It was sealed with a strange bulge in the middle. I opened it, reaching inside.

There was a note and... something else.

A rubber ear.

My mom recoiled and made an expression of disgust. "What on Earth?"

"It's a private joke," I explained, but nothing felt funny to me. Instead, the gift seemed imbued with life-and-death importance.

Written in black pen on the ear were the words, "Without you, it feels like a part of me is missing."

Moisture filled my eyes. "It's from Gray."

Unfolding the note, I read his words.

Dear Scarlett,

I'm not even sure how to begin this. I guess I'm sorry would be a good start. I wish I had told you sooner about my "secret career." I've been alone so long I guess I sort of forgot how to really let someone else in. I should have trusted my gut about you—all the way. If my failure to do that causes me to lose you, it'll be the greatest regret of my life.

I told myself I was going to just let you go, that you'd be better off without me and the baggage from my past. But then I thought, how does that make me any better than Bryce, who said he loved you then disappeared on you?

Speaking of that cocksucker, Viridian did a little digging and found out he's the one who put your picture online. He took my phone from the counter at the hospital. I guess his goal was to shame you, but I swear to God, that is the best piece I've ever created because you were the subject. You were and will always be the most beautiful woman I've ever seen. I took a picture of it because I wanted it for myself. I wanted you for myself.

Of course I never intended for it to go public. I'm so sorry that it happened, and you were embarrassed as a result. We made sure the proper authorities found out about it, and Bryce has been criminally charged under revenge porn laws. Because he stole the image and posted it with the intention of harassing you, he's being fined ten thousand dollars and is facing a prison sentence of five years.

As for us—and I hope there can still be an us—I'm ready to do anything you say to win you back. I'll quit my job with Viridian, I'll move to Minnesota and paint cows for the rest of my life.

I can live anywhere and create my art. I can live anywhere and expand my art program for incarcerated kids nationwide. But my heart can only be in one place—wherever you are.

Victoria told me what she did regarding her will, so I know you don't need anything I can give you financially. And now you know I don't need any of your money either. If you'll have me, I'll spend the rest of my life giving you the things money can't buy—fun, laughter, new experiences, sunsets, and sunflowers.

I know it's a lot to ask you to trust me again. I won't blame you if you say you can't. But if you'll at least try, I'll take whatever you'll let me have of you. You don't even have to marry me. We can keep all our assets separate so that if you want to, you can walk away at any time.

Of course I'll be praying every day that time never comes.

Please don't say no right away. Take a few days to think about it. The minute the auction is over this weekend, I'm getting on a plane and tracking you down the way I should have three years ago after "our" honeymoon. We can talk then.

I love you, with all my heart, forever,

Gray

By the time I finished reading, tears were streaming down my face.

Mom put her arm around my shoulders. "You love him."

I nodded rapidly. "I do. So much. And I forgive him—I *believe* him. But how can we possibly be together? My life is here. You're here, my job is here."

"About that..." David began then stopped and licked his lips, wincing.

"What?"

Mom put her arm through mine, pulling me toward the door. "Let's talk it over at lunch."

THIRTY-SEVEN

Anything You Want

Scarlett

The restaurant was one of those hot-dish and tater tot places —comfort food, comfortable surroundings. We sat in a booth with Mom and David on one side and me on the other.

Once we had our waters, he folded his hands on the tabletop in front of him. "Your mom and I thought it would be good to get away from the office for a little while so we could talk."

My hand came up to cover my mouth. "Oh my God, you're not getting a divorce, are you?"

She choked a laugh. "Heavens no. Why would you think that?"

"I don't know. You're just acting weird. You seem so serious. Wait—are you selling the company, David?"

He shook his head, smiling. "No, it's nothing like that. Your mom and I are fine, the company's fine. This is about you."

"Oh." I sat back a little farther in my seat.

"You've never seemed particularly excited about your work at Mixitall," he said. "I've always known you were trying your best, but honestly, honey, you kind of suck at it."

Mom nodded in earnest agreement. "You really do, Scarlett. And now that you're financially set thanks to your grandmother's will and the generous monthly stipend she's giving you until it takes effect..."

"Are you... firing me?"

"No," David said adamantly. "You're not *fired* but consider this your official invitation to move on to a job—and a life—that's better suited to you."

He *was* firing me.

My heart raced with the strangest combination of surprise, dejection, and elation.

My jaw hung open. "But I thought... I always thought you'd be devastated if I left. You talked about how important it was to have a 'family' business."

"It is important sweetheart," Mom said, "but your happiness is *more* important."

Reaching across the table, she drew my hands into hers. "Clearly you want to go back to Rhode Island and be with Gray. No offense babe, but why is it that you think everything will fall apart if you do what *you* want to do?"

The question gave me a little jolt. When I thought about it, it *was* rather conceited to believe I was so important no one could possibly get along without me or take my place.

"I'd miss you so much," I said.

"We'll miss you, too, but there are airplanes and phones. And we'll have someone to visit on the East Coast. David and I have even talked about moving to Cape Cod when we retire. That's not far from Rhode Island at all."

"The thing is, kiddo, this is your *life*," David said. "And I can tell you, the years go by pretty fast. All we want is for you to be happy. I don't think living here and doing the books for Mixitall is making you happy. Is it?"

I shook my head, finally admitting the truth to myself as well as to my parents.

Looking a little sheepish, David asked, "Do you think your roommate Julianna—the *accounting* major—might be happy at our company?"

My heart rate quickened. "Yes! And she's miserable in her waitressing job, but there haven't been many openings in accounting around here. Oh my gosh, this is the *best*. I'm going to text her right now."

I sent a text to Julianna who replied immediately with a mind-blown emoji followed by several hearts and some confetti.

I looked up at David and my mom. "I think you've got yourself a new bookkeeper."

We raised our respective water glasses and clinked them together just as our waiter arrived at the table.

"Hello folks. Looks like we're celebrating today. What's the occasion?"

I beamed at him. "I just got fired."

He angled one ear toward me as if to hear me better. "Hired?"

"No. *Fired*. And it's been a long time coming." I laughed. David and Mom joined me.

The confused waiter pasted on an uncertain smile. "And you're happy?"

"Ecstatic, actually," I told him. "What's your best bottle of wine?"

He whipped out a wine list and offered it to me, tapping the name of an expensive Chardonnay.

"That would be this one. It's a little pricey. The one below it is pretty good, too, if that's more in keeping with your budget."

"Budget is not a problem," I assured him. "And these two are worth it. They deserve the very best."

He smiled and rushed away, presumably before I had a chance to change my mind.

"You do too, sweetheart," Mom said. "I hope you'll allow yourself to have it. Because you can have anything you want now... as long as you know what that is."

"I do," I assured her. "I finally do."

THIRTY-EIGHT

Bidder 47

Gray

The auction had drawn an even bigger crowd than I'd expected, though maybe I *should* have expected it after all the publicity surrounding my "outing" as Inksy last weekend.

Once again, the ballroom at Indigo Point was full. Some of the same players were here, but there were many new faces, art investors from around the world who'd flown in with only a few days' notice.

Thankfully, Viridian had security well in hand, and the auction was going well.

Really well. The Renoir had just sold for seventy-eight million to a private phone bidder in the United Arab Emirates.

Victoria tugged on my jacket, and I leaned down to hear her whisper.

"Don't feel bad," she said. "In a hundred years, yours will go for twice that much. It's hard to compete with these dead guys."

I laughed. "I don't want to compete with them. I just want you to be happy and satisfied with the proceeds you're giving to the charities Scarlett picked out."

At Victoria's urging, I'd donated a few more of my pieces to the cause. They'd all sold for surprisingly high sums.

Only the one I'd given to Victoria remained. *Confluence*—Scarlett's favorite. The auctioneer's assistant was placing it on the block now.

"I'm sort of regretting selling that one now," Victoria said. Her expression was melancholy. "Maybe Shady Acres really would've put it on the dining room wall where I could see it every day."

"If you'd accept my offer to move into the townhouse on the harbor with me, you could be surrounded by my paintings all day long, every day."

She laughed. "How am I going to find a new sweetheart if I'm tied down to one man? No thank you. I'll be happier at the retirement home where I plan to acquire a harem of more age-appropriate beaus. Besides, you'll want privacy with your new bride."

If only. A painful spasm gripped my heart, bringing the never-ending longing back to the forefront of my mind.

I hadn't heard from Scarlett, though the florist in Anoka assured me she'd delivered the bouquet to her workplace and followed my other instructions to a T.

Victoria must have read my expression because she said, "Don't worry, son. She'll come around. All hope isn't lost."

The bidding began, and the selling price for *Confluence* quickly rose into the twenty million range. Glancing down and seeing the wistful way Victoria gazed at it, I excused myself to step out of the room, walking across the hall to a small private salon.

From behind its closed door, I dialed the auction company's switchboard and threw my hat into the bidding ring. If she wanted to keep the painting, by God she was going to have it—at any price.

Someone in the ballroom raised the bid by a million dollars, and I matched it, adding a million more. For a few minutes, bidder number forty-seven and I went back and forth, driving the price up.

When it reached thirty million, I started to sweat. I mean, yes, I was a billionaire, but was a painting of mine really worth *that* much? And who *was* this mysterious bidder number forty-seven? I had to see.

Phone still in hand, I crossed the hall again to the ballroom, scanning the crowd to locate the determined art collector. Whoever he was, he sure had a hard-on for my work.

The auctioneer spoke again. "I have thirty million. Am I bid thirty-five?"

I hit the button on my phone to bid thirty-five million then watched carefully to see who matched me.

There. A paddle went up in the middle of the room. It bore the number forty-seven. Ah, the art collector wasn't a *he.*

The hand belonged to a woman.

Moving swiftly toward the windows, I walked along the rows of chairs, craning my neck to get a look at her.

"I have thirty-five million for the Inksy original entitled *Confluence.* Do I hear thirty-six? Thirty-six?"

When I reached bidder forty-seven's row, she stood up and faced me.

Scarlett.

What was she doing here? And why was she throwing away her newly acquired fortune on my painting?

She shrugged, the tears in her eyes making them sparkle in the light of the chandeliers. "Inksy's my favorite artist. Some things really *are* worth it. They're worth everything you have."

"Thirty-five million going once, going twice..."

Before the auctioneer could bring down his gavel and end the auction, Victoria spoke up.

"Actually, I've decided to pull that item. The auction didn't meet my minimum reserve price."

"Madam, you didn't *set* a reserve price," the auctioneer, who was about to lose a hefty chunk of commission, pointed out.

"Son, this is *my* painting and *my* house, and I'm setting a minimum reserve price right now—it's priceless." She looked around the room. "Can anyone beat that?"

The bewildered auctioneer shot a helpless glance toward me and Scarlett.

"Too rich for my blood," I said, backing away with both hands raised.

"Me too. I'm out." Scarlett put her hand over her heart with a dramatic sigh. "Thank God."

There was laughter then applause throughout the audience.

To appease the auctioneer and the few disgruntled faces I saw —and to keep Victoria from being in legal breach—I made an announcement.

"I'll substitute another original if you want to start the bidding over. How about if I recreate the one I painted on the Providence wall that washed away?"

Immediately the faces in the crowd turned back to the auctioneer, and the room was filled with a roar of excited chatter. He took advantage of the fervor.

"What am I bid for the new Inksy original?"

Scarlett kept her paddle carefully lowered as she excused herself and made her way to the end of the row.

When she reached me, I took her in my arms. "What happened? Decided it wasn't so 'decent' after all?"

She stood on her tiptoes and whispered into my ear. "When it comes to Inksy, I decided I'm *much* more interested in his 'indecent' work."

My pants bulged with a very indecent reaction to that news.

"Let's get out of here, Red." I gave her my best smoldering look. "I've just had the strongest urge to do some finger-painting."

Epilogue

SCARLETT

Three months later

You can't really appreciate the meaning of the word "bliss" until you find yourself standing at the altar in a wedding dress in front of all your friends and family with the most handsome, most wonderful, most talented, and most loving groom imaginable.

Gray and I stood together in front of the flower-covered arch embedded in the stretch of green lawn between the beautiful deep-blue Atlantic Ocean and the four hundred wedding guests all trying their best not to cry as he spoke the wedding vows he'd written.

To one side were my bridesmaids and matron of honor, my sister Maddie.

Wilder Lowe, Badger, Sharkbait, and Volt stood on the other side, beaming at their friend, whom they would no doubt tease mercilessly for the tender words as soon as they could get him alone.

My niece Trina, the flower girl, had walked down the aisle ahead of me in the *right* direction this time, and Vivi had joined Mom and David in giving me away.

Now she was dancing—that's right, dancing—at the reception, looking about twenty years old instead of ninety. She'd ditched her wheelchair months ago.

Dancing with her was her new *age-appropriate* gentleman friend, Carl. They'd met at Shady Acres, where Gray's painting *Confluence* now hung in the dining room and where Vivi had gone to live when Gray moved into Indigo Point with me.

She'd persuaded me to keep the estate, though I had my qualms about living in a house the size of a Target store.

"You'll get used to it," she promised. "Besides, pretty soon there'll be children riding bicycles in the grand foyer and sliding down the banisters—just as it should be. Believe me, you'll be wondering if there's *enough* room in this old castle."

When we'd tried to convince her to live here with us, she'd turned us down cold.

"No offense, but I want to be with my peeps," Vivi explained. "I'm glad you'll be keeping the house—that way I can visit it anytime I like. But frankly, sweetheart, these old walls aren't as soundproof as you might think. And Carl and I can get pretty loud."

Though Vivi had designated me in her will as her sole heir, I'd earmarked most of my eventual inheritance to go to the charities I'd spent so much time researching.

For now, I was using my monthly stipend to expand Sweet Scarlett's. There were chain locations opening in Minnesota and Rhode Island with plans to open in several big cities nationwide.

Gray was taking his non-profit program, Arts Awake, national as well and had left Viridian to run it and work on his Inksy paintings full-time—when he wasn't painting *me*, that was.

"I can't wait for you to see the groom's cake," he said as we danced in the ballroom near Vivi and Carl. "I created the design myself and sent it to the cake decorator."

"Oh God, please tell me it's not called *Scarlett in Her Bridal Thong*," I begged.

He laughed. "No, but that's a great idea for a future piece. Come on, let's go check it out."

We left the dance floor and crossed the ballroom to the cake tables, where later we'd do the ceremonial cutting and feed each other the first bites.

The wedding cake itself was a gorgeous twelve-tiered red velvet with white cream cheese frosting, decorated with red and pink poppies.

On a separate table, the groom's cake was frosted around the sides to look like actual gray fur. The image atop it featured a woman in a red, hooded cloak sitting for a portrait while a wolf, painting at an easel, captured her likeness.

"It's incredible," I said. "I'm afraid someone's going to try to steal it or auction it off for millions of dollars before we get a chance to eat it."

"The room's full of Viridian bodyguards," he informed me. "The cake's safe. *You* however... are not."

Cradling my jaw, he lifted my face for a kiss. When it ended, his gorgeous green eyes were twinkling with mischief.

"You know... the design on the cake matches my new tattoo," he whispered.

"You got a new tattoo? Where?"

"Well, that's for me to know and you to find out," he teased. "I guess you'll have to go searching for it. It's a real work of art."

I rolled my eyes. "Oh my, what a big *head* you have, Mr. Wolf."

"You should see the other one—seriously, I've been hard all day seeing you in that white dress."

Laughing at his silly dirty joke, I followed as he backed away toward the ballroom door, beckoning me with a hand gesture and a seductive smile.

"Where are you going?"

"Somewhere I can steal a few minutes alone with you."

Realizing he was leading me toward the alcove under the grand stairway, I widened my eyes at him.

"Gray... there are hundreds of people in the house."

The sound of muffled explosions made us both look up.

"Not for long," he said as he took my hand and pulled me close. "I think the evening's *outdoor* entertainment has commenced."

Just then I heard Vivi's excited voice. "Come on outside everyone. Hurry! The fireworks are starting."

And they were.

Inside *and* out.

* * *

Thank you so much for reading **Scarlett and the Big Bad Billionaire**! I loved writing this story for you, and I hope you loved reading it. If you did, I'd be so grateful for a review on the retailer where you purchased it.

Want to find out where Scarlett and Gray went on their honeymoon? If you'd like to read a free **bonus epilogue** for this story, go to:

https://BookHip.com/SAPXXSZ

You'll be signed up for my Tru Tales VIP list and get a free novella set in the Eastport Bay story world. My list members are first to know about my new releases, sales, and the fun freebies I offer from time to time. I'd love to have you join us!

There's more love and laughter to come in Eastport Bay. My newest book is The Grumpy Billionaire, and I think you're going to love it! Find it on your favorite book retailers website or order it from your favorite bookstore and continue your stay in Eastport Bay. I'm so glad you're here!

Love,

Tru

<h1 style="text-align:center">Afterword</h1>

I hope you loved reading **Scarlett and the Big Bad Billionaire!** If you did, I'd be so grateful for a review at your favorite book retailer and if your fingers aren't too tired, on Goodreads too!

Reviews are so important for authors and they help other readers find great books.

There's more to enjoy in the world of Eastport Bay! There are six books out in the series now plus a holiday novella. All are of them can be read as standalones. They're connected in fun ways that makes them even more fun when read together, so I hope you'll try them all and love them.

Turn the page to check out my Also By page and be sure to join my Tru Tales mailing list! You'll get notifications of new releases, bonus epilogues, true stories of small town romantic comedy, excerpts, sneak peeks, giveaways, plus a FREE novella set in the world of Eastport Bay!

I'd love to have you join. Find the signup form at: https://trutaylor.com/tru-tales/

Award-winning romance author Tru Taylor writes romantic comedies to make you swoon, smile, and snort with laughter.

She runs on Coke Zero and dark chocolate, lives for lunches with her girlfriends, and drives to the town beach several times a week to watch the sun set over the water.

She loves LOVE and will attempt to turn any show or movie she's watching into a romance whether it is one or not. Star Wars? A romance. Lord of the Rings? Clearly a romance. The Expendables? Okay, well not even Tru can redeem that one.

When she's not writing, Tru enjoys watching movies and reading books with happy endings, spending time with her husband and two kids, and sneaking Hershey's Kisses from the top shelf of the freezer throughout the day. (Top shelf because... two kids. Enough said.)

Tru is the author of the Eastport Bay small town rom com

series and loves living in a small New England town where she's surrounded every day by the beautiful coastal setting you see brought to life in her books.

Learn more about Tru and her books at www.trutaylor.com.

Want fun email from Tru? Join her Tru Tales mailing list for true stories of small town romantic comedy, excerpts, sneak peeks, giveaways, and a free novella set in the world of Eastport Bay!

Sign up here: https://trutaylor.com/tru-tales/